PRAISE FOR
THE BILLIONAIRE SERIES

'A rip-roaring romp.' *Listener*

'A great whodunit which is almost as engrossing for adults as it is for children.' *Books+Publishing*

'Pure escapism…Magical writing, sharp dialogue and a plot with more twists and turns than a politican's speech.' *Dominion Post*

'Filled with secret passageways and deadly booby traps… you'll be on the edge of your seat!'
K-Zone

'Weird dreams, kidnapping, attacks by bandits, hectic chases and eerie explorations in archaeological sites… slapstick humour, verbal wit and a pervasive spirit of youthful exuberance.' *Magpies*

'An irresistibly fun-tastic tale that's virtually guaranteed to keep youngsters reading, chuckling and desperately waiting for the next book in the series.'
Independent Weekly

'From Roman emperors to murderous cults, Indian dynasties to secret fraternities, the adventures of Gerald and his friends will keep young readers turning the pages at lightning speed.' *Fiction Focus*

'A rollicking good yarn.' *Weekend Herald*

Richard Newsome lives in Brisbane with his family. He won the inaugural Text Prize for Young Adult and Children's Writing for *The Billionaire's Curse*, the first book in The Billionaire Series.

richardnewsome.com

THE
HOUSE OF PUZZLES

BOOK V *of*
THE BILLIONAIRE SERIES

RICHARD NEWSOME

TEXT PUBLISHING MELBOURNE AUSTRALIA

textpublishing.com.au
richardnewsome.com

The Text Publishing Company
Swann House
22 William Street
Melbourne Victoria 3000
Australia

First published by The Text Publishing Company, 2014

Cover and page design by W. H. Chong
Cover illustration by Simon Barnard
Typeset by J & M Typesetting
Printed and bound in Australia by Griffin Press, an Accredited ISO AS/NZS 14001:2004 Environmental Management System printer

National Library of Australia Cataloguing-in-Publication data:

Author: Newsome, Richard. 1964–
Title: The house of puzzles / Richard Newsome.
ISBN: 9781922147301 (pbk.)
ISBN: 9781922148346 (ebook)
Series: Newsome, Richard 1964– Billionaire series; book 5.
Subjects: Detective and mystery stories.
Dewey Number: A823.4

The paper this book is printed on is certified against the Forest Stewardship Council® Standards. Griffin Press holds FSC chain of custody certification SGS-COC-005088. FSC promotes environmentally responsible, socially beneficial and economically viable management of the world's forests.

This project has been assisted by the Commonwealth Government through the Australia Council, its arts funding and advisory body.

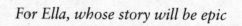

For Ella, whose story will be epic

Prologue

The man pulled a box of matches from his back pocket and struck one against the sole of his boot. The match head flared orange and red; the flame danced in the breeze that rolled off the River Seine. He cupped a hand and lit the unfiltered cigarette that dangled from his bottom lip. The tip glowed against the biting cold of the afternoon. Alphonse filled his lungs with the foul smoke and savoured the heat in his chest. It was good to be back in Paris.

He would have preferred the south of France (for the more pleasant weather) but winter in the city of lights was where the job had brought him. And when Sir Mason Green phones through an order, it takes a braver man than Alphonse Poulet to say no.

Alphonse took another drag. He rubbed one hand across his round belly and the other over his stubbled chin, then pulled a piece of paper from his coat pocket to study it for the umpteenth time. Mason Green's order was quite specific. Alphonse never queried the motives of his clients. In the world of international art theft it was wise not to ask too many questions. But even by the eccentric standards of his usual clients, this request was way out there.

Alphonse stroked his belly again, as if for luck. He took a final puff, tossed the cigarette butt to the gutter and crushed it under his boot. Then he joined the stream of people flowing into the courtyard of the Palais du Louvre and down an escalator to the main entrance of the most famous museum in the world.

Alphonse breezed through the metal detectors, brushed past clusters of tour groups and made his way to the second floor of the Denon wing. He entered a crowded, high-ceilinged gallery. Hanging on three of the walls were portraits and scenes from the Italian Renaissance—the works of masters, rich in colour and life.

No one was paying them the least attention.

More than three hundred people were crammed into the space and all of them were crowding around a single painting. It was the only piece that graced the gallery's fourth wall and it was no bigger than a large scrapbook.

The Mona Lisa: the most valuable painting in the world.

Alphonse elbowed his way to the front of the crowd where tourists pressed against a wooden barrier, trying to catch a glimpse of the portrait that hung behind a panel of bulletproof glass.

La Gioconda—the lady with the enigmatic smirk. Smiling. Beguiling.

Alphonse Poulet was entranced. There were times when his life as the Falcon—the greatest art thief of all time—was very good indeed. He checked through the corners of his eyes. A security guard the size of a small truck was parked by the door to the left of the Mona Lisa. Another guard, only slightly smaller and poured into his uniform like concrete into a mould, stood by the exit to the right.

Alphonse swivelled his gaze upwards. Security cameras were mounted along the length of the ceiling. More guards hovered at the rear of the room, watching every movement. If he was going to pull off this heist, everything was going to have to go exactly to plan.

Alphonse melted back into the crowd. He unbuttoned his coat, slid a hand inside the false belly strapped to his front and pulled out five ceramic cylinders, each one about the size of a torch battery. He looked left, then right, and dropped one of the cylinders into a woman's unzipped shoulder bag.

Alphonse ducked, then reappeared in the middle of the crush of people. He placed another cylinder into the drooping hoodie of a teenage girl. Seconds later he was at the rear of the room. He bent to tie his bootlace and placed two cylinders against the wall.

Alphonse squeezed his way through to the adjoining gallery and slipped the final cylinder into the truck-sized security guard's gaping trouser pocket.

Then he turned through an arched doorway and into a long room. Dull winter light seeped through glass panels in the ceiling high above. The blood-red walls were adorned with enormous paintings depicting scenes from French history. Alphonse strolled the wooden floor and stopped halfway along the room in front of an arresting image: a beautiful woman striding across the barricades of revolutionary Paris, her dress torn from her shoulders, a French tricolour flag clutched in one hand, a musket in the other. A messenger boy with a satchel over his shoulder stood to her left and a band of fallen fighters at her feet.

Alphonse scanned the massive canvas—three metres across and almost the same in height. Eugène Delacroix's *Liberty Leading the People*.

So beautiful. So much energy in its form. Such vitality in the golden light.

'Pity I have to destroy it,' Alphonse muttered. His right hand slipped inside his pocket. His fingers wrapped around a small remote control, and he pressed the button.

Sixty metres away, in the Mona Lisa gallery, five compact smoke flares detonated, breaking the museum silence like muffled fireworks.

Pop. Pop. Pop-pop-pop.

Then the alarms started. Great whooping sirens pierced the air. And all madness broke loose.

Alphonse took his eyes from the face of Liberty and glanced back towards the other gallery. Grey smoke billowed from the door. People stumbled through the haze, hands over their mouths, coughing and wheezing. The few tourists around Alphonse took one look at the mayhem and bolted for the far exit. Then what seemed like every security guard in the Louvre descended on the Mona Lisa gallery. They sprinted straight past Alphonse, boots clattering over the smooth parquetry.

Alphonse stood his ground. The sirens and screams wailed on. Within seconds he was alone, while all security focused on the priceless Mona Lisa. Again, Alphonse reached into the false belly beneath his coat. This time he pulled out two canisters, each about the size of a soft-drink can.

He popped the tab on one and rolled it across the floor towards the door on his left, then popped the other and sent it skittering to the exit on his right.

Both canisters sprang to life, spinning wildly and spraying a fine mist across the floor.

Alphonse observed his handiwork with a tight nod, then took hold of the bottom of the Delacroix painting. He lifted the ornate frame away from the wall and heaved. A shout came from the arched doorway. The truck-sized security guard was screaming at Alphonse in

French. Smoke poured from the man's pocket as if there was a clogged chimney in his pants. Alphonse barely glanced at him, then turned back to the painting. It was heavier than he had expected.

The security guard rushed into the gallery, still shouting. His foot hit the floorboards and the contents of the canister did its work. The man slammed onto his backside and skidded like a polar bear on a melting ice floe. He went to stand but his feet zipped out from under him. He scrambled onto his hands and knees, but that was as far as he could get.

Alphonse grinned. 'The Falcon comes prepared,' he said. The soles of his specially treated boots gripped firm on the slickened floor. He turned back to his task.

More security guards appeared in the doorway, flinging themselves into the gallery. They all ended up stranded on their backs with their legs waggling in the air like expiring cockroaches. Each time they tried to get up they fell, coating themselves in the lubricant from the canisters—slippery as soap in a sauna.

Alphonse knelt to gain better leverage and tugged again at the frame—this time the painting launched free from the wall. Like a giant kite, it caught the air and sailed out. Alphonse looked up at the inky underside of the canvas, seemingly floating in space.

Then it dropped.

The painting split over the top of Alphonse's skull with a shredding tear and came to rest on his shoulders, his head sticking through the hole. He blinked and looked down to find Liberty's bare breasts poking out in front of him, as if they had just sprouted from his shirt.

'Eep!' he cried.

The security guards sent reinforcements through the doorway like hockey pucks. They all fell short of the target and ended up on their backs. The gallery was fast resembling a turtle farm on prank night.

Alphonse rustled about in his fake belly. A ceramic blade pierced through Liberty's front and sliced another gash in the priceless canvas. Alphonse stepped through, stomping on the face of a dead revolutionary as he went.

'Sorry,' he muttered.

Another security guard sailed by.

Alphonse dropped to his knees and stabbed the blade into the painting, cutting out the messenger boy's satchel. He quickly rolled the thirty-centimetre-square piece of canvas into a cardboard tube and stowed it inside his coat.

He stood and looked back to the guards writhing on the floor. Their swearing was almost, but not quite, drowned out by the ongoing wail of the sirens. Alphonse waved them a cheery farewell and turned to the exit on his right.

There was a commotion from the opposite doorway. Two guards had a colleague by the hands and were about to launch him into the gallery.

Un. Deux. Trois!

The man soared into the room as if fired from a slingshot. He careered across the parquetry, his boots skating over the surface.

Alphonse set off, unconcerned, towards the other end of the gallery. The guard cannoned on, tucked up like a downhill skier. Then he reached for the taser on his belt.

Alphonse glanced back just as the guard fired the weapon. Twin electrodes spat from the barrel, as fast as a cobra's strike. They bit Alphonse square on his back pocket. Fifty thousand volts discharged straight into the box of 'strike anywhere' matches that Alphonse had stowed there.

The art thief's backside exploded in a ball of orange flames.

'EEP!' he cried and launched forward, yanking the Taser from the guard's grasp. His cries accompanied the clatter of the taser as it dragged behind him, still attached to the probes that were skewered into the seat of his burning trousers. His hands flailed, trying to beat out the fire that engulfed his buttocks. The taser bucked up and hit the floor hard, discharging another jolt down the wires. Alphonse soared into the air with a howl. He raced to the entrance and scrambled up the escalator, just as a platoon of ten armed gendarmes flew past him in the opposite direction.

The last of the police looked back at the shrieking man with the flaming trousers. He shouted a commanding

STOP! but Alphonse had already disappeared into the daylight. The gendarmes raced to the up escalator. But, by the time they reached the top, the Falcon had commandeered a passing motor scooter and was zipping away through the traffic.

Every few metres as he travelled along the Rue de Rivoli, Alphonse Poulet bobbed into view, smoke pouring from his pants and the taser blasting another jolt of electricity to launch him out of the saddle. His screams echoed through the winding laneways of the French capital well after the Parisian police had given up the chase.

Chapter 1

The convoy of luxury coaches rumbled off the narrow country road and passed beneath a weathered wooden archway. Automatic gates slid shut behind the last of them with the clanking finality of the delivery door at an abattoir.

Had it been summer and sunny and warm, the coach tyres might have kicked up a golden haze of dust across the words that were carved into the top span of the arch: *To strive, to seek, to find, and not to yield.* But as it was the dead of winter and it was Scotland, there was no sun and no warmth and no dust. There was just murk and drizzle and mud.

And cold.

Bone-shattering cold.

The five coaches continued along a winding tree-lined lane that finally opened out onto a broad driveway where they rolled to a stop in a chorus of hissing air brakes. The doors opened and the buses disgorged their passengers. Two hundred boys and girls stumbled out into the gloom, stretching their arms and rolling their shoulders, trying to ease out the cricks and folds of a long day on the road. Teachers staggered out after them, even more bent and creased than their students. They tried their best to get their charges into some version of order.

Sam Valentine paused at the bottom step of one bus and peered out at the dismal view that lay beyond. 'I don't like the look of this one bit,' he muttered. His head suddenly jerked backwards as he was shoved sharply between the shoulder blades and propelled out the door like a reluctant cannonball.

Ruby Valentine and Felicity Upham appeared in the bus doorway behind him, zipping up fleeces and yanking beanies over their ears. 'Don't be such a whinge pot,' Ruby said to her twin brother, rubbing her gloved hands together. 'This is going to be fun.'

Ruby and Felicity stepped down, straight into a pothole full of muddy water.

A moment later Gerald Wilkins tumbled out of the bus, wiping sleep from his eyes. His hair was a mop of neglect, and drool trailed from one corner of his mouth. He adjusted a sling that held his right arm and joined his friends at the side of the coach to collect his backpack.

Despite his arctic parka and cashmere scarf, the afternoon cold took Gerald's breath away. Even the youngest billionaire in the world could not arrange for much joy in a Scottish winter.

Somehow, the teachers from the St Cuthbert's School for boys and the St Hilda's School for girls managed to shepherd the milling mob of thirteen- and fourteen-year-olds inside a long wooden building and usher them towards a doorway at the far end.

Gerald fell into step beside Ruby just as Sam was getting wound up. 'All I'm saying is I thought going to a posh boarding school might involve a bit of luxury, that's all,' Sam said. 'Comfy beds and hot-and-cold-running servants. If I wanted to do hard labour in a highland jail I'd hold up the Bank of Scotland.'

Ruby prodded a finger into her brother's belly. It disappeared up to the second knuckle. 'You need to harden up,' she said. 'There's a few too many of Mrs Rutherford's sausage rolls packed in there. Ten weeks of camp food and outdoor activities might do you some favours.'

Sam gave a sullen grunt. The last thing he wanted was a diet of lukewarm baked beans and forest hikes.

They followed the sheep-trail of students into an enormous circular hall. A fire blazed in a large stone pit in the centre of the floor, embers shooting up to a conical chimney that hung like a brick stalactite from the ceiling. Sam unzipped his jacket and let the warmth wash over him. 'That's a bit better,' he said. He stared at the flames for a moment. 'I wouldn't mind some marshmallows, though.'

Teachers barked orders and pointed fingers. Finally, with everyone in the room and students wrangled into two concentric rings around the fire, a hush of anticipation fell over the assembly.

Into the midst of all this barely contained excitement strode a slight man. His sandy hair was cut short and was greying at the temples. His moustache was trimmed with military precision. He made his way through the seated students to the fire pit. He gripped a clipboard under one arm and held the other at his back, clamped in tight at the waistband as if he was worried his trousers were about to collapse around his ankles. The man cleared his throat and looked at the students over the top of his half-moon reading glasses.

Two hundred sets of eyes stared back at him. The only sound was the crackle of the fire.

The man cleared his throat again: a dry flinty rasp, as if from a crow suffering from asthma.

Ruby leaned in close and whispered in Gerald's ear, 'Who's this?'

Gerald nudged Ruby with his shoulder and gave her a look that unambiguously said *Shush!* Gerald knew only too well who the man was, and he had no desire to draw his attention.

But, like a guard dog raised on raw meat and

frequent beatings, the man sensed the movement. His head remained perfectly still but his eyes, twin spheres of fun detection, swivelled in their sockets and zeroed in on Gerald and Ruby. Gerald was sure he saw the man's nostrils flare.

For a third time, the man coughed. 'For those of you who do not know me,' he said in a tone of parade-ground clarity, 'I am Dr Crispin, headmaster at St Cuthbert's.' His eyes locked on Gerald's and remained there long enough to pass on the clear message: *Do not test me, boy.* To Gerald's enormous relief, the headmaster disengaged and turned a slow circle to eyeball the entire hall.

'Welcome to the young ladies of St Hilda's and the young gentlemen of St Cuthbert's to the annual Year Nine Highlands Retreat.'

Dr Crispin paused.

There was no response.

Finally, a teacher from St Hilda's started clapping and a ripple of applause swept the room.

Seemingly satisfied with that, Dr Crispin continued. 'This term in the Scottish highlands is the one time our two fine schools come together each year. It will be a great challenge for all of you, but also a tremendous educational experience. For the next ten weeks you will be tested in ways many of you will never have experienced before. For some the challenge will come in the form of a twenty-mile cross-country hike—'

Gerald felt Ruby shift by his side. He glanced around

to find her beaming at the prospect of a trek through the Scottish wilderness.

'—for others,' Dr Crispin continued, 'the challenge will exist in being cut off from the comforts of home: no television, no phone, no home-cooked meals or parents to serve you like little kings and queens.' There was a shuffling movement on Gerald's other side. Sam was staring at the floorboards, a look on his face as if someone had just cancelled Christmas.

'Whatever the challenge, you will emerge the better for it at the end,' Dr Crispin said. 'Miss Frobisher will now have a few words to you about discipline and—' Dr Crispin cleared his throat one more time, '—self-control.'

A tall woman crossed to the centre of the room. She was dressed in Burberry waterproofs, and Gerald thought she looked ready to embark on a twenty-mile hike there and then.

'Good afternoon, girls and boys,' she began brightly. 'I have the honour of serving as headmistress at St Hilda's, and I fully endorse Dr Crispin's comments. The term ahead will be the highlight of your time at school. Friendships will be forged that will last a lifetime. But a word of caution. We are all here together for the next ten weeks. Two hundred thirteen- and fourteen-year-old girls and boys living in close proximity, with less than the usual levels of supervision. It is a time of great excitement during a period in your lives when some of you are experiencing strong—' she searched for the right word, '—emotions. You must keep those emotions, and other urges, under control at all times.'

A light titter ran around the room.

Gerald leaned in to Ruby and whispered from the corner of his mouth. 'What's she talking about?'

Ruby whispered back, 'They don't want us snogging each other all term.'

Gerald's cheeks flushed red. It was at some stage during the next ten weeks that he planned on asking Ruby to be his girlfriend, with the expectation of a considerable amount of snogging to follow.

As the buzz from the assembly grew louder, Dr Crispin stepped forward. 'Quiet!' he snapped, his eyes burning. 'Just keep your blasted hands to yourselves.' The hall dropped into a dark silence. 'There is to be no hazing, teasing or bullying of any description,' Dr Crispin continued. 'Anyone who offends will answer to me.' He gave another look of total distrust to the students around him. 'Before you are allocated to your cabins, our new mathematics teacher, Mr Beare, has an announcement.'

Gerald looked with interest to where the headmaster was indicating. Since returning from Christmas holidays a week before, Gerald had found that a number of new teachers had been hired. Gerald was yet to meet his new maths teacher. A man stepped out from against the far wall and smiled. Where Miss Frobisher appeared ready to launch herself up Ben Nevis at a moment's notice,

Mr Beare looked like the effort of ordering a pint at his local pub would require a lie down and a damp cloth across the forehead. Broad of girth and multiple of chin, he appeared to be the outcome of a science experiment involving a middle-aged man and an excess of pork buns.

'Hello everyone,' he said, almost running out of breath from the effort. 'I will talk to you all in more detail about this later, but I want to let you know about a special event that will take place during the time we're all here at the Captain Oates Outdoor Education Centre.' He paused again, as much for effect as out of necessity, and took a deep breath. 'Every year at this camp the schools run the Triple Crown.'

A flutter of recognition sounded from some in the room.

'Some of you may have heard of it. It involves three challenges that follow the camp motto: *To strive, to seek, to find*. I'm told that in the one hundred years that St Cuthbert's and St Hilda's have been conducting these camps, no one has ever successfully completed the Triple Crown. To be the first would be an extraordinary honour. I encourage you all to participate and to participate with vigour.' Mr Beare ended with an exhausted wheeze and staggered back to his stool by the wall.

Dr Crispin waited for the buzz to die down. Ruby didn't say a word, but Gerald could almost feel the excitement radiating from her body.

'Remember,' the headmaster said, 'this term is the

opportunity of a lifetime. Do not squander it.' With that, he dismissed the students into the care of their teachers.

Gerald was happy to find that he and Sam would be sharing a cabin with four other boys. Gerald and Sam agreed to meet up with Felicity and Ruby at teatime in the dining hall and went to collect their packs. Gerald winced as he slung his bundle onto his shoulder. 'This busted collarbone is going to slow me down,' he said to Sam. 'Why don't you go ahead and grab us a bunk together?' Sam agreed and jogged off in search of their cabin.

Gerald adjusted the sling on his arm and followed after him. It was only five o'clock in the afternoon, but the Scottish night had dropped over the camp like a sodden blanket. Gerald stepped into the starless evening and shivered at the bite in the air. The pack dragged on his shoulder and he grimaced. The injury still hurt from his adventure a fortnight ago on the Swedish island of Ven when he had gone head-to-head with a mercury-addled madman who thought he was a 450-year-old Danish astronomer. Gerald shook his head at the memory. Since inheriting a fortune from his great aunt, his life had become somewhat complicated.

He shouldered his pack more evenly and trudged down the path. Excited boys rushed past him in search of their cabins. The girls were housed on the far side of the camp, supposedly beyond the range of 'strong emotions'. Soon Gerald found himself alone, hauling his pack into the night. Despite the cold and the twinges of pain, a smile spread across his face. Ahead of him was the prospect of ten whole weeks away from normal school, and away from his bizarre life. And the chance to spend a whole lot of time with Ruby Valentine…

Oh yes, indeed, on that count Dr Crispin was right. Gerald had no intention of squandering this opportunity.

The path ahead turned to the left, skirting a grove of trees. Gerald reached the bend, and suddenly everything went black. A bag was dragged over his head. Rough hands grabbed him by the collar. Before he could do or say a thing, the world's youngest billionaire was crash-tackled to the ground and bundled into the trees, swept from sight as if he had ceased to exist.

Chapter 2

White-hot pain flared in Gerald's right shoulder. It felt like a branding iron had seared into his flesh. His pack went flying as he was slammed onto the muddy ground, jolting his injured arm. Lights burst inside Gerald's eyes, a barrage of fireworks detonating in his brain. A knee crushed into his chest, squeezing out whatever air remained in his lungs.

Gerald tried to move but strong hands held him down. Another shunt on his shoulder and he howled in agony.

Then a voice sounded in Gerald's ear.

'Do not go out for the Triple Crown.'

The voice was haggard, short of breath.

'Do not go out for the Triple Crown or you're dead.'

Gerald's eyes popped open in surprise. In the dark he could barely make out the cloth that shrouded his face. Gerald had been terrorised before. But this voice in his ear, threatening his life, was truly astonishing.

It was a boy.

Gerald stopped struggling and lay back in the muck. The cold crept through his clothes like a million burrowing ice worms.

'D'you understand?' The voice demanded an answer. 'Do not try for the Triple Crown.'

Gerald nodded. But with his head inside a bag, his attacker could not see the response.

'Well?' The boy pushed harder against Gerald's shoulder.

Gerald cried out. 'Yes!' Then he swore, a broad Australian curse that would strip the paint from the back of a ute.

'Good,' the boy said.

Then the knee lifted from Gerald's chest and the hands released his shoulders.

Gerald sat up and pulled the bag from his head. It took him a moment to realise it was a pillowcase. He blinked to clear his vision and looked to a gap in the trees. But, in the smudgy darkness of a winter's evening, there was no sign of his attacker.

'Someone seriously blindfolded you with this?' Sam held up the pillowcase. It was still soiled with mud and rotting leaves from Gerald's roll in the mire.

'Yep,' Gerald said. 'I couldn't see a thing.' The clatter of knives and forks on plates rang around the cavernous dining hall where Gerald, Sam, Felicity and Ruby, along with the rest of the year nine students of St Cuthbert's and St Hilda's, were eating their evening meals.

'But it's got Hello Kitty all over it,' Sam said. He screwed up his face. 'Who threatens somebody with a Hello Kitty pillowcase? It's not natural.'

Felicity nibbled on a carrot stick and frowned at Gerald. 'And you're not going to tell a teacher about this?' she said. 'This is just the type of bullying that Dr Crispin was talking about. You could have rebroken your collarbone, or worse. Don't you agree, Ruby?'

Ruby held a forkful of macaroni cheese in front of her mouth and shrugged. 'In my experience, getting Gerald to do anything sensible is like trying to teach a monkey to read or a crocodile to see reason. It doesn't matter how much you tell him to do the smart thing, he'll just go ahead and do the boy thing. It's genetic—it's what they do. Besides, as if anyone would actually kill him just for taking part in some school camp challenge.'

'That's ridiculous,' Felicity said. 'He was attacked. He was threatened. He was—'

'Blindfolded with a Hello Kitty pillowcase,' Sam said, interrupting. 'Do you really think Gerald wants everyone to know that he's frightened of someone who attacked him with a brushed-cotton pussycat?'

Felicity regarded Sam blankly. 'You are kidding, aren't you? He won't report it because it will somehow make him look like a bit of a wuss?'

'Actually,' Sam said, shoving a spoon-load of peas into his mouth, 'it would make him look a colossal wuss. A prize princess. He may as well dress in a lilac tutu with matching tiara for the next ten weeks.'

Felicity looked to Ruby in exasperation, but Ruby just laughed. 'It's simple mathematics, Flicka,' Ruby said. 'Boy equals stupid.'

Felicity turned her frustration back onto Gerald. He held up both his hands, as if defending a punch. 'What do you want me to do?' he asked. 'I have no idea who attacked me. I didn't see a thing.'

Sam leaned over and patted Gerald on the arm. 'Is that because the nasty pussy cat had his ickle wickle paws over your eyes?'

Felicity gave him a filthy glare. 'You are not helping,' she said.

Sam shrugged and took another mouthful of peas. 'I'm just giving him a taste of what to expect if he tells a teacher about this. He won't be able to move for all the purring and the meowing.'

Gerald cracked a smile. If he was honest with himself, his shoulder did not hurt that much from his wrestle in the woods. The greater injury was to his pride. Besides, he was quite enjoying being the subject of some pity. Not that Ruby was doing quite as much pitying as Gerald would have liked.

'I didn't even recognise the voice,' Gerald said. 'All I can say for certain is that it was a boy.' He thought for a moment. 'Or a really strong girl with a head cold.'

Ruby swallowed her macaroni cheese and gazed around the room of diners. 'So who among this lot would be so desperate to win the Triple Crown that they'd threaten your life?' she asked.

'Apart from you, you mean?' Gerald said.

Ruby gave him a 'Who, me?' look.

'Don't try to pretend,' Gerald said. 'I saw you when Mr Beare was talking about the Triple Crown. You were ready to kick down the door. You're not exactly hard to read, you know.'

Ruby's cheeks blossomed pink. 'Maybe I might like to be the first to complete it,' she said. 'Maybe not. But I do know one thing, Gerald Wilkins.' Ruby opened her blue eyes wide and leaned in close to Gerald.

Gerald's heartbeat ratcheted up a notch. 'And what's that?' he said.

'I'm not going to be beaten by some sooky boy wearing a Hello Kitty head-dress.' Ruby flashed her fingernails and murmured, 'Meow…'

Fortunately, Gerald's response was drowned out by Sam and Felicity's laughter.

Gerald adjusted his sling and stifled a wince at a

twinge in his shoulder. He looked around the dining hall at the other campers, clustered on benches at long wooden tables, scoffing their way through their first meal together. Someone in that crowd had tackled him to the ground, covered his head in indignity and made some stupid threat about—what?—a school camp scavenger hunt? Gerald shook his head. After all he had been through over the past eight months, the stakes could not possibly be any lower.

After dinner, the students split into groups of twenty for some get-to-know-you activities. Gerald was more than happy that he and Ruby were in the same group as they and eighteen others gathered in a cosy room lined floor-to-ceiling with bookcases. All the tables and chairs had been pushed back and everyone formed a circle on a colourful Indian rug on the floor.

A slender woman, her black hair cut in the style of a 1920s flapper, sat in the middle of the circle and smiled at the students.

'For those who don't know me, I am Miss Davenport,' she said. 'I have been a teacher at St Hilda's for five years.'

A boy sitting opposite Gerald piped up. 'What do you teach?'

Miss Davenport arched an eyebrow and peered across at the boy. 'I teach young girls how to become young ladies, part of which involves teaching them not to interrupt people.'

The boy wriggled in his place. 'But what if I don't want to be a young lady?' he said, winking at his friend next to him.

Miss Davenport arched her other eyebrow. 'And who might you be?' she asked the boy.

'I'm Charlie Blagden,' he said, grinning.

'Well, Charlie Blagden,' Miss Davenport said, 'if you agree not to interrupt me, I'll agree not to turn you into a young lady. Surgically, or otherwise.'

Charlie's grin faded a touch, but he nodded nonetheless.

'Excellent,' Miss Davenport continued. 'The next ten weeks will bring a lifetime of memories. The people in this room will be your camp group for the term. We'll take classes together and do extra-curricular activities together. Now is the chance to get to know a little bit about each other. I'd like each of you to introduce yourselves to the group. Tell us who you are, one interesting thing about you and what you want to achieve in life.' She clapped her hands together and pointed to a blond boy sitting across from Gerald. 'You can start.'

Gerald had only been at St Cuthbert's for a single term so he was yet to meet everyone in his year level. But he knew the boy well enough by reputation alone.

'I'm Alex,' the boy said, casting his eyes around the circle. 'Alex Baranov. But I expect a few of you from St Hilda's know that already.' A knot of girls sitting near Ruby started to giggle. Alex smiled at them. 'An interesting thing about me? Well, my family owns a few oilfields in Siberia so I guess you could say we're pretty well off. In fact,'—he looked straight at Ruby and winked—'we're *really* well off. Put it this way, my father's a member of the Billionaires' Club and they don't invite you to join that place just because you're good looking.' He paused for a moment to comb his fingers through his hair. 'Though, as luck would have it...' The girls next to Ruby giggled again. Alex tilted his head their way. 'When I leave St Custard's I want to be just like my father: good looking and stupendously wealthy.'

He sat back with a satisfied grin.

Ruby leaned close to Gerald's ear and whispered, 'Ten whole weeks?'

Gerald smothered a smirk.

'Thank you, Alex,' Miss Davenport said. 'That was very...revealing. Now, Ruby, you're new to Hilda's this term. Let's hear from you.'

Ruby propped onto her knees and clasped her hands in her lap. 'Hello everyone,' she said. 'My name is Ruby Valentine and I've only been at St Hilda's for a week. I was at school in London before, but I'm really enjoying my time so far. I love gymnastics and I'm going to try everything I can to be the first person to achieve the Triple Crown—whatever it is we're supposed to do.'

'That's terrific, Ruby,' Miss Davenport said. 'And what do you want to achieve after you leave school'— she cast a glance at Alex—'other than being rich and good looking.'

Alex chucked his chin towards Ruby. 'She's halfway there already,' he said. The girls next to Ruby sniggered.

Ruby blushed deeply and stared at the rug in front of her knees. 'I'm not sure what I want to achieve just yet,' she said, 'but whatever it is, it will be something I do through my own efforts, not something that's been handed to me by someone else.'

Gerald looked across to Alex. The smug grin had frozen on the boy's face like a death mask. His eyes never left Ruby. 'That's a bit rich,' Alex said at last, 'coming from someone whose boyfriend inherited everything that he's worth.'

A crisp silence settled on the room, like a frost over an apple orchard. Miss Davenport narrowed her eyes on Alex Baranov and was about to rebuke him when Ruby spoke up. 'Three things,' she said, directing her gaze straight at Baranov. The boy cocked his chin and returned the icy glare. 'First,' Ruby said, 'Gerald is not my boyfriend, though he is possibly my best friend. Second, he is worth more than any sum of money that even someone as shallow as you could possibly dream of. And third, shut your stupid face.'

The group burst into hysterics, with most of the girls loudly applauding Ruby. Alex Baranov's cheeks burned red, making his ice-blue eyes glow even brighter.

Gerald sat silently as the catcalls and jeers rained around him.

His insides were aglow. He was *possibly* Ruby's best friend? How good was that! He managed to blithely overlook the ease with which Ruby had dispatched the boyfriend question. That was a minor detail, a mere speed bump in the highway of his plans to ask her to be his girlfriend.

'You're *that* Ruby Valentine?' The voice broke through the hubbub. A boy sitting opposite Ruby was studying her face intently. Gerald recognised him from his French class: Kobe Abraham.

'You were in the newspapers over the Christmas break,' the boy said, his eyes growing wider. 'Did someone really try to cut out your heart?'

The room could not have gone more quiet had a penguin walked in and asked for directions to the sauna.

Every eye was fixed on Ruby. Even Miss Davenport, who appeared to be a stickler for maintaining control in the classroom, was reeled in by Kobe's question.

Ruby cleared her throat with a tight cough. 'I may have had a run in with someone...' she began.

'It was in a torture chamber under a farm on an island off Sweden,' Kobe said, his gaze intensifying. 'That's right, isn't it?'

Ruby raised her eyes to look at the boy. 'You must have read a lot of newspapers on the holidays,' she said.

Kobe nodded eagerly. 'I like to stay up to date,' he said. 'The man who attacked you wanted to use your heart in a potion that could cure all known diseases, right?'

Ruby's eyes returned to the rug.

One of the girls who had been giggling at Alex chirped up. 'What's the matter? Couldn't he find it?' Her friend emitted a sharp snort. 'Or is it because your heart already belongs to Gerald Wilkins?' The two girls collapsed in laughter again.

Miss Davenport found her voice. 'That is enough Millicent. You and Gretchen, control yourselves.'

The girls smiled sweetly. 'Yes, Miss Davenport,' they chorused.

The get-to-know-you session dragged on for an hour, during which the campers got to know about Kobe's obsession with current events ('If you're not in the know, you're in the nowhere.'), Millicent's fascination with fashion ('Those hiking boots are so last season.'), and Charlie's desire to open the batting for the English cricket team ('I'll run, but I'll never walk!').

Finally, it was Gerald's turn.

After an hour of sitting cross-legged on the rug, he unhooked his feet and stretched out, accidently kicking Ruby. 'Sorry,' he said, patting Ruby on the knee. This prompted a barrage of smooching noises from Millicent and Gretchen.

'Thank you, ladies. That will do,' Miss Davenport said. She looked at Gerald. 'Please, go on.'

Gerald gave a curt nod. 'My name is Gerald Wilkins,'

he said, 'and I'm—'

'The richest kid in the world!' Kobe could not restrain himself. He was bouncing with excitement. 'He inherited twenty billion pounds from his great aunt who was killed on the orders of Sir Mason Green, not that Green was ever convicted because he faked his own death right in the witness box at the Old Bailey and escaped, but then Gerald caught him again in Greece and he was locked up in jail, but he escaped again and was involved in the kidnapping of a whole bunch of people from the British Museum and the theft of some ancient document that once belonged to an old European emperor and supposedly had the recipe for a cure-all medicine that required someone to rip out Ruby's heart, but she got away by stabbing a guy in the head with his own nose!' Kobe paused to take a breath. He looked at Gerald with wide eyes. 'Did I miss anything?'

Gerald chewed his bottom lip for a moment. 'You forgot the Indian death cult and the woman with the poison blowgun, but apart from that I think you pretty much got it all.' He looked at Miss Davenport. 'Is that enough?'

'Is all that true?' she asked, her eyes bulging in their sockets.

Gerald shrugged. 'Yeah,' he said. 'I guess it is.'

'Of course it is,' Kobe said. 'See? That's why you've gotta read the papers. To stay informed.'

Then another voice chimed in.

'So how is your friend from the museum? The professor who went missing. Have you heard from him?'

Gerald looked across to Alex Baranov, who was eyeing him intently. In one term and one week at St Cuthbert's, that might have been the first time Alex Baranov had spoken to him.

'He's still missing,' Gerald said through thin lips. 'The police are looking for him and the other people from the museum.'

Alex wrinkled his nose. 'You must feel terrible,' he said. 'You know, the way you're the reason he went missing.'

Gerald muttered under his breath, 'Ten whole weeks.'

Miss Davenport, clearly glad the session had come to an end, wished everyone a good night and ushered them towards their cabins. Gerald was making his way to the door, mumbling to Ruby about what a jerk Alex Baranov appeared to be, when he was grabbed by the shoulder. He shouted a loud 'Ow!' and swung around to find Millicent and Gretchen scowling at him.

'Where did you get that?' Millicent demanded. She was pointing to the mud-smeared pillowcase that Gerald still had tucked into his sling. He had completely forgotten he was carrying it around.

'This is yours?' he asked, pulling out the pillowslip.

Millicent snatched the grubby cloth from Gerald's fingers and flipped it inside out to reveal a nametag sewn into the lining: *Millicent Corfield*. 'Have you been snooping around in our cabin? 'Coz if you have, it takes just one word to Miss Davenport and you are on the first bus home.'

Ruby slid in front of Gerald like a shield before a knight. The tip of her nose was just millimetres from Millicent's face. 'It was given to him by a coward who was too afraid to show his face,' Ruby said. 'Now, does that sound like anyone you might know?'

Millicent's jaw tightened but she said nothing.

'Besides,' Ruby continued, 'I would hate to be the girl who ran to teacher on the first night of camp just because her precious Hello Kitty pillowcase got some dirt on it. You know, especially because all the stress threatened to bring on her chronic bedwetting problem. That would be a terrible thing to live with. For ten weeks.'

Millicent's eyes shot wide. 'I don't have a bedwetting problem!' she said, her face glowing red. A few heads turned their way and Millicent dropped her voice to a thick whisper. 'That's a complete lie!'

Ruby gave an idle shrug. 'Maybe. But you know how these stories get around.' She gave Millicent and Gretchen a look of disdain. 'See you for breakfast, ladies.'

Ruby turned on her heel and strode out the door, leaving Gerald behind. He looked first to Millicent and then to Gretchen, aware of the death stares they were directing his way. 'Um, it's probably best not to get on Ruby's bad side,' he said with a nervous chuckle. 'She can be a little…stubborn.' He nodded towards the pillowcase in Millicent's hand. 'Have a good sleep,' he said, then, as an afterthought, 'Meow.'

Gerald turned tail and bolted out the door to catch up with Ruby.

Chapter 3

When Gerald finally managed to drop off to sleep, he dreamed a giant, insanely grinning kitten was attacking him. He sat upright with a gasp, almost waking Sam in the bunk beneath him.

Gerald rolled onto his back and moved his right elbow across his belly to the only position where the pain in his shoulder would ease. He stared at the ceiling and sighed. The cabin contained three sets of bunks. The buzz of five sleeping boys seemed to make the air vibrate. Gerald was sharing with Charlie Blagden and Kobe Abraham from the get-to-know-you session, as well as Nic Lloyd and Giles Spofforth, who both played in Gerald's school rugby team, and Sam. It was a good cabin to be in. Certainly better than having to share with

Alex Baranov and his cronies, Gerald thought.

'Little blond twerp,' Gerald mouthed into the darkness. His cheeks burned at how rude Alex had been to Ruby. And as for him saying that it was Gerald's fault that Professor McElderry was still missing, well that was absurd. It was hardly Gerald's fault that Mason Green had ordered the professor's kidnapping. Besides, what could Gerald do about it? Just because everyone he got close to seemed to end up on the receiving end of Mason Green's wrath wasn't Gerald's doing. At least, Gerald frowned into the darkness, not *entirely* his doing.

A movement at the window caught his eye. He rolled his head to get a better look.

Snow.

Gerald kicked his legs from his sleeping bag and dropped silently to the ground. He stepped across to the window in his thick woollen socks and peered outside.

The air was alive with snowflakes, white wintry fluff dancing across a blackened stage. Gerald stared at the scene with wonder. The ground was carpeted. Tree branches stripped bare of leaves cradled thick clumps of snow in their arms. It was a postcard.

Perfect.

The setting was just what Gerald wanted for his grand plan to ask Ruby to be his girlfriend.

He had it all figured. It would be on a night just like this one. As the other students made their way to the various after-dinner activities that the teachers had prepared for them, Gerald would take Ruby by the arm and hold her back until they were alone. It would be snowing and a few flakes would settle on the tip of Ruby's nose. He would brush them away, then say some special words (still to be determined—possibly a limerick) and give her a gift with a ribbon tied around it. Ruby would be overjoyed by the gesture and would agree to the whole girlfriend arrangement on the spot. Then it would be a warm embrace and kisses and she would gaze at him in wonder and hug him again and squeeze his hand and laugh and everything would be a blur of pulse-thumping perfection.

Too easy.

Dr Crispin would *hate* it.

And Gerald had already bought the perfect gift: a brand new copy of *Zombie Viscera Quest V* for X-Box. And if Ruby didn't like it, Gerald could always play it. Win–win.

Now all Gerald had to do was go through with the plan.

Breakfast the next morning was a rowdy affair as two hundred hungry and excited students crammed the dining hall. The clatter of cutlery on crockery echoed in the rafters.

Gerald and Sam eased onto a bench seat and put their

plates, piled with bacon, fried mushrooms, tomatoes and eggs, on the long wooden table. Felicity emerged from the kitchen and wandered over to join them with a small bowl of porridge and a fruit salad.

Sam looked at Felicity's breakfast and wrinkled his nose. 'Have they run out of food already?' he asked.

Felicity stabbed a piece of kiwi fruit with her fork and popped it in her mouth. She peered at the mound of bacon that was congealing on Sam's plate in a shimmering swamp of fat and gristle. 'One can only hope, Sam, that your life will be as rich and full as your arteries are going to be,' she said.

Sam stuffed a rasher of bacon into his mouth. 'You're funny,' he said through his mouthful.

Felicity blanched and looked away. 'That is terribly sick-making.'

Gerald upended a tomato sauce bottle over his plate, drowning its contents in thick red goop. 'Where's Ruby?' he asked. He was excited about his plan and already had a good line on a limerick. Another day of drafting and it should be ready for the big event.

Felicity bit into a strawberry and looked back towards the kitchen. 'She was only a few behind me in the queue. She can't be far away.'

Gerald spotted her across the hall in her St Hilda's maroon and navy tracksuit with her blonde hair pulled into a ponytail. She was talking to a boy who had his back to them. Then Gerald realised who it was.

'Why is Ruby talking to Alex Baranov?' Gerald asked.

And more importantly, Gerald thought, why is she smiling?

Felicity shifted along the bench to make space for Ruby as she joined them. 'Good morning everybody,' Ruby said, cradling a bowl of honey-drizzled porridge in one hand and a mug of tea in the other. 'It's so beautiful outside. All that snow last night—'

'What did Baranov want?' Gerald asked, cutting her off mid-sentence.

Ruby looked at Gerald with surprise. 'And good morning to you too, Ruby,' she said in her best teacher's voice.

'Huh?'

'I said, 'good morning'. It is polite to respond in kind.'

Gerald looked at her blankly. His excitement of a few moments before had evaporated. 'Uh, good morning,' he mumbled.

'Better,' Ruby said. 'As for Alex—'

'Oh, so you're best friends with him now, are you?'

Ruby took a long sip of tea then fixed Gerald with a penetrating stare. 'Maybe not best friends,' she said. 'But friendly, anyway.'

'What's happened? Last night you sounded like you wanted to break his legs,' Gerald said. 'And that went double for his buddies, Millicent and Gretchen.'

Ruby dipped a spoon into her porridge and blew across the bowl. 'Oh, don't worry about Millie and Bletchen,' she said. 'I'm still gunning for them. That stupid Hello Kitty creature and her friend can sleep uneasy knowing that.'

'What about Baranov?' Gerald said. 'He was well out of order with what he said about Professor McElderry. And about you. How come you're all smiley-smiley with him today?'

Ruby put down her spoon. 'Because Alex had the decency to come up to me this morning and apologise for his behaviour last night,' she said. 'He was sorry that he'd got off on the wrong foot with me and wanted to start over. I may have misjudged him.'

Gerald choked on his bacon. 'Misjudge Alex Baranov! You can misjudge a basketball shot or a golf swing, or even Sam's ability to think about anything other than food, but you can not misjudge people like Alex Baranov. It is just not possible. What you see is what you get and what you get is one hundred per cent jerk.'

'And you made up your mind on that from one interaction last night?' Ruby said.

Gerald simmered. 'I've met his type before.'

Felicity leaned over and bopped Gerald on the point of his nose with her finger. 'I do believe you are jealous,' she said.

The fork slipped from Gerald's fingers and clattered to the tabletop. 'Jealous?' he said, with a little too much force. 'Me? That's ridiculous.'

Felicity flicked a long plait over her shoulder and arched an eyebrow at Gerald. 'Oh, come off it,' she said. 'You don't seriously think we've forgotten about the Christmas Eve snog you two had at the chalet in California? If those bandits hadn't attacked we would have had to throw a bucket of water over you.'

This time it was Ruby's turn to glow red and sputter out a protest. 'Snogging? Gerald? Who saw what now?'

Felicity returned to her breakfast. 'Oh yes,' she said. 'There's nothing going on here.'

Gerald struggled to think of something to say. He panicked, turned to Ruby and blurted out, 'There once was a girl named Valentine...'

Ruby looked at him as if he had gone insane. 'What are you going on about?'

Gerald opened his mouth but what came out sounded like a gagging goldfish. He was saved by Kobe Abraham, who wandered past and dropped an envelope onto the table in front of Gerald, narrowly missing the lake of tomato sauce on his plate.

'Mail call,' Kobe said. 'Someone thinks you're worth writing to.'

Ruby nodded at the copy of the *Economist* that Kobe had tucked under his arm. 'Keeping up with world events, Kobe?'

Kobe flashed her a smile. 'You're either in the loop or in the soup,' he said with a finger to the side of his nose.

'I thought Rice Crispies said there was no contact with the outside world while we're at camp,' Sam said.

Kobe peeled the wrapper from his magazine. 'It also pays to have sources in the right places,' he said. 'And it looks like Gerald is one who does.' He brandished another envelope. 'And he's not the only one, as it happens.'

Ruby tilted her head to the side. 'Who else?'

Kobe tapped his nose again. 'Ah, that would be telling, toots. Cheerio.' He turned and wandered deeper into the dining hall.

Ruby and Felicity looked at each other. 'Toots!' they chorused, and fell into giggles. 'He's a strange one,' Ruby said.

Sam grunted. 'You think he's strange, you should meet nearly everyone else at St Custard's. The place is overflowing with strange.'

'Better than overflowing with custard,' Ruby said, watching Kobe as he weaved among the grid of tables.

'Who's Rice Crispies?' Felicity said.

Gerald wedged a mushroom into his cheek. 'That's Dr Crispin's nickname,' he said. 'Don't let him hear you using it though.'

'Well, there's an interesting thing,' Ruby said, still gazing across the hall.

'What's that?' Felicity asked.

'Kobe just delivered the other letter.'

'And?'

Ruby turned back to the three others at the table.

'To Alex Baranov.'

Gerald spat out a moist *pffft*. 'Probably the latest issue of *Rich and Good Looking* magazine.'

Felicity patted Gerald on the arm. 'Don't worry. I'm sure Ruby will be able to resist his charms.'

'Felicity!' Ruby glared at her friend.

'What?' Felicity said. She looked across to Alex Baranov's table. 'He is quite cute.'

'Oh for goodness sake,' Ruby said, then she turned to Gerald. 'What's so vitally important that you get a letter in the mail?'

Gerald studied the business-sized envelope. It was addressed to his house in Chelsea in London and had been forwarded to St Cuthbert's. He recognised his mother's handwriting on the front: *URGENT. Must be sent to school camp in Scotland OR ELSE!*

The envelope was made with a thick linen paper with an embossed *B* on the flap. Gerald ran a finger under the seal.

'Oh, it's from the Billionaires' Club,' he said, holding up a single sheet of paper. He looked up to be met by three blank stares. 'You remember,' he said. 'The club that Jasper Mantle and Tycho Brahe wanted me to join.'

'You mean the butterfly collector and the certifiable lunatic who tried to slice the still-beating heart from my chest for a chemistry experiment?' Ruby said. 'Yes, I vaguely remember them.'

Felicity took a sip of tea. 'It's in New York, isn't it?'

Gerald scanned the letter. 'It says that the initiation for membership to the Billionaires' Club will be held during the mid-term break.'

'How are you going to manage that?' Ruby asked. 'We're supposed to spend the break here.'

Gerald's eyes lit up. 'It says that Mr Mantle has arranged with Dr Crispin for me to take time off for a long weekend in New York City!'

He looked up to Sam's disbelieving face. 'You get to spend a long weekend in some six star hotel in New York—with room service and a comfy bed—while we're stuck here freezing our buns off in some godforsaken place that if it's not the end of the world you can at least see if from here?'

Gerald leaned over, plucked a rasher of bacon from Sam's plate and took a bite. 'There's got to be some benefits to being a billionaire,' he said.

Chapter 4

The Captain Oates Outdoor Education Centre bristled with anticipation as two hundred students gathered in the reception hall. Burning logs crackled in the fire pit, providing some relief from the bitter cold that clawed at the windows like an impatient house cat demanding to be let in.

Dr Crispin stood with his back to the flames and held his hands up for silence. 'Tomorrow you will embark on the first stage of the Triple Crown.' He stared at the assembled faces like a lion scanning the savannah for lunch. 'I have no doubt that by the end of the day there will be tears and not a little heartbreak. That is how it should be. These three tasks are about pushing yourselves to the limit. I like to think of them in alignment with my life philosophy: If it's not hurting, it's not working.'

Sitting with his back against a wall, Sam whispered to Gerald, 'Is this supposed to inspire us?'

Gerald shook his head and stared back at the St Cuthbert's headmaster as he droned on about personal mission statements and key performance indicators. He gave the distinct impression of a general saying farewell to his troops as they prepared for battle, before he popped back to headquarters for a snifter of brandy and a three-course meal.

Dr Crispin swivelled his head towards Sam and Gerald. His nose twitched, as if picking up a scent. 'I expect at least a third of you to fail,' he said in a tone redolent of dawn runs and ice baths. 'The remaining two tasks will sort the rest of you out.'

If there had been any enthusiasm left in the room at that point it was sucked up the chimney with the smoke.

Gerald looked over to Ruby and Felicity sitting with a group of St Hilda's girls. They all seemed appalled at what they had just heard. Ruby glanced up and caught Gerald's eye. Her expression said, 'Is this guy for real?'

Gerald raised his eyebrows, as if to say, 'Sadly, yes.'

The headmaster snapped his fingers like a rifle shot, and looked to where Mr Beare was sitting in a chair. 'If you please, Mr Beare.'

The maths teacher lifted himself up and crossed to the centre of the room. He ran a hand over his chins and smiled at the upturned faces before him. He pulled a large envelope from his jacket and held it above his head.

'I have here the instructions for the first leg of the Triple Crown.' He paused for a moment. 'Shall I read them?'

Enthusiasm bubbled back into the room. 'Yes!'

Mr Beare made a dramatic event of ripping open the envelope and removing a sheet of paper. 'In a moment you will sort yourselves into teams of four: two members from St Cuthbert's and two from St Hilda's. These will be your teams for all the Triple Crown challenges, so choose wisely.'

A buzz spread around the students. Gerald and Sam turned and pointed at each other.

'Team?' Sam asked.

'Team,' Gerald replied.

Gerald looked up to where Felicity and Ruby were sitting and was surprised to see Alex Baranov deep in conversation with Ruby.

Gerald did not have a good feeling about this.

Mr Beare called for quiet. 'You will have time to assemble your teams shortly. First, let us find out about tomorrow morning's task.'

A hush descended on the hall.

Mr Beare unfolded the sheet of paper and read. 'Starting at 8am, groups will depart at five-minute intervals on an overnight hike. Each team will be given a map, a compass and coordinates for a checkpoint. At the checkpoint you will find an ink stamp that you must apply to your map to prove that you made it there. You will camp overnight and hike back in the morning. As the night descends quite early this far north, some of the teams may have to camp overnight before arriving at the checkpoint.'

Sam and Gerald looked at each other. 'Seems simple enough,' Sam said.

'There is one complication,' Mr Beare said, raising his voice to be heard over the excited rumble that filled the hall. The noise died down, and heads turned his way. 'The maps you will be given are not entirely accurate. All of the compasses have been adjusted to be at least five degrees off, and the checkpoint is twenty miles away.'

Gerald and Sam looked at each other again. 'Twenty miles, a dodgy map and a next-to-useless compass counts as one complication, does it?' Sam said. 'Is he having a joke?'

Mr Beare raised his hands for calm. 'The more mathematically minded students will have already calculated that a five degree discrepancy over a twenty mile hike will have you about two miles adrift of your target for the checkpoint. So we have included in your kitbags, together with food and a four-man tent, a series of clues to help you. Now do not forget to stamp your map, because you will need the checkpoint symbol for the second challenge of the Triple Crown.'

Mr Beare checked his watch. 'Right, you have ten minutes to form your teams. Anyone not in a team of four by then will be disqualified. Go!'

Two hundred boys and girls leapt to their feet and scrambled in all directions. It was as if someone had thrown a cat into a chicken coop. Sam grabbed Gerald by the elbow and dragged him towards where Ruby and Felicity had been sitting.

'Ow!' Gerald protested. 'Easy on the arm pulling.'

In the mad jostling of bodies Gerald lost sight of Ruby. He finally spotted Felicity, who was up on her tiptoes and waving her arms above her head at them. Gerald and Sam pushed past a cluster of girls who were negotiating with Kobe and Charlie about pack-carrying duties.

'Where's Ruby?' Sam asked, searching for her face among the crowd. 'I thought she was with you.'

'She was,' Felicity said. 'But she got waylaid.'

'Waylaid?' Gerald said. 'By what?'

Felicity nodded towards a group of bodies. 'Not by what,' she said. 'By whom.'

Gerald looked to where Felicity had gestured and saw Ruby talking with Alex Baranov. He pressed his lips together and pushed his way towards them.

'Ruby?' Gerald said, making a point of shouldering his way between her and Alex. 'What's going on?'

Ruby blinked up at him and her voice caught in her throat. 'Oh, Alex was just asking me something,' she said, somehow avoiding looking Gerald in the eye.

'Asking you what?' Gerald said.

Alex Baranov fixed Gerald with an electric stare. 'I've asked Ruby to join my team for the Triple Crown, Wilkins. I was just telling her that my friend Owen is an orienteering champion. He can read a map and compass better than anyone I know. This first challenge will be a doddle for my team.'

Gerald's mouth fell open. 'Join your team? You're too late. Ruby's on my team.'

Ruby pulled her shoulders back and jutted out her chin. 'I don't believe I've agreed to be on anyone's team yet,' she said. 'Alex had the good manners to actually ask me.'

'What's that got to do with anything?' Gerald said. 'Obviously you're on my team.'

Ruby straightened even further. 'You've made that decision for me, have you?'

Gerald realised he might have gone a step too far. 'No,' he said, 'I would never do that.'

'Because you know how much that would annoy me, don't you,' Ruby said, narrowing her eyes.

'Yes, of course,' Gerald said, backpedalling as fast as he could manage. 'I never meant to annoy you.'

Mr Beare's voice cut through the hubbub in the hall, 'Two minutes, everyone!'

A calculating smile settled on Ruby's lips. She looked first to Alex, then to Gerald.

'If I was to join your team,' she said, 'what would the team motto be?'

'Our what?' Gerald said.

'Our motto. Our slogan,' Ruby said. 'What would be the guiding principle that defined our team?'

Alex puffed out his chest. 'Simple,' he said. 'It would be the same as the Baranov family crest: *Victoria Super Omnia*: Victory above All.'

Ruby considered this for a second. 'Strong,' she said. 'I like it.' She turned to Gerald. 'What do you have for me?'

Gerald started to perspire. 'Uh, I don't know. I'd have to ask Sam and Felicity.'

'One minute!' Mr Beare called.

Ruby raised an eyebrow. 'You better hurry,' she said.

Gerald's forehead was awash. If he couldn't convince Ruby there would be no time to find another teammate: he, Sam and Felicity would be disqualified and out of the Triple Crown.

'Uh—*Ruby Is Always Right*,' Gerald said in a rush.

Ruby pricked up her ears. 'Say that again,' she said.

Gerald blinked. 'Ruby Is Always Right.'

'Hmmm,' Ruby said. 'I like the sound of that.' She pondered for a moment,

'Thirty seconds!' Mr Beare called.

Again, Ruby looked from Gerald to Alex. 'All right,' she said. 'I choose…Gerald's team.'

Gerald pumped his one good fist just as Mr Beare called time.

Ruby put a hand on Alex's forearm. 'I'm sorry, Alex,'

she said. 'Does that mean you don't have a full team?'

Alex did not look at her, but stared daggers at Gerald. 'Oh no. Owen and I paired up with Millicent and Gretchen days ago.'

Ruby looked confused. 'Then why did you ask me to join?' she asked.

Alex grinned. 'I was going to punt Gretchen if you said yes. And I figured if you did join us that would leave Wilkins one person short and then he'd be out of the challenge. I guess Gretchen owes you a favour.' He gave Ruby a wink. 'Shame—you could have been a winner.' Alex turned his back, walked over to Owen, Millicent and Gretchen, and threw his arms around their shoulders.

Ruby grinned up at Gerald. 'That was a bit of fun,' she said brightly. 'I reckon our team will go really well.'

'What was that all about?' Gerald demanded.

'Now, what's the team motto?'

'Don't you—'

'Team motto?' Ruby repeated.

Gerald groaned. 'Ruby is always right,' he said.

A broad smile spread across Ruby's face. 'It's music to my ears,' she said.

Chapter 5

Felicity sat slumped on her backpack and checked her watch for what seemed the hundredth time that day. 'This is taking forever,' she grumbled.

Sam lounged on the ground beside her, his legs splayed in front of him. He wore a beanie on his head and a bored expression on his face. 'Why did Mr Beare make us the last team out?' he asked.

'Because we were the last ones to form a team,' Gerald said. He was leaning against a doorway overlooking the empty car park. He sent a pebble skittering across the driveway. 'I wonder whose fault that was.'

Ruby sidled up to Gerald and tossed him an apple. 'Quit griping,' she said. 'People might think you're not having a good time.'

Gerald caught the apple in his good hand and took a bite. 'Being the last of fifty teams is hardly an advantage, is it?' he said. 'We'll only have a few hours of light before we have to make our camp.'

'So what?' Ruby said. 'We'll have a nice night around a campfire, sing some songs and make it to the checkpoint in the morning. It's no big deal.'

Gerald kicked at another stone. 'I've heard your singing,' he said. 'All I'm saying is—'

'No, no,' Ruby said. 'Team motto?'

Gerald, Felicity and Sam sounded a laboured chorus of, 'Ruby is always right.'

Ruby grinned from ear to ear. 'That never gets old.'

Mr Beare popped his head around the doorframe. 'All right you lot,' he said. 'You can head off now. Best of luck.'

Felicity raised herself from her pack and took Sam's hand, pulling him to his feet. 'Let's go before my legs seize up entirely,' she said.

The four of them hoisted their packs to their shoulders and trudged across to the tree-lined lane that led to the road.

The day was grey and still, with clouds sinking into the surrounding hilltops.

'So, how long is this going to take?' Sam asked.

'Probably six or seven hours, depending on how flat it is,' Ruby said. 'By the look of this map, we have to cross a fair amount of open country.'

Sam adjusted his pack on his shoulders. 'Try to avoid the hilly bits then.'

They reached the wooden arch that spanned the front gate and Gerald looked up at the words carved into the top span. 'To strive, to seek, to find, and not to yield,' he read out loud. 'Seems a pretty good motto.'

Ruby clicked her tongue. 'Not as good as ours,' she said. 'But I suppose it might work for some people. Now, according to the map we should head north up the road for a mile or so then north-west across a field.'

'How will we know when we've gone far enough?' Felicity said. 'I don't fancy walking any further than we have to.'

Ruby nudged Sam with her elbow. 'Do you have those clues from Mr Beare?'

Sam dug in his pocket and unfolded a sheet of paper. 'Let's see,' he said. 'The dead centre of town.' He looked up, confused. 'There's a town near here? I thought we were in the middle of nowhere.'

Ruby looked at the map. 'Strange,' she said. 'There's no town marked.'

Gerald crossed the road. 'We'll just have to see what we find,' he said. For a while he walked along lost in thought. His brain buzzed about his friend, Professor McElderry. Alex Baranov had managed to get under Gerald's skin about that, and Gerald could not dodge the feeling that maybe, in some small way, he was responsible for the professor's disappearance.

Gerald looked up as Ruby fell into step alongside him. 'So,' he said. 'Your mate, Alex Baranov.'

Ruby thrust her thumbs under the shoulder straps of her pack. 'Yeah? What about him?'

'Do you reckon he might be the Hello Kitty bandit?'

Ruby laughed. 'What makes you think that?'

'Twice now I could have been knocked out of the Triple Crown,' Gerald said. 'Baranov tried to poach you for his team and that would have left me high, dry and disqualified from the challenge.'

'And?'

'And the Hello Kitty attack on the first night. Whoever did that was determined that I not even sign on for the Triple Crown.'

'But why would you think Alex was responsible for that?' Ruby asked.

'He seems pretty tight with Millicent. He could have taken the pillowcase from her pack, easy.'

Ruby thought for a moment. 'Not everything is about you, Gerald. Why would Alex want to knock you out of some school camp challenge? It's not like there's much at stake.'

Gerald trudged on, his brow furrowed. He caught a glimpse of Ruby's face from the corner of his eye. As far as he was concerned, there was a lot at stake.

Three short pips of a car horn sounded from behind. They stood to the side of the road as a dirty green Land Rover slowed next to them. The passenger-side window wound down to reveal Mr Beare at the wheel. 'Have fun,' he called. 'I hope I'll see you at the checkpoint tomorrow.'

Sam gave him a cheeky grin. 'Any chance of a lift then, sir?'

Mr Beare laughed and drove off.

'Come on,' Ruby said. 'It can't be much further till we go cross country.'

Felicity looked ahead—all they could see were flat fields with a ribbon of low stone wall snaking along either side of the road. 'It doesn't look like there's any town up ahead,' she said. 'Are you sure we're going the right way?'

Ruby walked on. 'This is the only way,' she said.

'This doesn't feel right,' Sam said. 'No trees, no buildings, no sign of civilisation at all. We should have seen something by now.'

Ruby spun around and snapped at him. 'If you're such a geographic genius, you have a go then.' She shoved the map and compass into Sam's hands. 'Let's see how you go.'

'Keep your teeth in,' Sam said. 'I just meant this first clue doesn't seem to be helping us.'

Gerald put a hand on Ruby's shoulder. 'Look, there's a big pile of rocks in that field. Maybe we'll see something from the top of it.' He sat on the low stone wall, flipped his legs onto the far side and led the way across the meadow.

The rocks were piled neatly to form a rounded pyramid about twelve metres across and four metres high.

Sam ran up behind Gerald, starting the inevitable race to see who could get to the top first. Gerald shrugged his pack from his shoulders and scrambled up the rocks, with Sam matching him step for step.

They both claimed victory at the top.

'I win!' Sam said.

'In your dreams,' Gerald said, catching his breath.

Felicity called up to them. 'Can you see anything?'

'No,' Sam called back. 'Just more of the same: open countryside and some trees on a hill way over that way.'

'There's no town, that's for sure,' Gerald said. 'What should we do?' He looked down to Ruby, who was standing near the base of the rocks. 'Ruby?'

She was on her haunches, holding up a square sheet of metal. 'I'm just reading about this rock pile of yours,' she said. 'This sign must have fallen over. You do realise it's a cairn, don't you?'

Gerald and Sam looked at each other and shrugged. 'What? Like a tin can?' Sam said.

'No, you idiot,' Ruby said. 'A cairn. It's a pile of rocks—'

'No kidding,' Sam said, then turned to Gerald. 'And she calls me an idiot.'

'— used by Scottish highlanders as a burial marker,' Ruby continued. 'You're standing on somebody's grave.'

Sam was halfway down the side before Gerald could move.

'What's the matter with you?' Gerald asked when he reached Sam back at the bottom.

Sam blinked at him. 'Zombies,' he said.

'Are you serious?' Gerald said. 'Look, people can not come back from the dead. They—' He stopped, and turned to Ruby. 'The dead? Do you suppose this is the dead centre of town?'

Ruby snatched the map back from Sam. 'That has to be it,' she said. 'Which means the checkpoint should be on the far side of that hill with the trees on top. I say we head there.'

Felicity turned to pick up her pack and found Sam standing behind her, looking pale and nervous. 'Are you quite all right?' she asked.

Sam's eyes remained fixed on the cairn. 'As long as you stay between me and that, then yes, I'm all right.'

Felicity smiled in pity, then threw her head forward with a sudden, 'BOO!'

Sam fell flat on his backside in the mud as if clocked on the chin by a prize fighter.

Felicity laughed. 'Come on, hero,' she said, helping Sam to his feet. 'Before you wake the dead.'

Ruby folded the map and put it in her pocket. 'What's the next clue?' she asked.

Sam gave Felicity an injured look, then consulted the note. 'Where the sun no longer shines.'

'That could be anywhere around here,' Gerald said. 'It's not exactly Bondi Beach on a summer's day, is it?'

They set off across the field, Ruby and Sam in front, Gerald and Felicity following them. The afternoon sky had darkened to a slate grey, and a penetrating wind sliced across the stunted heather. A winter numbness set in as the group of hikers made its way through marshy lowlands and across the occasional stream.

Gerald was deep in thought, watching his boots slosh, slosh, slosh across the boggy ground, when he looked up and was surprised to find that he and Felicity had fallen a good fifty metres behind Ruby and Sam.

'You're being very quiet,' Felicity said. 'You're not still plotting revenge for Hello Kitty?'

Gerald stifled a half laugh. 'No, I'm just worried about Professor McElderry,' he said. 'To be honest, I've also been thinking about something else.' Gerald had a sudden thought. 'Can I ask your advice?'

Felicity smiled. 'Of course.'

'It's like this,' Gerald began. 'I want to ask Ruby to—you know—be my girlfriend. And I want to recite a poem when I do it.'

Felicity arched an eyebrow. 'Good idea,' she said.

'The only thing is,' Gerald continued, 'I'm finding it hard to come up with the right words. And the rhymes are killing me.'

Felicity thought for a moment. 'All right. What rhymes with Ruby?'

'Um…booby?' Gerald said.

Felicity failed to hold in her laughter. 'Somehow, I don't think she'd appreciate that.'

'I didn't think so,' Gerald said. 'And finding a rhyme for Valentine is even worse.'

'Why? What have you got?'

'Frankenstein.'

'Maybe poetry isn't such a great idea after all.'

They both looked up at the sound of Sam shouting to them.

'Come see this!' he called. He was standing at the top of the hill. Felicity and Gerald scrambled up the sharp rise and ran along a line of wind-beaten trees whose roots clung to the rocks with their last reserve of life.

They found Ruby studying the map. She pointed to a valley in the distance. 'If I'm reading this correctly, that is Hell's Glen. We have to go through there to get to the checkpoint. I'd say it's another ten miles.'

'Hell's Glen?' Sam said. 'That doesn't sound very welcoming.'

'Take a look at the valley,' Felicity said. 'I'd say that's a place where the sun doesn't shine.'

Ruby scanned the horizon. 'We better get moving,' she said. 'Those clouds look like snow. We'll need to find somewhere sheltered to put up the tent.'

Sam suddenly squeaked. Ruby turned to her brother; his face had gone as drab as the landscape around them.

'What's the matter?' Ruby asked.

Sam's eyelids peeled back to the point where his eyeballs looked like they were about to be ejected from his head. He wrestled his pack to the ground and tore open the top.

'What is it?' Felicity asked as Sam ripped out a flurry of shirts and socks. He stared down into the belly of the pack then up to his three friends.

'The tent,' he managed to say. 'I've forgotten the tent.'

A band of crows scattered from the trees around them as Ruby informed her brother, in abbreviated terms, of her exact feelings regarding his revelation about the tent. The caws and cries of the fleeing birds spread across the countryside.

Ruby scooped up her pack, threw another disgusted look at her brother and set off into the valley. Gerald stumbled after her. 'What are we going to do if we don't have a tent?' he asked.

'We'll have to find a barn or a tree to sleep under,' she said, muttering more furious thoughts under her breath.

'Don't be too hard on Sam,' Gerald said. 'I've got the tent poles in my pack. That's something,' he said.

Ruby grunted. 'True enough,' she said. 'At least I'll have something to beat him with.'

Gerald swallowed. He wasn't sure that Ruby was entirely joking. And then, just to ensure Ruby's mood could sink no lower, it started to snow.

Heavily.

Chapter 6

Snow flew into their faces in thick, unrelenting bursts. The wind whipped across the frozen ground as if running late for a funeral.

Padded parkas and gloves held out some of the cold, but the line of four hikers cut a forlorn path across the open countryside as they trudged towards the wooded glen below them.

Gerald's teeth chattered staccato as he wiped the slush from his face. His head was down and his eyes were trained on the back of Sam's pack bobbing along in front of him. Felicity followed behind Gerald, and Ruby brought up the rear. No one had said anything, but it seemed to be decided naturally that keeping Sam and Ruby as far apart from each other as possible was probably a good idea.

A shiver ran down Gerald's spine. He glanced past Sam's head. The trees leading into the dark valley seemed no closer, and the day's light was fast expiring. He reached out and tugged on Sam's pack. 'We need to figure out what we're doing tonight,' Gerald said. 'We can't just keep walking in the dark.'

'Hey, I've got an idea,' Ruby said, drilling a glare in her brother's direction. 'Let's set up the tent and get nice and cosy warm inside.'

Sam stared at the ground. 'I said I was sorry,' he mumbled.

'And yet that brings us precisely no closer to finding shelter for the night,' Ruby said.

'And neither does all your complaining,' Felicity snapped. 'How about you give it a rest?' Ruby's lips froze shut. 'I'm cold, I'm tired and I'm hungry,' Felicity said. 'We've got about ten minutes of light left and I've had it with both you Valentines.' She turned to Gerald. 'I can't imagine what you see in her.'

The wind whipped down from the hilltop, flapping the hood on Gerald's jacket about his ears. He couldn't see the expression on Ruby's face, but he had the feeling it was not all warmth and sunshine.

'Let's get down into the valley,' Gerald said. 'Maybe we can find some shelter there.'

There was no debate. There was no other choice.

This time Gerald took the lead. He agreed with Felicity. Sam and Ruby could tear each other apart—all he wanted was to get out of the cold.

As they descended into the valley the snowfall intensified. Gerald stared into the dying day.

His heart sank.

Beyond a line of stumpy trees, for as far as he could see, there was heather and bracken beaten down by the Scottish winter into a brown carpet that was fast disappearing under a smothering of white.

His shoulders dropped. He turned back to Ruby and Felicity.

'Anything?' Ruby asked.

Gerald shook his head. 'We could try to build something under those trees but they're so stunted. They don't offer much cover.' A pit opened up in his stomach. People died of exposure on nights like this.

'Or we could try that house down there,' Sam said as he joined them.

'What house?' Gerald said.

'The one down there,' Sam said, pointing into the gloom.

Gerald, Ruby and Felicity strained their eyes into the near darkness as the blizzard swirled around them.

'I can't see a thing,' Ruby said. 'Are you sure?'

'Of course,' Sam said. 'What's the matter with you?'

'Apart from my terminal lack of a tent?'

Gerald grabbed Sam by the arm before another domestic dust-up broke out. 'Take us there, will you? You and Ruby can yell at each other later.'

Sam shrugged agreement and led the way down a snow-covered slope. Gerald could barely see. He felt a hand fall on his shoulder and realised Ruby had grabbed hold so she wouldn't get lost in the murk. He hoped Felicity was doing the same to Ruby. He reached out and took Sam's shoulder and, like a line of baby elephants walking trunks to tails, they cut a path through the bleak night.

Before long, Sam stopped. Gerald walked right into the back of him. Ruby and Felicity stumbled into Gerald. It was a four-body pileup.

'Why did you stop?' Gerald asked, pulling his face free from where it had buried itself in Sam's pack.

'Because we're here,' Sam said. 'Why else would we stop?'

Gerald looked up and could just make out the outline of a two-storey stone building against the night sky.

'How did you even see this place?' Felicity said. 'You're amazing.' An inch of snow had settled on her head and shoulders.

'You can erect a statue to him after we get inside,' Ruby said through chattering teeth.

'The front door must be round here,' Sam said. He led the way up three steps to the shelter of a covered porch. Gerald dumped his pack onto the stone paving. 'We could always climb into our sleeping bags right here,' he said. 'At least it's out of the snow and wind.'

Ruby tossed her pack next to Gerald's. 'I have

marshmallows,' she said. 'And I won't be happy until I'm toasting one over an open fire. Let's get inside.'

The last of the day's light disappeared, sinking them into abject darkness.

'I can't see a thing,' Gerald said. 'It's like swimming in ink. Ow!'

'What is it?' Ruby's voice came through the dark.

'I banged my shin on something.' Gerald held his glove to his nose and could barely make out his fingers. 'This is ridiculous.' He scrabbled about and his hands found a large iron ring. 'I think I've found the door!' he called out. He tugged on the handle. 'Locked.' Gerald muttered an oath under his breath.

'There must be a window we could try,' Felicity said.

'Ow!' Gerald howled again.

'Now what?' Ruby asked.

'Shin,' Gerald said. 'Something.' He held his hands out in front and inched along. 'Glass! I think I've found a window.'

'Told you,' said Felicity.

'It's locked,' Gerald said. 'Should we break it?'

'Of course!' Ruby said. 'We could freeze to death out here.'

'What can I break it with?' Gerald asked.

There was the sound of someone rustling around in their pack. Then Sam said, 'Here, use this.' Gerald waved his hand around until he felt a heavy cylinder fall into his palm, like a relay baton.

'Thanks,' Gerald said. 'This feels solid enough to do some damage.' He gripped the tube like a hammer and tapped it against the glass to get his bearings. 'What is it?'

Sam's voice came from the blackness. 'My torch.'

There was a long silence.

'Your torch?' Ruby said.

'That's right,' Sam said.

'You idiot.'

Gerald fumbled for a moment. Then a beam of light pierced the night, enough for everyone to see Sam looking sheepishly back at them. 'Whoops,' he said.

Gerald shook his head and turned back to the window. A sharp tap with the metal torch smashed a hole large enough for him to reach in and unlock the sash. A minute later all four of them were inside.

Felicity and Sam ventured down a long hall while Gerald and Ruby gathered the backpacks in the spacious entryway.

'Nice job,' Ruby said.

Gerald nodded a thanks, and then he saw it: a snowflake on the tip of Ruby's nose.

The moment had arrived.

Gerald reached out his gloved hand and brushed the snowflake clear.

'Oh,' said Ruby in surprise. Her eyes smiled at him. A sudden warmth glowed in Gerald's chest.

Limerick time.

He cleared his throat.

'There once was a girl named Ruby…'

A quizzical expression formed on Ruby's face. Before Gerald could say anything more, Sam rushed up to them. 'Come and see what we've found!' He grabbed Ruby by the hand and dragged her. 'It might even stop you whinging. And hating me.' Gerald watched as the Valentine twins scampered down the hallway. He sighed and trudged after them.

'This must be a hunting lodge, closed for the winter,' Sam said as he led the way down the wood-panelled corridor. 'Ruby, I think you're going to like this.'

They burst through a doorway into a roomy lounge and came to an abrupt stop. A huge smile spread across Ruby's face. 'Oh, this is perfect,' she said.

A massive stone fireplace in the far wall was set with kindling and chopped wood. The panelled walls were hung with mounted stag heads and stuffed trout. A brown leather chesterfield, complete with tartan rugs, sat in front of the hearth like a tired uncle after too much Christmas lunch.

Ruby looked at Sam. 'You are almost forgiven,' she said. 'Almost.'

Within minutes, a fire crackled in the grate and Ruby and Felicity sat, legs outstretched on the hearthrug, poking marshmallows onto long toasting forks. Their boots were kicked to the corners and their wriggling toes defrosted in the glow of the flames. Outside, the wind howled like a lovesick wolf.

'I wouldn't fancy camping in a tent on a night like this,' Sam said from a plush armchair. His face was suffused with utter contentment. 'Lucky I found this place, isn't it?' He paused for a moment as the girls turned the marshmallows on their forks. 'Imagine all those sorry sods between here and the checkpoint, freezing in their tents. Who'd want to be in a tent tonight, eh?'

There was a long silence, broken only by the crackling of the fire.

'Tents—' Sam continued.

'All right!' Ruby said. 'You've made your point. Well done. Congratulations. Leaving that tent behind was an act of genius. What do you want? A medal?'

Sam leaned back in his chair, his hands clamped around the back of his head, exuding smugness.

Felicity popped a toasted marshmallow into her mouth. 'This is so good,' she said. 'Do you want one, Gerald?'

Gerald knelt at a coffee table where he had set up their camp stove. A pot of baked beans was just beginning to bubble. 'Yes please,' he said, stirring the brownish goop with a wooden spoon. 'There might be no electricity but we've got candles and beans. What more could you want?'

Ruby tossed a toasted marshmallow to Sam and prodded another onto her fork. 'Do you know what this reminds me of?' she said. 'That night in the caretaker's cottage at Mt Archer in California. All of us bunking down in front of a fire while a blizzard raged outside.'

Gerald scooped a spoonful of beans onto a plate. 'At least this time we're not on the run from a bunch of gun-toting kidnappers,' he said.

Ruby laughed. 'That was Christmas Eve,' she said. 'That was a fun night.'

'It was,' Felicity said, 'Right up to the moment when the bandits attacked.'

Gerald felt the warmth spread through his chest again. That was also the night that he and Ruby had somehow ended up in each other's arms when the lights went out. He took a plate of beans across to Ruby and sat beside her.

'Thanks,' Ruby said, smiling at him.

Gerald cleared his throat.

The time was right.

'There once was a girl named Ruby—' he began.

Ruby looked mildly concerned. 'What are you doing?' she asked.

Then the door to the lounge room exploded open, the force almost knocking it from its hinges. Ruby dropped her plate and cried out.

Standing in the doorway was a tall, silver-haired man with a gun in his hand.

Gerald recognised him in an instant.

'Good evening to you all,' said Sir Mason Green.

Chapter 7

The fire smouldered in the grate, sending fingers of smoke twisting up the chimney to the frigid night outside.

There was no such easy escape for Gerald, Sam, Ruby and Felicity. The four of them stood in a tight huddle on the hearthrug.

Sir Mason Green held the pistol in a steady hand. He was a desperate man on the run from the law, wanted on two continents for murder, forced into a life of skulking in shadows. Then why, Gerald wondered, did Mason Green look like he had spent the past month lazing by a tropical lagoon? He was positively aglow.

'You—uh—look well,' Gerald said, not sure of the etiquette for coming face-to-face with someone who had tried to kill you on half a dozen occasions.

Mason Green stepped into the room and leaned with theatrical flourish on his walking cane. 'Do you know something, Gerald? I *feel* well. I've shed a few pounds, I go swimming every day, and I take an evening walk to soak up the last of the sunshine. I can't remember the last time I felt so alive. And I have you to thank for it, my boy.'

Gerald did not try to hide his displeasure at hearing this news. 'Me?' he said. 'What did I do?'

Green waved towards the couch. Gerald, Ruby, Felicity and Sam looked at each other uncertainly, then squeezed onto the chesterfield.

Green smiled down at them, creasing his suntanned face. 'You freed me, Gerald,' he said. 'Freed me from the daily grind of the city, of pursuing riches as a pastime. For that, I thank you.'

Ruby glared at Green through narrowed eyes. 'Aren't you meant to be hiding from the police?' she said.

Sir Mason settled in an armchair opposite them. 'That is what I find so invigorating, Miss Valentine. There is nothing better to sharpen your wits than keeping a step ahead of Constable Plod. It's quite liberating, in every sense of the word.' Green placed his gun on a table by his elbow and clasped his fingers over the handle of his walking cane. 'And, I believe, I owe you an apology.'

Ruby shifted in her seat and eyed the man cautiously. 'What for?' she asked.

'The rather unfortunate behaviour of my former associate, Tycho Brahe. I do hope you are all right. Such a frightful experience.'

Ruby moved her gaze to the fire and said nothing.

Gerald stared at Green. The flames painted the man's silver hair with a strawberry tinge. 'You haven't come all this way to say sorry to Ruby,' he said.

'You are surprised to see me, then?' Green said. 'That is tremendous news. That means Inspector Parrott and his colleagues from the Met are highly unlikely to come sniffing around here. I have found that the best place to hide is where people least expect to find you.'

'But your tan,' Ruby said. 'Taking a daily swim— that doesn't sound like a winter in Scotland.' Then, after a second's thought, 'It doesn't even sound like a summer in Scotland.'

Green's mouth curled into a smirk. 'Believe me, Miss Valentine, I am merely in Scotland for a visit.'

Gerald's eyes flicked to the gun by Green's side. 'What do you want?' he asked. 'And where is Professor McElderry?'

'You Australians,' Green said with a sweep of his hand. 'Always to the point. I have certainly not risked coming all the way here simply for a pleasant reunion with friends.'

'We're not friends,' Gerald said flatly.

'And this really isn't pleasant,' Ruby added.

Green stood up and crossed to the woodpile by the

fireplace. He rolled a fresh log into the flames. Sparks leapt up the chimney. 'You'll begin to make me feel unwelcome,' he said. 'And we have so much to talk about.' He returned to his chair and eased himself into the cushions. 'Such as how you managed to break into my apartment in San Francisco and destroy an historic relic.'

Gerald, Ruby, Felicity and Sam sucked in a collective breath.

'I may be on the run from the law, but I'm not completely clueless,' Green continued. All the warmth leeched from his eyes. 'You lied your way into my apartment and smashed a bottle. I understand that Miss Upham was the one responsible.' He fixed Felicity with a rapier stare.

Felicity gasped.

'How did I know your name and the circumstances behind your act of vandalism?' Green did not pause for a response. 'I'll leave you to ponder that in the spare moments you have while completing a task for me—a task that you are in no position to refuse.' He laid a casual hand across the pistol at his side, stroking it as if it was a spoiled cat.

Gerald clenched his teeth and forced out the question, 'What do you want?'

Green smiled. 'There was a message hidden inside that bottle. I believe you have it.'

Gerald shifted in his seat. 'Is that all you want? It's

in my sketchbook back at the outdoor centre. Take it. It's no use to me.'

Green locked his eyes on Gerald's. 'But you do have a use for it, Gerald. The message is written in code, if you recall. A message from Jeremy Davey.'

Gerald's mind flashed back to the message that had been hidden inside the old bottle. It was scratched in faded ink on the back of a page torn from the Voynich manuscript. 'It was just a bunch of random letters,' he said.

Green's eyes grew dark. 'Then I suggest you figure out how to render them less random,' he said. 'Solve that code and tell me what the message is.'

Gerald lifted his chin in defiance. But before he could say anything, Green continued. 'Don't start with the tired *What if we refuse?* gambit. If you refuse then someone dies. It's as simple as that.'

Green turned his head towards the lounge-room door and called out, 'You may enter now.'

The sound of shuffling feet came from the hall. Then a figure appeared in the doorway. The red beard was straggly and the eyes were dull, but there was no mistaking the shambling presence of Professor Knox McElderry.

Gerald jumped from the couch and took a step towards the professor. In one fluid movement, Sir Mason Green leapt from his chair, unsheathed a sword from his walking stick and had the tip at McElderry's throat.

'Slow down, Gerald,' Green said. 'That is, unless you want to witness something quite distasteful.'

Gerald froze. He looked in despair at the professor. The old man's clothes were crumpled and his hair was unbrushed. His shoulders were slumped and his head tipped to the side like a cow perplexed by something that had wandered into the paddock. The professor's expression, normally so animated and engaged, was blank. Sedated.

'Professor McElderry?' Gerald said. 'Are you all right?'

The professor did not respond. His eyes drifted to a window in the far wall, as if looking for a visitor who was long past due.

'Professor?' Gerald repeated. He turned to Green. 'What's the matter with him?'

Green moved the point of his sword towards Gerald and gestured to the couch. Gerald reluctantly resumed his seat. 'The Voynich manuscript that you so kindly tracked down for me on the island of Ven is throwing up all manner of interesting secrets,' Green said. 'I can see why Emperor Rudolph II was so keen to get his hands on it.'

'What's that got to do with the professor?' Sam asked. 'He looks like he's only half here.'

McElderry stood awkwardly in the doorway, like a scarecrow that had faced one too many tornados. A look of smug success washed across Green's face. 'The Voynich isn't so much an ancient manuscript as a cookbook for the ages—for the Middle Ages anyway,' he said. 'The professor and his colleagues from the British Museum have been helping to unlock its mysteries.'

'But I thought the manuscript only had the recipe for the universal remedy,' Ruby said. 'At least, that's what Brahe was using it for.' Her voice trailed off.

Green lowered his sword and leaned on it with both hands. 'Yes, our friend Tycho was fixated on prolonging his days on earth. He failed to see that it's not the number of days you have, but what you pack into them. He missed the vast wealth of wonder that the Voynich contains. Just look at what one recipe has produced.' He waved a hand towards Professor McElderry. 'Observe,' Green said. 'Food!' he barked at McElderry.

'Haggis!' the professor barked back, his head lolling across to the other shoulder.

'Drink!' Green called out.

'Whisky!' the professor bellowed, as if last drinks had been called at his local pub. 'Single malt!'

Ruby bristled. 'What are you doing?' she cried at Green. 'Don't be awful!'

Sir Mason raised an eyebrow and chuckled. 'Oh, Miss Valentine, do not despair. The concoction of rare tropical plants and crushed insects that I have fed him merely makes him susceptible to suggestion. It's a nice warming bowl of hypnosis soup. Imagine if I mass produced it and sold it tinned in supermarkets. I could rule the world.'

'What do you mean?' Gerald said. 'The professor will do anything you tell him?'

'Precisely,' Green said. 'And if you fail to solve that coded message, I will tell him to do something most unfortunate.'

Gerald wanted to stop himself from asking the question. He knew nothing good could come of it. But the words forced their way out.

'Like what?'

Green stared at Gerald for a moment then picked up the pistol from the table by the armchair. He took McElderry's wrist and placed the gun in his hand.

'Professor,' Green began, 'I want you to shoot yourself. In the head, please.'

'No!' Gerald yelled. Sam jumped to his feet, but Green whipped the sword to the boy's face. 'Be still,' Green said in a chill whisper. He turned back to McElderry. 'Now.'

Gerald watched in dumb horror as the professor lifted the pistol to his temple. His forefinger tightened on the trigger.

McElderry's eyes registered nothing as the hammer fell with a dull metallic *clack*.

Gerald was almost sick on the rug.

Green retrieved the pistol and lowered the professor's hand to his side. 'Naturally the gun was not loaded,' Green said as he slid it into his jacket. 'But I think you have an idea now of what will happen if you do not solve that code for me.'

Felicity buried her face in Ruby's neck and sobbed.

'And you can imagine what will happen if you tell anyone about my being here,' Green continued. 'You do not want the consequences on your conscience, I can assure you. And Gerald?'

Gerald glared up at the man with barely controlled rage. 'What?'

'I understand someone tried to convince you to quit the Triple Crown challenge.'

Gerald's stomach tightened. 'How could you possibly know about that?' he asked.

One corner of Green's mouth turned up into a sickly smile. 'You must remember, I have eyes everywhere. There is nothing you can say or do that will not find its way back to me. You must continue with the challenge and for the sake of your friend's life, you will complete it. What's more—'

The pounding of a fist on the front door cut him off. The sound was followed a moment later by a man's voice. 'Gerald Wilkins! Sam Valentine! Are you in there?'

Green scowled in the flickering light. He raised the tip of his sword to Gerald's throat. 'Not a word about me,' he hissed through clenched teeth.

Green took hold of the professor's elbow and dragged him into the hallway, through a side door and out into the snow-strewn night.

Chapter 8

The front door banged open and a howl of wind blasted inside. Heavy footsteps thudded down the corridor, and a burly figure lumbered into the lounge.

'Mr Beare!' Gerald said. The St Cuthbert's maths teacher was the last person he had expected to see. 'What are you doing here?'

Mr Beare smiled cheerily. 'Well, hello,' he said, brushing snow from his shoulders. 'You've set yourselves up nicely, I must say.' He strode to the fireplace, tugging his gloves off with his teeth. 'Far better than all the miserable sods under canvas tonight, that's for sure. I've just been doing the rounds to make sure everyone is all right. That snow is really coming down out there. You'll be happy to know all your classmates are accounted for, though none of them have fires and marshmallows and soft beds like you.'

Mr Beare turned around to the four faces staring up at him. Felicity was sobbing quietly.

'What's the matter with her?' Mr Beare asked. 'You lot have the least to be sad about.'

Ruby glared at him. 'Ghosts,' she said flatly. 'We've been telling scary stories. One of them upset Felicity.'

Mr Beare looked at Felicity as if she was about to detonate. 'I'm not used to dealing with girls,' he said. 'Things tend to be a bit more straightforward with chaps. Right, Gerald?' Mr Beare clapped him on the shoulder, triggering a sharp cry of pain.

Mr Beare's eyes shot wide and he took a pace backwards. 'Everyone's on a short fuse tonight. Just to let you know, the time limit for the first leg of the Triple Crown has been extended because of the snow. You can have another crack at it next weekend if you like.' He looked at Felicity with mild concern. 'Um, I might hop back in the Land Rover and bunk down at Oates. I'll leave you lot to your ghost stories. Good night.' He plucked a marshmallow from the packet and popped it in his mouth then made his way back up the hall.

Ruby helped Felicity to the couch and sat with an arm around her shoulders. Gerald and Sam looked at each other, then at the girls.

Nobody spoke.

There was nothing to say.

It was a grim breakfast of leftover baked beans.

Gerald poked his spoon around his plate with no real appetite, shifting beans from one pile to another.

'The professor looked so miserable,' he said.

'Wouldn't you?' Ruby said. 'Stuck in some hypnotic fog and made to perform like a trained seal by that horrible man.'

'Well, that horrible man has given us something to do,' Gerald said. He dropped his plate onto the table. 'I say we hike back to Oates and start on that coded message.'

'What about the checkpoint and the Triple Crown?' Felicity said. 'Green made it very clear that you need to complete that as well.'

'He doesn't ask for much, does he?' Sam said. 'How are we supposed to do both?'

'We'll try for the checkpoint next weekend,' Gerald said. 'I get the feeling this code is going to take some time to solve.'

The blizzard had eased overnight, and they tramped four hours through snow-covered fields back to Oates.

The dining hall was only half full when they arrived just in time for lunch. Ruby watched with distaste as Sam demolished his second serving of shepherd's pie.

'How was it?' she asked.

Sam shoved the final forkful into his mouth. 'Could

have used a bit less shepherd,' he said. He wiped the back of his hand across his lips. 'So, what do you think, Gerald? Can we solve this thing, or should I get some pudding to keep me going?'

Gerald cleared some space in the lunchtime debris on the table and unfolded a sheet of paper.

Another group of hikers arrived in the hall, full of stories of snow and tents and wandering lost in the dark. Gerald, Sam, Ruby and Felicity ignored them, concentrating on the note in front of them. The paper was creased and grubby from being unfolded and refolded so many times, but the letters were still quite clear:

Xers blu c axtb pxfbi pab cilbnixg hxracib jl snbeebg xis rjiocuibs cp pj pab sbkpao eqp hy rjiorcbirb co cgg xp nbop c xh lclpy hcgbo ib jl rqgkbkkbn cogxis c sj ijp fijv cl c sbobntb nborqb oj c nbgy ji pab dqsuhbip jl pab jib vaj lciso paco hbooxub hxy yjqn ojqg eb nxcobs ji eqppbnlgy vciuo.

Midshipman Jeremy Davey, October 1835. May God have mercy on his humble servant's soul.

Sam took in a long breath. 'Well, that makes no sense at all.' He pushed his chair back. 'Anyone fancy some dessert? They've got hot chocolate pudding and custard.'

Ruby did not look up from scribbling in a notebook. 'Sam, is it possible for you to forget about food for just five minutes? This is important.' She tapped the end of a pencil against her teeth and looked up to her brother. 'Actually, that does sound pretty good. I'll have one.'

'Me too,' said Gerald.

Felicity said a polite, 'No thank you,' and Sam wandered off to the kitchen. Felicity nodded at the coded message. 'Where do we even start in trying to solve that?'

Ruby consulted her pad again. 'Our mum and dad used to leave coded messages in our school lunches,' she said. '*Ruby, work hard and be the best you can be. Sam, don't be such a colossal arse your entire life.* That type of thing.'

Gerald grinned. 'How did you go about solving them?'

Ruby held up her pad for Gerald and Felicity to see. On it she had drawn a rough grid:

A	B	C	D	E	F	G	H	I	J	K	L	M	N	O	P	Q	R	S	T	U	V	W	X	Y	Z

'They were simple substitution ciphers,' she said. 'They had to be if Sam was ever going to solve them. You just replace one letter for another. So A might become B, B becomes C, C becomes D and so on.'

Gerald grunted. 'So all we have to do is substitute the right letters using the grid and it solves itself.'

'That's the theory,' Ruby said. 'But every combination I've tried has gone nowhere.'

Sam arrived back at the table with a tray of steaming pudding bowls. He glanced at Ruby's notepad as he handed around the plates. 'That looks like the notes mum and dad used to put in our lunches,' he said. '*Sam, today is the first day of the rest of your life. Ruby, try not to be such an insufferable know-it-all.'*

Ruby ignored him. 'Sometimes, to make it more challenging, mum would use a keyword. Those ones were really tough.'

'How did that work?' Felicity asked.

Ruby scribbled into the grid in her pad. 'Say the keyword was RUBY. You fill in the first squares with those letters, then complete it in alphabetical order, so it looks like this.'

A	B	C	D	E	F	G	H	I	J	K	L	M	N	O	P	Q	R	S	T	U	V	W	X	Y	Z
R	U	B	Y	A	C	D	E	F	G	H	I	J	K	L	M	N	O	P	Q	S	T	V	W	X	Z

'Here—try to decode this.' She wrote down: *Prj fp r yliq*

Gerald took the pencil from Ruby and a few moments later declared, 'Sam is a dolt.'

'Hey!' said Sam.

Ruby retrieved her pencil. 'If you and the person you're sending the note to are the only people who know the keyword, then the code is almost impossible for anyone else to crack. There are just too many combinations.'

'Unless you can guess the key,' Gerald said. His mind was spinning at a million miles an hour. The odds were long, but at least it was a start. 'I think we need to find out a bit more about Jeremy Davey,' he said. 'He might give us a clue to finding the keyword.'

Sam and Ruby nodded, but Felicity did not look convinced.

'What's the problem, Flicka?' Gerald asked.

Felicity tucked her hands under her thighs and rocked gently on the bench seat. 'I've heard you talk about Sir Mason Green before,' she said. 'I knew he wasn't a nice person. But when I saw him for the first time last night…' She grew quiet, tucking her hands in deeper.

Ruby put an arm around Felicity's shoulders. 'I know,' she said. 'He is completely vile.'

Felicity sniffed back a tear. 'Would he really injure the professor? Would he actually do that?'

Ruby squeezed her arm tight. 'He would absolutely do that.'

Felicity dropped her gaze to the tabletop.

'The last time we saw Mason Green he was trying to find a way to control the future,' Sam said, 'like he was a god, or something. Whatever he does, he doesn't do it by halves.'

Felicity sniffed again. 'Then what is he doing this time? What could be so desperately important about this code that he would actually kill someone to solve it?'

Gerald chewed on the tough skin at the end of his thumb. 'You can bet it's more potent than a few recipes from the Voynich manuscript,' he said.

Gerald yelped in pain as a heavy hand clamped onto his right shoulder. He looked up to find Alex Baranov beaming down at him. 'If it isn't Gerry Willy and his happy crew,' Alex said, his eyes sparkling. 'I hear you guys actually had a comfy time of it last night. Half your luck. We were stuck in a leaky tent and had to dig our way out of the snow this morning.' He looked straight at Ruby. 'I wouldn't have minded sharing an open fire and some marshmallows with you.'

Gerald glanced at Ruby. She was biting the end of her pencil and he was sure her cheeks had turned pink.

He brushed Alex's hand off his shoulder. 'It was an interesting night,' Gerald said. 'Hot food, soft beds…all the comforts of home.'

Alex gave an indifferent shrug. 'Who cares. At least we got this.' He dropped a map onto the table. There was a large red stamp in the middle, shaped like an egg with a band of stippled dots running around it.

Felicity picked up the map. 'Is this it? The symbol we're meant to find?'

The twinkle returned to Alex Baranov's eye. 'That's it,' he said. He looked again to Ruby. 'That's the first leg of the Triple Crown done. You should have joined the winning team. It's not too late, you know. After a night in a tent with Gretchen, I'd be happy to dump her.'

'You would do that?' Ruby said.

Alex nodded. 'You would not believe the snoring.'

Gerald plucked the map from Felicity's fingers and shoved it back at Alex. 'You'll just have to get used to the noise,' he said. 'Our team won't be changing.'

The corners of Ruby's mouth flickered upwards.

'You seem very sure of that, Gerald,' she said. 'What makes you so confident?'

Gerald pursed his lips and frowned. 'Because you chose to be on this team and I am reliably informed that you are always right.'

A broad smile broke out on Ruby's face. 'Quite right. Sorry, Alex. It looks like I'm stuck with this bunch.'

Alex tilted his head. 'Ah, well. That is my loss. I suppose I'll see you on the second leg—that is, if you manage to finish the first one.' He turned to go. But just as Gerald was preparing to unleash his thoughts about Alex Baranov and his team, the blond boy swivelled in his tracks. 'Oh, Gerry Willy,' he said, clamping his hand on Gerald's shoulder again. 'I almost forgot. You and I have to go and see Rice Crispies.'

Gerald spun around and jumped to his feet, coming nose to nose with the other boy. 'Stop calling me that,' he said.

'Oh, I don't think so. It's a bit like Gretchen's snoring,' Alex said, a snide smile on his face. 'You're going to have to get used to it.'

Chapter 9

Gerald Wilkins and Alex Baranov sat outside the closed door of the headmaster's office, waiting. Alex spent the time regaling Gerald with tales of his summers in the south of France. Gerald spent the time ignoring him.

A woman at a tidy desk on one side of the room typed at a computer. She looked up from her work. 'I'm sure Dr Crispin won't be too much longer,' she said.

'That's not a problem,' Alex said. 'Gerry and I can entertain ourselves.'

The woman returned to her typing.

Gerald shifted uncomfortably in his chair. 'I've told you to stop calling me that,' he said, trying not to let the woman overhear.

'Not a chance, Gerry Willy,' Alex said. 'I've made it my mission to have everyone in this camp calling you Gerry Willy by the end of our time here.'

Gerald's face flushed red. 'If you keep calling me that then your time here might not be very long.'

Alex sat back in mock horror. 'Gerry! Is that a threat? Because now I'm scared.' The snide smile returned. 'Willy, willy scared.'

Gerald clenched his jaw. He knew he couldn't get into a dust-up outside the headmaster's office so instead he launched headfirst into his suspicions. 'You'd know all about threats, wouldn't you?' he said. 'You attacked me the first night here. Maybe I should mention that to Dr Crispin.'

Alex picked up a copy of *Field & Slaughter* magazine from a coffee table and leafed through the pages. 'I have not the slightest idea what you are talking about,' he said, and, as if to add a point, 'Gerry.'

Gerald was about to fire a barrage of abuse when the door to the office popped open. With it came something quite unexpected from any headmaster's office: the sound of laughter.

Dr Crispin stood in the doorway with a look of almost manic delight on his face. 'Ah, here are the two young scamps. Come in, lads. There are some people here you might like to see.'

Gerald gave an uncertain glance to Alex, then another one to the headmaster. He'd had a few experiences of being called to the principal's office at his school in Sydney. One of them involved his old school buddy Ox, a dozen eggs and a blender in the home economics room. It had not ended well. Since then, Gerald had made a point of having as little as possible to do with head-masters and their offices.

Gerald followed Alex through the door and had a tentative look inside. To his astonishment, he found his mother seated on a couch with the self-assurance of a queen on her throne.

'Gerald!' Vi Wilkins trilled with delight when she saw him. She rolled out of her seat and wrapped him in her arms. 'My little man!'

Through a curtain of silk blouse Gerald caught a mooshed-up vision of Alex Baranov looking at them with undisguised glee.

Gerald struggled to extract himself from the embrace. 'Mum! Please!' he said, muffled in the stranglehold. Then, in a lower voice, 'You're embarrassing me.'

'Embarrassing you!' Vi said in a not-at-all low voice. 'How strange you are, darling. As if I could possibly embarrass you. Come, let me see you.' She released her hold and clamped her hands over Gerald's cheeks. 'But you're wasting away, dear boy.' She turned to Dr Crispin. 'Headmaster, I do hope that little contribution I just made to the school's building fund might include some extra tuck for my little boy.'

Gerald's eyes swivelled across to Dr Crispin. The

headmaster had taken a seat behind his large wooden desk. What looked like two cheques lay on a blotter in front of him. The headmaster reached out and tucked the slips of paper into his breast pocket. 'I think we might be able to arrange seconds for Gerald and Alex, given the circumstances,' he said in velvet tones.

It was only at that moment that Gerald realised there were other people in the room as well. Standing beside Alex was a man who could only have been his father. He was a taller, broader and, if possible, blonder version of his son.

'I thought we weren't meant to see our parents at all during this term,' Gerald said.

Dr Crispin patted his top pocket. 'I am nothing if not flexible,' he said, his moustache bristling.

Alex thrust his chin towards Gerald. 'Father, this is the boy I was telling you about,' he said.

The man looked at Gerald as a thoroughbred might regard a mule. He stepped forward and took Gerald in a crushing handshake.

'Sergei Baranov,' the man said in a mild east-European accent. 'You are Gerry?'

Gerald had known Sergei Baranov for all of five seconds and already he hated him with a white-hot intensity. 'Actually,' Gerald said, 'my name is Gerald. Your son, Lexie, has a tremendous sense of humour. Everyone at camp laughs at him.'

Sergei Baranov stared at Gerald with eyes of blue ice.

The handshake continued for another awkward moment before Gerald's mother came to the rescue. 'Imagine anyone calling you Gerry,' Vi said with a birdlike laugh. 'How terribly amusing. And of course, you remember Jasper Mantle from the Billionaires' Club.'

Gerald wrenched his hand free and turned to find Mr Mantle standing by the headmaster's desk. He greeted Gerald warmly. 'We haven't seen each other since the afternoon at my butterfly house,' he said. 'You were with a friend. Miss Upham, yes?'

'That's right,' Gerald said. 'And you were with a friend too. Tycho Brahe.'

Jasper Mantle's complexion reddened. 'You have a good memory,' he said flatly.

'He made a big impression,' Gerald said.

Sergei Baranov settled into a plush armchair and declared, 'Enough with pleasantries. Let us get to business. What is the latest with the initiation plans?'

Gerald had that feeling of helplessness that always occurred when other people made decisions for him.

'Do I get any say in this?' he asked his mother.

Vi responded with a glare, then turned to Jasper Mantle and lavished him with an ingratiating smile. 'I'm sure Gerald is very much looking forward to New York, Jasper, even if he isn't showing it.' She dropped her voice to a whisper. 'Teenagers.'

Mr Mantle gave a knowing nod. 'We all had our rebellious stage,' he said. 'I seem to recall bunking off school to spend the occasional afternoon down by the riverbank.'

'To have a sneaky cigarette?' Vi said. She leaned across and placed a hand on his arm. 'I'll bet you were quite the wag in your time.'

'To catch butterflies, actually,' Jasper Mantle said. He stared wistfully out the window. 'Heady days.'

Gerald looked at him blankly. 'Butterflies?'

'My collection had to start somewhere, Gerald. But that's the collector's lot—once you start you have to keep going. It's a bit like eating peanuts. It's impossible to stop at one. I'm still searching for the elusive Xerxes Blue all these years later. It's a lifelong pursuit.'

'I'm the same way with shoes,' Vi said, nodding in sympathy. For a moment, she too gazed wistfully out the window. 'So much leather, so little time. Now, do tell us about the initiation. It has us all intrigued.'

Gerald squeezed in next to his mother on the couch. Jasper Mantle took a sip from a china teacup and coughed lightly into his closed hand. 'The Billionaires' Club is an institution of long-held traditions,' he said. 'Once you become a club member, you are a member for life.'

'What about Mason Green?' Gerald's head was slumped between his shoulders, his eyes trained on the floor. 'You booted him out.'

Jasper Mantle shifted in his chair. 'Those were exceptional circumstances,' he said, his neck stiff as a gatepost. 'Murder is most definitely not a tradition we hold dear.

However, one man's fall from grace is your opportunity, Gerald.'

Vi clamped her hand onto Gerald's knee and squeezed. 'Mr Mantle is right, dear. This is an important opportunity for all of us. Certainly not one to be squandered.'

'Ow!' Gerald yelped. He rubbed his knee where Vi had dug in her fingernails. His mother gave him one of her *button your lip if you know what's good for you* looks.

'It's not at all onerous,' Mr Mantle continued. 'All you have to do to become a full member in good standing is spend a night in the Billionaires' Club in New York.'

Gerald looked sceptical. 'That's all?'

Jasper Mantle smiled. 'That is all.'

Gerald narrowed his eyes. 'What's the catch? Is it haunted, or something?'

Vi emitted a trill of laughter. 'Oh, Gerald—I hardly think Jasper would put you up in a haunted house!' A sudden look of concern washed across her face. She turned to the butterfly collector. 'Would you?'

Jasper Mantle spread his hands wide. 'We all have skeletons in the cupboard, Mrs Wilkins, but not so many ghosts. Our founder had quite the sense of humour. He designed a house to explore his whims and fancies. Have you heard of him: Diamond Jim Kincaid? He made his pile in railroads and property speculation in the United States, and he established the Billionaires' Club in 1830.

He was quite the eccentric, I'm told.' Jasper Mantle clapped his hands together with gusto. 'And now we can welcome two new members into the fold.'

There was a sudden sickening lurch in Gerald's stomach. 'Two new members?' he said. He looked aghast at Alex Baranov, who was sitting smugly next to his father.

Jasper Mantle gave him a patient smile, as if he was house-training a particularly dense labrador. 'That's right, Gerald. Two new members. It is such a piece of luck that young Alex can attend the initiation as well, following the, uh, resignation of Tycho Brahe.'

'Someone else who didn't hold with club traditions,' Gerald said.

'Quite.' Mr Mantle dabbed a handkerchief at the corners of his mouth. 'The members were more than happy to offer the spot to Sergei's son. All part of the renewal and revitalisation of our group—it will certainly bring the average age of the membership down.'

'To a hundred and eight,' Gerald muttered under his breath.

'What was that, Gerald?' Jasper Mantle asked.

'I said, "I can hardly wait." I'm sure Alex and I will have a wonderful night together.'

Jasper Mantle beamed at the two boys. 'That's the spirit. The more the merrier. You see, Diamond Jim embedded a number of puzzles into the house. Part of the charm of this initiation night is seeing how many of them you can solve. They have tested some of the finest minds for generations. Working together, who knows what you might turn up. But I'm sure you'll become jolly good friends forever.'

Alex glared at Gerald. 'Oh yes. Jolly good friends.'

Gerald returned the glare. 'Forever,' he said.

Gerald zoned out as the details were discussed. The only detail he was worried about was the one that had him sharing a night with Alex Baranov. As the meeting wrapped up and his mother gave him a parting hug, Gerald was pulled to one side by Sergei Baranov. The tall blond man stooped to speak quietly in Gerald's ear.

'My son has been teasing you, yes?' Baranov said. 'About your name?'

The note of sympathy in Mr Baranov's voice took Gerald by surprise. 'I suppose,' he said. 'But it's no big deal.'

Sergei Baranov shook his head. 'Alex can be a bit of a bully, I'm afraid,' he said. 'His mother and I...' He stared at the floor and shook his head again. 'We try our best. But sometimes a person's character, it cannot be changed. No matter what you try.'

Gerald wasn't sure how to respond.

Sergei Baranov stroked a hand across his chin. 'Has Alex threatened you regarding this Triple Crown challenge? Told you not to try?'

Gerald's eyes were drawn in to the man's hypnotic gaze. He nodded.

Again, Sergei Baranov ran a hand across his whiskered chin. 'I see.' He moved his mouth close to Gerald's ear. 'This is one time I agree with my son.'

Gerald's head jolted. 'I beg your pardon?' he said.

Sergei Baranov's voice deepened. 'If you know what is good for you, you'll quit this challenge and walk away. The same goes for the initiation at the club. You have nothing to gain here, Gerald Wilkins. Spare yourself the trouble and some very real pain.'

Gerald took a clumsy step backwards, bumping into the corner of the headmaster's desk. He looked wide-eyed at Sergei Baranov, not sure if he had heard right. But the look on the man's face told Gerald there had been no mistake.

'So nice to meet you, Gerry,' Sergei Baranov said in a voice of Siberian frostiness. 'I do hope to have the pleasure again very soon.'

Chapter 10

Gerald chose a desk near the back of the classroom as a stream of students flowed inside. Felicity tossed her bag on the floor by his feet and settled in next to him.

'I'm looking forward to this,' she said. 'Scottish history in Scotland. What a treat.'

Gerald watched Felicity insert a pencil into a sharpener and give it a twist. 'You were more fun on holidays,' he said.

Felicity withdrew the pencil and pursed her lips to blow away any stray shavings. 'And you run the risk of being very boring indeed if you keep up that attitude.'

Gerald rested his chin in his palm until his cheek squished up to his eyeball. 'More boring than Scottish history?'

Felicity did not bother to respond.

Gerald's initial excitement at being away at camp had quickly flattened when he realised that his days were still going to be full of school lessons. Sergei Baranov's threat and Mason Green's insistence that he crack the coded message from Jeremy Davey had made him anxious. That anxiety was only compounded by the relentless drudge of algebra, French vocab and the periodic table. And, worst of all, Scottish history.

The remainder of the students filed in. Ruby was the last through the door. Gerald raised his hand to beckon her across, when her path was intercepted.

'Will you look at that?' Gerald said.

Felicity glanced up. 'At what?'

'Blinking Alex Baranov has just asked Ruby to sit next to him.'

'And?'

'She said yes!'

'I don't think that's illegal,' Felicity said. 'She can sit wherever she wants.'

'I know,' Gerald said in a low grumble. 'But Alex Baranov? That's just revolting.'

Felicity screwed up her nose to mirror the look on Gerald's face. 'So is jealousy.'

'I am not jealous,' Gerald said. He paused while he sharpened his narrow-eyed scowl at Alex. 'I just really hate that guy.'

A hush fell over the room as a short woman in a

tweed skirt and starched white blouse marched into the class. 'Settle everyone, please,' she said, in equally starched tones. 'It's thinking time.'

Felicity wriggled upright in her chair. 'Oh goodie,' she whispered to Gerald. 'It's Miss Whitaker. She's one of my favourite teachers.'

Gerald squinted at the woman at the front of the class and tried to reconcile the concepts of 'favourite' and 'teacher'.

Miss Whitaker rubbed her hands together and beamed. 'Today we are going to talk about the life of King James VI of Scotland. Now, can anyone tell me something interesting about James VI?' she asked.

She was met by a sea of blank faces.

She scoured the room, looking for signs of intelligent life.

'Anyone?' she asked.

Gerald was not surprised to see Ruby's hand in the air.

'Yes, Miss Valentine?' the teacher said. 'What can you tell us?'

Ruby's spine straightened. 'King James VI of Scotland was born in 1566 and died in 1625. He became the king of England after the death of his cousin, Elizabeth the first, who was the daughter of the Tudor king Henry VIII, thereby bringing together the realms of England and Scotland to form the United Kingdom.' Ruby cast a smug look back at Gerald and Felicity. Gerald screwed up his face in response.

Miss Whitaker tossed her hands in the air. 'Oh, dates and deaths—how very dull. I want something interesting. Something that will light the fires of our imagination. Did you know that James kept a hunting estate just up the road? That's at least a little bit interesting. Surely one of you knows something more interesting than Miss Valentine's vomited-up calendar bile.'

At that moment Gerald would have gladly signed away half his fortune in exchange for a photograph of Ruby's face. Felicity leaned in close to Gerald and whispered, 'I told you she was one of my favourite teachers.'

Miss Whitaker strode down the centre aisle between the desks. 'Come along! Give me something to *chew* on!'

Kobe Abraham raised his hand. 'Wasn't he, like, a little baby when he became king?' he said.

'Yes!' Miss Whitaker cried in a voice that would have been heard from the front gates. She spun on her toes and advanced on Kobe. 'How old was he? Do you know?'

'Uh, maybe a year old?' Kobe replied, his eyes registering alarm at Miss Whitaker's sudden burst of speed and enthusiasm.

'Thirteen months,' she said. 'King of Scotland and still filling his nappies. Can you imagine it?' Miss Whitaker turned her attention to Sam, who was daydreaming at the next desk. 'You! Boy!'

Sam jolted upright. 'Yes? What?'

Miss Whitaker descended upon him like a vampire at sunset. 'Who invented the submarine?'

Sam blinked up at the teacher. At the back of the room, Gerald suppressed a laugh. Even by Sam's standards, that was a particularly random question.

'Go on. Who invented the submarine?' Miss Whitaker said.

Sam wrinkled his nose. 'Um…King James of Scotland?'

'No! Of course not,' Miss Whitaker barked. 'He was the monarch, boy. Not a bloody inventor. What a ridiculous response. Naturally King James didn't invent the submarine, but he hired the man who did. Cornelius Drebbel, a Dutch dabbler of no fixed address, became a great friend of King James. He was appointed royal inventor and even took James for a ride in his submarine in the River Thames in London. He was the first ruling monarch in history to travel underwater.' Miss Whitaker stood with her feet apart and fists planted on her hips in triumph, as if she had just felled a charging rhino with a single shot and the force of her convictions. 'Now, how's that for interesting?'

At the back of the class, Gerald's head rose from where it had been resting in the cup of his hands. His eyes glazed as the gears in his head spun. Something Miss Whitaker had said sent his mind whirring.

Sam beat him to it.

'Cornelius Drebbel?' Sam said. 'Didn't he invent a

perpetual motion machine?'

The cogs in Gerald's brain engaged with a jarring *clunk*, which could probably be heard from the front gates.

Cornelius Drebbel.

Gerald's mind shot back to a night a few weeks before in a snow-frosted village in the Czech Republic, to a small hotel and a fireplace and an old man telling ghost stories while his wife hung a string of garlic from the front door. The old man talked about Cornelius Drebbel.

Miss Whitaker swooped on Sam like a seagull on a hot chip. 'Yes! That is also an interesting fact,' she said. 'Among Cornelius Drebbel's many employers was the Bohemian emperor Rudolph II. Now, Rudolph was a fascinating character—a man obsessed with collecting. He amassed a cabinet of curiosities that was the envy of every ruler in Europe, and part of the collection was rumoured to be a perpetual motion machine built by Cornelius Drebbel.' Miss Whitaker prowled down the aisle. Every eye in the classroom was on her. 'Cornelius left Rudolph's castle in Prague under strange circumstances and along with him went his amazing machine. It was suspected, but never proved, that Drebbel gave King James the world's first and only perpetual motion machine as a gift. But its location, if it ever existed, has been a mystery ever since.'

The teacher crossed to where Ruby and Alex were sitting and gave Ruby a look laced with meaning. 'You see, Miss Valentine? Your brother has the right approach. There is more to history than simple regurgitation of birthdays. Do you know another quite interesting thing about King James?'

Ruby's lips were pulled tight across her teeth. 'I'm sure we're about to find out,' she said.

Miss Whitaker's eyes flashed wide. 'The King made a trip to Copenhagen in his younger days, to collect his bride to be, a young lady named Anne of Denmark. Can you guess who he met when he was there?'

Ruby looked at Miss Whitaker with scathing eyes. 'I have no idea.'

Miss Whitaker smiled pleasantly at Ruby. 'Why Tycho Brahe, of course,' she said. 'Isn't that interesting?'

Ruby's response earned her a Saturday detention.

Chapter 11

That night, after dinner, Ruby could barely string together a coherent sentence.

'I'll tell you something interesting,' she said in a passable imitation of Miss Whitaker's Scottish trill. 'Here's something I bet you didn't know. I've got a big bum face. That's right. My face looks exactly the same as my bum. That way you don't know whether I'm coming or going. Ha!'

Everyone around the table stared at Ruby like she was a blocked kettle about to blow its top.

'You heard right,' she said, taking a moment to regather the strands of her rage. 'Bumface!'

Gerald gave Felicity an encouraging nudge. Felicity swallowed tightly then reached out a hand to pat Ruby on the arm. 'It's only a detention,' she said, as if she was negotiating with a sugar-loaded toddler carrying a bulging water balloon. 'It's not the end of the world.'

Ruby turned manic eyes to Felicity. Gerald had never witnessed the actual moment a normal human transformed into a flesh-guzzling zombie, but he expected it would look pretty much like Ruby at that moment.

'Only a detention?' Ruby said. Her eyelids drew back to reveal more eyeball than was comfortably necessary. 'You don't understand: I never get detentions.' She clamped a hand on Felicity's arm. 'Never.'

Felicity's mouth formed a tight O shape. 'Ow! You're hurting me.'

Ruby gripped tighter. '*Never ever.*'

'Fingernails!' Felicity squeaked. 'Fingernails!' She whipped her arm free, rubbing a neat semicircle of talon marks.

Sam looked up from a notepad where he had been keeping himself busy with a pencil, a compass and a ruler. 'This detention will be a first,' he said. 'It's been a point of pride for Ruby, like a perfect driving record. This will be her first ever speeding ticket.'

Gerald looked back to Ruby. Her arms clamped her knees to her chest, and her breathing came in shallow pants.

'Is she going to be all right?' he asked Sam.

Sam studied his sister for a moment. 'Who knows—we're entering uncharted territory. You know those old maps that showed the edges of the explored world with drawings of hideous winged beasts and the warning, *Here there be dragons*?'

'What about them?'

Sam cocked his head towards Ruby. 'Dragon.'

Gerald, Sam, Felicity and a shell-shocked Ruby sat in a collection of mismatched armchairs around a coffee table in one of the many lounge rooms at Camp Oates. There were similar clusters of beanbags and couches around the room, all warmed by the well-stocked fireplace. Outside, a frigid gale clawed at the window-panes.

Felicity gave her forearm another rub. 'We don't have a lot of time,' she said. 'Professor McElderry is in real danger. And we have to finish the Triple Crown as well as solve the code. Mason Green was very clear on that.'

'And Sergei Baranov was equally clear that we shouldn't finish the Triple Crown,' Gerald said. He tossed his pencil into a nest of screwed-up balls of paper and empty mugs. 'I don't know what's driving me more nuts: the Baranovs or this stupid code. Unless we find the keyword we'll never solve it.' Gerald stretched his arms wide to ease the crick in his back. 'All I can think of is poor Professor McElderry. It was like he was lost in time.' He looked over to Sam who was drawing circles with his compass. 'What are you working on?'

Sam rubbed an eraser on his pad, sending a shower

of bits across Gerald's shirtfront. 'Sorry about that,' he said, not sounding the least bit sorry. He held up his notebook, revealing a sketch of an elaborate piece of machinery.

'What is that supposed to be?' Felicity asked.

Sam rolled his eyes as if it was the most ridiculous question he had ever heard. 'It's a perpetual motion machine,' he said. 'I'm designing one.'

Felicity reached over and patted him on the arm. 'Of course you are.'

'It's based on magnets, see? A whole series of them on a tiny ferris wheel. And what do we know about magnets?'

Felicity narrowed her eyes. 'Opposite poles attract,' she said.

'Very good,' Sam said, as if talking to a three-year-old. 'So when we set the wheel spinning, the magnets around the outside are attracted to this magnet that's fixed at the top. But when they get close, the influence of the opposite pole takes over and pushes the wheel around. The wheel will keep turning forever and ever.'

Felicity's eyes narrowed further. 'I topped my year in science, Sam. You do know that, don't you?' she said. 'Perpetual motion is not possible because it violates the basic laws of thermodynamics.'

Sam looked at her as if she was blowing spit bubbles. 'Turning forever and ever and—ow!'

Sam clamped his hands over the spot on his forehead

where Ruby had cracked him with a teaspoon. 'Don't be such a wally,' Ruby said. 'Felicity is way smarter than you could ever hope to be.'

Sam glared at his sister. 'You've crawled out of the dragon's nest, have you?'

'I've been thinking, dopey drawers,' Ruby said.

'Really?' Sam brandished the blueprint for his machine. 'And what do you call this?'

Ruby glanced at the drawing. 'Daycare for kindergarten kids,' she said. She turned to Gerald, all business. 'I'm sorry for being so insensitive about Professor McElderry. A weekend detention doesn't even begin to compare with what he is going through. Now, this is what we should do. On Saturday, Gerald and Felicity are going to find that symbol for the Triple Crown. I'm stuck in detention but I think I can get Miss Bumface to give me access to the library. Maybe I can find out something about Jeremy Davey that will help crack the code. With a bit of luck we can complete both tasks on the same day.'

Sam gave his forehead another rub and inspected his fingers for any sign of blood. 'What about me?' he said. 'What am I doing?'

Ruby leaned across and patted Sam on the arm. 'Why don't you spend the day in the camp workshop and see if you can build your perpetual motion machine?'

Sam's face lit up. 'Great idea!' he said.

Ruby took a slow breath. 'Weekend daycare,' she muttered to herself.

Professor McElderry visited Gerald's nightmares that evening. And the dreams grew increasingly gruesome as the week wore on. In them, the professor blundered across a bleak landscape. Gerald tried to guide him to safety, but every time Gerald thought he had his friend out of harm's way, the professor would slip his grasp and be swallowed by a billowing fog. If that wasn't disturbing enough, the thing that most freaked out Gerald was McElderry's eyes. They were sealed shut, leaving him blindly shuffling through an endless night of despair. Gerald got to the end of the week having had almost no decent sleep.

'You look terrible,' Ruby said as she joined him in the breakfast queue on Saturday morning.

Gerald stared ahead through hard-boiled eyes. 'Thanks. And your face could stop a clock,' he mumbled.

Ruby smiled to herself and nudged Gerald with her shoulder. 'You're in a great state to find that checkpoint today.'

Gerald blinked. It was like someone had lined his eyelids with sandpaper. 'You seem ridiculously happy for someone about to do a day's detention,' he said.

They moved forward in the queue. Ruby rose onto her tiptoes to see what was on offer for breakfast. 'It's not so much a day lost indoors as the chance to find out more about Jeremy Davey,' she said.

'More?' Gerald said.

'All right,' Ruby said. 'Something. In fact, anything would be better than what we've got now.'

Gerald took a plate and asked the woman behind the counter for scrambled eggs and a double serve of bacon.

'Busy day ahead, dear?' the woman asked as she piled rashers onto a mound of watery eggs.

'It has disaster written all over it,' he replied.

'That's nice, dear,' the woman said.

Ruby filled a bowl with porridge and followed Gerald to a table.

Gerald picked at his eggs. 'Do you really think you'll find anything about Jeremy Davey in the library. It's a long shot, isn't it?'

'Put it this way,' Ruby said. 'I've got a better chance of doing that than Sam has of building a perpetual motion machine.' She shook her head. 'He is a lovable dolt.'

Gerald shifted in his seat and accidentally brushed up against Ruby's leg.

'Sorry,' he said.

Ruby flashed him a smile. 'That's all right.'

A familiar warmth flooded Gerald's chest. It dawned on him that the two of them were alone.

No interruptions.

No distractions.

'This is nice,' he said.

Ruby glanced at the grey splodge of warmed-up oats in her bowl. 'I've had better.'

'Not the breakfast,' Gerald said. 'This. You. And…
you know…me.'

Ruby bit her bottom lip and her cheeks deepened a
shade. 'Oh…'

There was an awkward pause.

'*I once knew a girl named Ruby—*'

Ruby turned to face Gerald front on. 'Look, what
is it with all the attempts at limericks?' she asked. 'It's
a bit bizarre.'

It was Gerald's turn to blush. 'They're poems,' he
said. 'They're meant to be charming.'

Ruby thought about that for a second. 'No, they're
just bizarre. What are they for?'

'For?' Gerald said, louder than he had intended.
'They're for you. But every time I start we get interrupted
or a madman with a gun bursts through the door.'

Ruby pressed her lips together. 'That's very sweet,' she
said, not daring to make eye contact. 'Can I hear one?'

Gerald shuffled in his seat. 'All right. It's still a bit
rough.' He cleared his throat and stared hard at his plate
of bacon.

There once was a girl named Ruby,
Who played video games like a newbie
She could hike miles and miles,
And just one of her smiles,
Makes my stomach go scooby-dooby-doo-bee…

There is nothing as dead as the silence that follows
a love poem in the form of a badly rhyming limerick.

Gerald raised his eyes expectantly towards Ruby.

Ruby was pressing her lips together really hard.

Finally, Gerald broke the silence. 'Ruby, I'd really like it if you would be my—'

Ruby shot out a hand and clamped it over Gerald's mouth. '*Mmmmwwmmfffmm*,' he said.

Ruby spoke slowly and distinctly, as if talking to someone who had lost his hearing aid. 'I have to go to my detention now,' she said. 'I can't be late. You have a good day with Felicity and come back with that stamp, okay?' Ruby's hand tracked up and down as Gerald slowly nodded his head. 'Good,' she said, her cheeks deepening another shade. 'Good. We can talk about your...um...poetry later. Oh, crumbs.' And then she was off, weaving through the maze of tables and out of the dining hall.

Gerald blinked after her.

Then a broad smile broke out on his face.

'She didn't say no,' he said out loud.

Gerald's reverie was broken by the appearance of Felicity. She crooked her elbow through his and yanked him to his feet. He looked at her with dazed surprise. 'What's the matter?'

'Change of plan,' Felicity said. She looked around, as if anxious not to be noticed as she guided Gerald towards the door. 'There's a beautiful girl out here who is desperate to meet you.'

Chapter 12

Gerald gazed into two large brown eyes. He stood mesmerised.

'Isn't she gorgeous?' Felicity whispered in Gerald's ear. 'I know you two are going to fall deeply in love.'

Gerald blinked. The big round eyes staring back at him did not.

'But,' Gerald said in a voice soaked in doubt, 'I hate horses.'

The chestnut mare, sensing Gerald's unease, unleashed a lip-flapping blast of hay breath straight into his face.

Gerald struggled to keep his breakfast in his stomach. 'That is disgusting,' he said.

Felicity stepped between Gerald and the horse and

ran a hand down the length of the mare's face. 'Don't be foul, Gerald,' she said. 'You'll hurt Marjory's feelings.'

'That's another thing,' Gerald said. 'The name. Can't you find one called Flash or Lightning or Thunderbolt?'

Felicity glanced sideways at Gerald. 'I think Marjory is just about perfect for you.'

Gerald and Felicity stood outside one of a line of horse stalls inside the Oates stable complex. Marjory tilted her head and gently took a sugar lump from Felicity's cupped hand.

'This is the genius of it, Gerald,' Felicity said. 'We ride out to the checkpoint to find that stamp and we can be back in time for dinner tonight. No camping in the snow. No sore feet at the end of the day.'

Gerald looked with uncertainty at Marjory, then ran a hand over his backside. 'It wasn't my feet I was worried about,' he said. 'Aren't we meant to hike out there? Isn't that all part of the deal?'

Felicity pulled a carrot from her pocket and clamped the thick end between her teeth. Marjory latched onto the other end and chomped it out of Felicity's lips.

Gerald put a hand over his mouth. 'That is truly disgusting.'

'Don't be such a boy,' Felicity said. 'Look, the way I figure it we've already done the hike, or most of it. It doesn't seem fair that we have to do it twice because of that snowstorm. If we get caught we just say we didn't know there was a rule against it, and there's no harm done. But if we don't get caught—and we won't—then the first leg of the Triple Crown is done, we keep Mason Green happy and we can concentrate on solving that coded message. Plus, I get to take you on that ride I've been promising. Tell me that's not a good plan.'

Gerald screwed up his nose. 'And I have to take Marjory.'

'Well, technically she'll be taking you. She's the oldest and most sedate of the horses at this camp, so I can't imagine you'll cause her too many problems.'

'Me cause her problems?' Gerald almost choked. 'Have you not seen her? She's bleeding enormous. The only camp she should be at is a weight-loss camp.'

Felicity clamped her hands over Marjory's ears. 'Shush! You'll hurt her feelings.'

Gerald snorted. 'You'd have to turn her hearing aid on first.'

Felicity spent the next half hour giving Gerald a quick riding lesson in the mounting yard. He soon relaxed, and the mare responded to the gentle pressure of the reins and the tap of his heels.

'You're a natural,' Felicity called from astride her horse. 'I think we're ready to find that checkpoint.'

Felicity led the way to a narrow path that ran away from the stables and across rolling countryside. Gerald trotted up level with her.

'We can avoid the driveway and the front of the camp, and any curious eyes, by going this way,' Felicity said. 'I'm guessing we should come out quite close to that big pile of rocks that you and Sam climbed. We know the way from there.' She gave Gerald a playful glance. 'See if you can keep up with me and Belle.' Felicity nudged her horse and they cantered forward, leaving Gerald staring after them.

Gerald looked down at his horse as she plodded along the path. 'Let's see what you're made of, Marjory.' He dug his heels in.

Marjory twitched her ears.

'Oh come on,' Gerald said. 'I could go faster than this on my own. Move!' He banged his boots harder into Marjory's ribs and finally got her to lift the pace to a brisk walk.

Gerald looked ahead. Felicity and Belle had disappeared over a hillock.

'We'll never catch up at this rate,' Gerald said. He flailed the reins up and down. This prompted a mild annoyance from Marjory who continued her easy gait.

They rounded a bend and Gerald could make out the edge of a lake through a tangle of bare trees. The path dipped and Marjory carried Gerald into the woods.

The air was still. Gerald was suddenly aware of the sound of the horse's hooves in the mush of half-melted snow and decayed leaves on the path. There was no bird song. No other sound at all. Just the steady clop, clop, clop of the hooves. Gerald lost sight of the lake. The trees were closer together, branches snared over the top of the path like entwined fingers.

Marjory's ears flickered and turned backwards. Gerald felt a movement roll through his thighs, as if the horse had shivered.

Then he heard something—a sudden fizzing.

Marjory cried out as if she had been whipped. Gerald's eyes shot wide as the horse reared. He gripped on tight, his fingers clutching at a handful of mane as Marjory rose high, stabbing her forelegs at the air.

Gerald's breath caught in his lungs. His thighs clamped in hard. Then Marjory landed heavily. Gerald slid forward in the saddle, the fork of his jeans snapping tight and sending a lump to his throat. Tears sprang from his eyes; his face exploded purple. A high-pitched cry spilled from his lips.

Then Marjory took off.

Bare branches whipped at Gerald's face as he thundered through the wood. Each hoof-fall sent a jolt of pain through his shoulder and a hammer blow further south.

'Whoa, Marjory!'

The horse shot clear of the trees and galloped along the lake path. Gerald caught a blurred glimpse of Felicity as he bolted past. He looked up in time to see he was heading straight towards a stone wall.

He scrabbled with the reins, hauling at them.

'Whoa! Marjory!'

Gerald felt the horse's rear legs coil. He was shocked at the power they unleashed as he went sailing into the air. Gerald was sure he saw two squirrels squabbling over a chestnut on top of the wall. Marjory's hooves barely cleared the edge. He seemed to hang in the air for an age before the horse landed on the other side. Gerald hit the saddle hard.

A second lump joined the first one in his throat. His eyes bulged.

'Gerald! Lean back and pull on the reins!'

Gerald took a moment to register that Felicity was riding alongside him, the two horses neck and neck streaking across the open field. He rattled his head to regain his senses. He gripped the reins and pulled.

But nothing was going to stop Marjory.

She galloped on, oblivious to Gerald's cries and his attempts to pull her up. Felicity urged Belle forward, struggling to keep pace. She leaned out and tried to grab Marjory's bridle. The ground beneath them was a blur. But Marjory flicked her head to the side and strode on, relentless. They were fast approaching another stone wall. It was twice as high as the one Marjory had only just cleared. Gerald's eyes popped.

'Whoa! Bloody well whoa!'

The wall loomed ahead, ancient stones seemingly held in place by thick ropes of ivy.

'Stop, dammit! Stop!'

Gerald heaved back on the reins but he had no effect. He threw his arms around the horse's outstretched neck, desperately holding on.

The wall rose in front of them. Gerald had a vision of Marjory hitting it at high speed, but at the last second she lurched to the right, sending Gerald sprawling to the side. He struggled to stay in the saddle as the horse charged on. He managed to right himself to find Marjory was galloping alongside the wall.

Towards the lake.

Felicity surged across the field on Belle, trying to cut them off.

'Gerald! Hold on!'

Great advice, thought Gerald. What else was there to do?

He clung on, his thighs screaming.

The lake was only twenty metres away.

Marjory galloped on, as if a pack of ravenous wolves was at her heels.

Then, at the water's edge, she stopped. And her rider was catapulted out of his stirrups over her head. He landed with a skidding crash.

The lake was frozen solid.

Gerald slid like a hockey puck across the ice.

He finally came to a stop, flat on his back and staring up at the grey sky. 'Well that's just great,' he said.

After a moment he sat up and looked back to the shore. Felicity was holding both horses by their reins. Gerald carefully rolled onto his hands and knees and climbed to his feet. He only fell over seven times before he got back to land.

'What happened, Gerald?' Felicity helped him up the bank. 'What did you do?'

'What did I do?' Gerald said. 'I didn't do anything. The stupid horse just reared up and bolted.'

Felicity gave him a curious look. 'Are you sure?' She moved across to the horse and ran a hand down her flank and over her legs. 'She seems all right.'

'Well thank goodness for that,' Gerald said, sweat cooling on his face. 'I wouldn't have been able to sleep if she'd done a hamstring or rolled an ankle.'

'Don't be rude, Gerald,' Felicity said. 'She's been through an ordeal.'

Gerald was about to inform Felicity of his definition of an ordeal, when she suddenly straightened. 'Oh, what's this?' she said.

'What's what?'

Felicity ran a finger over a large welt on Marjory's rump, showing red through her dark coat.

'It looks like she's been stung by something.'

'A wasp?'

'It's too big for that,' Felicity said. 'No wonder she bolted. It must really hurt.'

Gerald clamped a hand over his groin to make sure everything important was still in the right place. He would tell Felicity about real pain but he did not have the energy.

'She seems all right,' Felicity said. 'Let's keep going before she gets cold.'

Gerald wiped ice from his jeans and jacket. 'Yeah, that would be a tragedy,' he said.

They led the horses back across the fields. They were in the heart of the woods, where the branches formed a canopy overhead, when Gerald said, 'This is where she took off. It would have been better if I'd fallen here. It would have saved me some hassle. And before you say anything about how brave Marjory was, I—'

Gerald stopped. He handed the reins to Felicity and squatted.

'What is it?' Felicity asked. She peered over Gerald's shoulder. The two horses nuzzled each other behind them.

Gerald held up a bright red sphere about the size of a marble. He turned it between his thumb and forefinger. 'This doesn't look like it belongs here, does it?' He scanned the area. 'There are boot prints in the mud over here. They lead off into the trees.'

'So?'

Gerald went back to the horses and held the ball next to the welt on Marjory's rump. 'Do you think this could be what set Marjory off?' he said.

'Could be,' Felicity said. 'But it would have had to hit her really hard to leave a mark like that. Do you think someone was hiding by the trees and threw it?'

'You'd have to have an arm like a slingshot to throw it that hard,' Gerald said. He paused. 'Maybe it was a slingshot.'

'Why would someone come all the way out here to hurt a beautiful horse like Marjory?'

'I don't think they were out to get Marjory,' Gerald said. 'I think they were trying to hurt me.'

'Oh, Gerald,' Felicity said. 'Don't be paranoid.'

He tucked the ball into his pocket and shivered. 'Felicity, one thing I've learned over the past year is that when you're paranoid, you're seldom disappointed.'

Gerald took Marjory's reins and led the way out of the woods and back to the path. Someone had tried to knock him off the horse, he was sure of it. And he had a sneaking suspicion that the Hello Kitty bandit might be involved.

By the time Gerald and Felicity reached the checkpoint Gerald's backside felt like an over-ripe strawberry.

'Sore! Sore! Sore!' Gerald yelped as he rolled out of the saddle and dropped to the ground. He hobbled towards a stout A-framed hut nestled in a stand of trees. The place was deserted. Gerald spotted a wooden bench outside the hut and flopped onto it. Instantly, he sprang to his feet. 'Sore! Sore! Sore!' he yelped again.

Felicity found Gerald draped face first over a picnic table, doing a jig. 'What exactly are you doing?' she asked as she tied the horses to a tree trunk.

'I'm trying to get the blood back into what used to

be my bum,' Gerald said. He rubbed his hands across the most sensitive bits. 'What exactly is it that you enjoy about this riding thing?'

Felicity grinned to herself. 'It gives me a legitimate way to torture boys every now and then,' she said. She tugged the riding gloves from her hands and pushed open the door to the hut.

Gerald raised his head. 'Is the stamp in there?' he called.

A second later and Felicity was out the door and pulling her gloves back on. Gerald looked at her with surprise. 'You've got it?'

'Yes,' Felicity said as she breezed past him and unwound the horses' reins from the tree trunk.

'You mean that's it?' Gerald said. 'There's nothing else we need to do?'

Felicity fitted her left boot into a stirrup and hoisted herself into the saddle. She led Marjory over to Gerald and gave him the reins. 'What were you expecting?' she asked.

Gerald looked at the length of leather in one hand and ran the other once more over his tender behind. 'A bit more of a rest?'

Felicity looked down at him with a complete absence of pity. 'Toughen up, toots. We've got a twenty-mile ride ahead of us and these horses will need to be stabled before dark.'

Gerald closed his eyes and took in a deep breath

to steel himself for the ordeal ahead. He turned to face Marjory. She let out a light nicker and nuzzled against his shoulder.

'See?' Felicity said. 'She likes you.'

Marjory let out another lip-flapping burst of hay breath right in Gerald's face. He raised his eyes to Felicity. 'Best friends forever,' he said.

Gerald slotted a boot into a stirrup and threw his other leg over Marjory's back. He settled tentatively into the saddle. 'Sore,' he said. 'Sore. Sore. Sore.'

Felicity gave Belle a nudge in the flanks and led the way back along a narrow path towards the valley. Gerald trotted up next to her, wincing at each thump of his backside against the saddle. 'So let's see it then,' he said.

Felicity pulled the map from her jacket and tossed it to Gerald. He caught it on his chest. In the middle of the map was a large red stamp. It was shaped like an egg with a stippled band of dots around its perimeter.

'What's it supposed to be?' he asked.

Felicity retrieved the map and tucked it back into her pocket. 'I'm not sure it's meant to be anything,' she said. 'But it does mean we've completed the first leg of the Triple Crown, which is something.'

'It's a pretty distinctive shape,' Gerald said. 'I wonder why we need it for the next stage.'

The sound of an approaching vehicle cut through the still winter air. The rough country path was no place for a car. Gerald looked up just as a Land Rover painted camouflage green came over the hill and thundered towards them. He tightened his grip on the reins. He was determined not to take a return journey on the Marjory express.

The chunky four-wheel drive rocked to a stop about ten metres in front of them, blocking the path.

The driver's door popped open.

Out climbed Sir Mason Green.

'Hello there,' he called. 'Fancy bumping into you two all the way out here.'

Chapter 13

A shrill whistle erupted from the kettle on the camp stove. Sir Mason Green looked up from his stool and nodded towards a teapot on a foldaway picnic table. 'Professor?' he said, 'Be a good chap and do the honours, will you?'

Professor Knox McElderry shuffled across to the stove and lifted the kettle from the gas burner. Fingers of steam curled from the spout as he filled the teapot.

Gerald and Felicity sat in a glowering funk on a fallen log while the professor readied the afternoon refreshments. The horses were tied up a dozen metres away, their ears upright and alert.

'Are you sure you won't have a cup, Gerald? Miss Upham?' Green asked as the professor handed him a steaming mug. 'He makes a very good brew, for a Scot.'

Gerald's hatred for the silver-haired billionaire had never been so intense. 'Don't treat him like that,' he said, his eyes like daggers. 'He's not your slave.'

'Says the thirteen-year-old with his own butler,' Green said, blowing gently on his tea. 'Such hypocrisy.'

'Mr Fry is an employee,' Gerald said. 'That's not even close to being the same thing.'

'It's only a question of degree,' Green said. 'Now, have you solved that code yet?'

Gerald looked down at the ground. 'We're getting close,' he lied.

Green stared at him, then slid his blade an inch from its scabbard. 'You'll need to do better than "close",' he said.

Gerald's pulse raced.

He had to give Green something.

Anything.

'We think it's a keyword cipher,' he said. 'Ruby is trying to find out more about Jeremy Davey today.'

Green pushed the sword back into place. 'Good thinking.' He looked at the professor, who stood staring into a stand of trees. 'I need hardly remind you of what is at stake.' He placed his mug on the ground and reached into a leather satchel by his feet. He pulled out a cardboard tube and tossed it to Gerald.

'You recall we were rudely interrupted in our last conversation,' Green said. 'I was about to ask you a favour.'

'A favour?' Gerald said. 'Since when do you ask for favours?'

'Favour. Order. Whichever makes you feel more comfortable,' Green said. 'You are going to New York in a few weeks to the Billionaires' Club, I believe?'

Gerald screwed his eyes shut. 'How could you possibly know about that?'

A thin smile creased Green's face. 'As I have told you, I have eyes and ears everywhere.'

Gerald felt a great weight press down on his shoulders. 'What do you want?'

'I assume that old fluff Jasper Mantle has told you about the club's founder, James Kincaid? About his acquisitive habits and strange collections? He was a latter-day Rudolph II with his cabinet of curiosities. You remember Rudolph, I'm sure.'

Gerald said nothing.

'Yes, I thought that might be the case,' Green continued. 'When you have your night in the Billionaires' Club, you must find something that is hidden there and bring it to me. The coded note should provide the information you need, along with the contents of the cylinder in your hand.'

Gerald's eyes fell to the cardboard container in his fingers. 'What is it I'm meant to be looking for?' he asked.

'You remember my room at the Rattigan Club?' Green said.

Gerald's mind shot back to the musty old clubrooms in London, where he first learned of Mason Green's obsession with his family. 'What about it?' he asked.

'On my desk there was a wooden box. It was painted a gloss black. Do you recall it?'

Gerald's stomach turned. He knew the box only too well. 'There was a human skull inside it,' Gerald said flatly.

'That's the chap,' Green said. 'Somewhere in the Billionaires' Club in New York there is an identical box. I want you to find it and deliver it to me.'

'What's in it?' Gerald asked. 'It's not another skull, is it?'

'You do not need to know the contents,' Green said. 'Just bring the box to me, and then your friend the professor walks free. We will be in New York waiting for you.'

Felicity stared hard at Green. 'Aren't you meant to be on the run?' she said. 'How are you going to get to New York?'

Green flashed her an oily smile. 'You underestimate my genius, young lady.'

Gerald turned the tube in his hands. 'What's in here?' he asked.

'A little something with an interesting history,' Green said. 'Open it up.'

Gerald slid a thumbnail under the red plastic cap at one end and was about to flick it off when the sound of singing floated through the air. Green turned his head to look down the path. 'We have company,' he muttered. 'Some of your fellow hikers, I expect.' Green snapped his fingers at the professor. 'Come, McElderry. Into the vehicle.' He pulled the car keys from his pocket and spun around to face Gerald. 'You know what will happen if you don't find me that box.'

Green climbed into the Land Rover and the four-wheel drive roared off the path and over a hill. A moment later, Kobe Abraham, Charlie Blagden and two girls Gerald recognised as Cailyn and Emma rounded the bend. The four of them pulled up short at the sight of Gerald and Felicity sitting at a fold-up picnic table in the middle of the path, sharing a pot of tea.

Gerald held up a mug. 'Cup for you, Kobe?' he asked.

Chapter 14

The cardboard tube sat in the middle of the table with the unassuming presence of a stick of dynamite.

The other students had filed out of the dining hall for after-dinner activities, leaving four disconsolate figures seated around the latest offering from Sir Mason Green.

'I suppose you should open it,' Ruby said. She gave the tube a prod. It rolled across and stopped in front of Gerald.

Gerald blinked at it. 'I suppose I should,' he said. He made no move to pick it up.

'What's stopping you?' Ruby asked.

Gerald reached into his shirt pocket and pulled out the red marble that he found on the trail where Marjory had spooked. 'Someone is doing all they can to stop me from doing the Triple Crown,' he said. 'First the Hello Kitty mugging on our first day here; then this morning someone tried to knock me off a horse by firing this into its rump.'

Ruby looked at the red ball curiously. 'What happened?'

'Let's just say I got to see a bit more of the Scottish highlands than I'd planned,' Gerald said.

Sam reached out, took the marble from Gerald's palm then popped it in his mouth.

Ruby wrinkled her nose in disgust. 'What are you doing?'

Sam tilted his head and smiled at her. 'Peppermint,' he said. 'My favourite.'

'It's a sweet?' Felicity said.

'Sure,' Sam said, chewing. 'Red Bombs. I love 'em.'

'Someone tried to knock you off a horse with a peppermint?' Ruby said. 'Who would do that?'

'Someone who wants me to quit the Triple Crown,' Gerald said. 'And we can rule out Mason Green as a suspect in that mystery.'

Ruby clicked her tongue. 'I'm sick of mysteries.' She picked up the tube, flicked off the end cap and tipped it up. A rolled bundle fastened with brown string slid out. She untied the knot and a square of rough canvas, about thirty centimetres across, unfurled on the table.

'What is it?' Felicity asked. She shuffled closer to Ruby to get a better look. 'Is that…paint?'

Ruby ran her fingertips across the surface of the material: an expanse of dull blue with a gold crest in the centre.

'See?' Felicity said. 'That looks like brushstrokes.'

Ruby suddenly snatched her hand back.

'What's the matter?' Sam asked.

'Oh my gosh,' Ruby said, her eyes widening. 'It's from that painting.'

'What painting?'

'The one from the Louvre,' Ruby said. She reached out a finger and prodded at the canvas as if to make sure it was dead. 'The one that was vandalised.'

Sam looked at his sister as if she had recently arrived from Mars. 'What are you talking about?'

'Don't you ever read the newspapers?' Ruby asked.

'Nothing past the sports pages.'

Ruby gave him an exasperated look. 'It was in the news just before we left for Scotland. A man sliced a piece from a famous painting at the Louvre in Paris.' She prodded the canvas square again. 'This piece.'

'What painting was it?' Felicity asked. She stared at the canvas square in wonder.

Ruby closed her eyes and a wrinkle crawled across her forehead. 'Oh, what was it?' she muttered. She turned to Felicity. 'You know the one: a woman is holding the French flag during the Revolution.'

Sam blinked at his sister. 'Do you mean *Liberty Leading the People* by Eugène Delacroix?' he asked.

Gerald, Ruby and Felicity looked at Sam as if a baboon had sauntered up to the table and asked for directions to the public library.

'What?' Sam said. 'Gerald might doze his way through history lessons, but I find all that stuff interesting. Weren't you listening to Mr Bassingthwaighte in the first week of term? The second uprising of the French people against the monarchy? That's what that painting is all about—there's a picture of it in our textbook.'

'There is?' Gerald said. 'I really have to stop sleeping in class.'

'Who's Mr Bassingthwaighte?' Ruby asked.

'Our history teacher back at St Custard's,' Sam said. 'He was banging on and on about the three glorious days of July 1830 and the people revolting against the crown.'

Gerald nodded as he remembered the lesson. 'It was a pretty miserable story, actually,' he said.

Felicity stared at the canvas square and tightened her jaw. 'Shouldn't we tell someone that we've got this?' she said. 'I mean, doesn't this count as being in possession of stolen goods, or something?'

Gerald picked up the hank of canvas and inspected it. 'If we're not going to bother contacting the police when a crazed billionaire threatens to kill Professor McElderry, then I hardly think being on the receiving end of a bit of high-end vandalism is too much to worry about.'

Felicity did not look convinced. 'We have a piece of one of the most famous paintings in the world and we're about to do a favour for the man who probably ordered it to be sliced up like a Christmas turkey. What happens to us if someone finds it?'

'I think it's a safe bet that the French police are not going to raid a school camp in the back blocks of Scotland as part of their investigation,' Gerald said. 'Don't worry so much. I've got it under control.' He flipped the painting over and found the back was covered in a mottled pattern of black ink. He grunted. 'It looks like somebody used this to mop up an oil spill. How is this supposed to help us find that black box for Green?'

'Maybe the coded message will give you a clue,' Felicity said. She stared at the piece of the Delacroix painting like it was a ticking time bomb. She turned to Ruby. 'Did you find out anything about Jeremy Davey?'

Sam barely managed to control a grin. 'Yeah? How was your very first detention?'

Ruby glanced at Sam the same way she might inspect the sole of her shoe if she had stepped in something revolting. 'Time spent in a library is never wasted,' she sniffed.

'You mean you actually found something about Jeremy Davey?' Gerald asked.

'Don't be ridiculous. Of course not,' Ruby said. 'It's a library at an outdoor education camp in the wilds of Scotland, not the Bodleian. The only books they've got here are about tying knots, shooting deer and salmon fishing.'

'So how was it not a waste of time?' Sam asked.

'Because, beetle brain, the one useful thing they do have is an old encyclopaedia.'

'What? Made from paper?' Sam said.

'A real paper set of books,' Ruby said, shaking her head in wonder. 'There was so much dust in them I almost popped a lung from the sneezing. So while Miss Whitaker sat there planning her lessons for next week, I flicked through the volumes and came across a history timeline. Do you know what was happening around the world in 1835 when our friend Jeremy was throwing his bottle into the ocean?'

Felicity, Sam and Gerald waited in anticipation.

'Not a whole lot, actually,' Ruby continued. 'It was a pretty dull year. Someone tried to shoot the American President, Charles Darwin sailed to the Galapagos Islands and the city of Melbourne was founded in Australia.'

'Melbourne was founded?' Gerald said. 'You're right. That was a dull year.'

'What help is any of that to us?' Sam asked.

'None at all,' Ruby said. 'But it helped to pass the time. Speaking of which, what did you achieve, mastermind? Solve the secrets of perpetual motion, did you?'

Sam gave his sister an indignant look. 'I'll have you know I have made significant advances. Take a look at this.' He ducked under the table and retrieved a cardboard box. He carefully took out an elaborate assembly of cogs, flywheels and gears.

Gerald, Felicity and Ruby leaned in to get a better look. 'What's it do?' Gerald asked.

Sam beamed. 'Watch this and prepare to be amazed,' he said. He put it on the table and extended a finger to start a flywheel spinning. The wheel whirred in place, setting the contraption into a gentle hum. Then a large cog on one side started to rotate. That in turn wound a spring tighter and tighter. Two other gears sprang into motion, and soon Sam's invention was a buzzing blur of activity.

Then a sprocket shot out the top and pinged off Sam's right eyebrow.

'Ow!' he yelped.

The machine burred into a frenzy, bouncing on the table, shedding bits in a metallic storm of self-destruction. Felicity dived under the table and Ruby grabbed Gerald for a human shield as bolts, springs and sprockets sprayed everywhere. Gerald wrapped his arms over his face to ward off the flying machine parts until Sam's invention farted out its final flywheel, leaving a scene of devastation across the table and floor. Felicity emerged from her hiding place, Ruby released her death grip on Gerald's shoulders and Gerald unwrapped his arms from around his head. They all stared at Sam, who sat unmoved in his seat, his front littered with metal debris.

'I may have wound it a bit too tight,' he said.

Ruby shook her head. 'You are a loveable doofus.'

'You certainly got the motion going,' Gerald said as

he swept a pile of bits into the cardboard box. 'But you might need to work on the perpetual bit.'

Sam plucked a large spindle from his hair and dropped it with the other remnants. 'I probably should be helping you solve that code,' he said. 'But it's a bit hard when all you've got is a message from 1835 and a torn piece of painting.'

Ruby paused in her cleaning up. 'Sam, when did you say that revolution took place in France?'

'The three glorious days?' Sam said. 'In July 1830.'

Ruby thought for a moment. 'And Gerald, when did you say the Billionaires' Club was formed?'

Gerald thought back to the meeting that took place in Dr Crispin's office with Jasper Mantle. 'I'm pretty sure Diamond Jim Kincaid started it in 1830,' he said.

'It's interesting that the note from Jeremy Davey, the Delacroix painting and the Billionaires' club all came into being round about the same time, don't you think?'

There were many things that Gerald had found interesting since arriving at the Oates Outdoor Education Centre: being attacked by Hello Kitty for a start, the return of Sir Mason Green, the threat to Professor McElderry's life. The seeming coincidence of dates around a coded message, a vandalised French masterpiece and the club he was about to join would just have to go on the bottom of the list.

Chapter 15

Mr Beare stood with a pointer in his hands before a large map on the wall and waited for the teams to settle.

A buzz of excitement ran through the room as students, gathered in their tight clusters of four, craned their necks in search of classmates among the crowd of expectant faces.

'Where is everyone?' Sam said to Gerald. 'Half the camp isn't here.'

'They didn't complete the first leg in time,' Gerald said. 'I hear they have to stay back and do extra maths lessons.'

'They ought to be doing geography,' Felicity said with a sniff. 'Honestly, it wasn't that hard.'

Sam scoffed. 'Says the person who rode there on a horse.'

Gerald slapped at the back of his neck as if a giant wasp had just stung him. 'Ow!' he yelped. He spun around in time to see Alex Baranov whipping something at him from across the room. Gerald flung a hand out and snatched the object out of the air.

He unfurled his fingers. A bright red mint rested in his palm.

Gerald jumped to his feet and barged across the room to where Alex was sitting with his teammates. 'It was you!' Gerald said, his eyes ablaze. 'I knew it was you.'

Alex Baranov stood up, his smile bright and bold. 'Of course it was me,' he said. 'Me and a slingshot. A bloody good shot it was too. You should be thanking me. I was doing you a favour.'

Gerald couldn't believe what he was hearing. 'Doing me a favour?' he said.

'Of course,' Alex said. 'You could do with a mint. Your breath is toxic—especially if you're going for a romantic horse ride in the woods with Miss Snooty.'

Gerald weighed up the benefits of smacking Alex Baranov square in the mouth, but before he could wind up and unleash, Mr Beare called for quiet. 'Be so good as to join your teammates, Mr Wilkins, and we'll get underway.'

Gerald scowled at Alex and shuffled back across the room. He ignored the boy's parting call of, 'Say hello to

Miss Snooty for me.'

Felicity took hold of Gerald's arm as he sat next to her. 'Did he just call me Miss Snooty?' she asked. Gerald dismissed the question with a grunt.

Mr Beare waited for silence. 'Congratulations to you all for making it this far. As you can see we have lost half of your number already. We are down to twenty-five teams and I expect to lose half of you again on this next leg. For those of you who do succeed, you can be well satisfied that you have shown resilience and intelligence of an extremely high order. For those of you who fail… there will be extra history lessons with Miss Whitaker.'

Sam leaned in close to Ruby. 'Lucky you,' he said. 'You can't lose.'

'One day I'm going to send you to the vet to get fixed,' Ruby replied. Sam shrank back into his seat.

Mr Beare raised his voice again. 'The second leg of the Triple Crown starts today. As soon as we finish here, coaches will take you to the ruins of an ancient castle.' He stabbed the pointer at the map, which showed the outline of a vast medieval complex: moat, battlements, castle keep, bailey, towers, stables, orchards. 'Miss Whitaker tells me it was once a summer house of the boy king of Scotland, James VI. We are very fortunate to have access to the site as it has been closed to the public for decades. Hidden somewhere in the ruins is this.' He held up a large picture of the red stamp that Felicity had found at the checkpoint: an oval surrounded by a band of dots. 'The reason you are here and not becoming more familiar with Pythagoras's theorem is because you found this symbol in the first challenge,' Mr Beare said. 'This same symbol is located somewhere in the confines of the castle complex. Each team will be given a satellite locator. You must record the exact longitude and latitude of the location of the symbol. Those teams who get it right will go on to the third leg of the challenge and the opportunity to make history as the first team to ever complete the Triple Crown. The others will have an appointment with their history books. Are there any questions?'

Sam stuck a hand in the air.

'Yes? Valentine?'

'How long do we have to find it, sir?' Sam asked.

'Good question. You will have twenty-four hours from your arrival at the castle. Camping equipment will be waiting for you there.'

Sam put his hand in the air again. 'So we don't have to pack a tent?' he asked.

Mr Beare arched an eyebrow. 'No, as I said camping equipment will be provided.'

'Terrific,' Sam said, flicking a glance at Ruby. 'Just wanted to be sure.'

Mr Beare brought his hands together with a thunderous clap. 'Be out in the driveway in ten minutes. The buses will leave on time. No exceptions.'

There was a rush of bodies towards the cabins as people scrambled to collect warm clothing for the adventure ahead. Gerald was trailing Sam out the door when he was collared from behind and shoved hard up against a wall.

Alex Baranov gripped Gerald's shirtfront with white knuckles. Gerald could feel the heat of the boy's breath on his face.

'What is your problem, Baranov?' he said, struggling to lift his shoulders away from the wall.

'Maybe I haven't been clear enough,' Alex said coolly. He lifted Gerald away from the wall then slammed him back against the timbers with tooth-rattling force. 'Or maybe you don't hear so well. You will *not* try for the Triple Crown.'

Bang. He slammed him into the wall again.

'Or the Billionaires' Club.'

Bang.

Alex Baranov's eyes narrowed to a laser-sharp intensity. 'You do not need anything more, all right?' he said. 'Your fortune is assured.'

Gerald stopped his struggle. 'What are you talking about?' he said. 'What's my fortune got to do with this?'

Alex drew his mouth into a taut line. He tightened his grip on Gerald's shirt. 'You know as well as I do what that symbol represents,' he said. 'And what it's worth. You don't want to get in my way of finding it.'

Then Gerald sensed someone had joined them.

'What are you pair up to?' It was Mr Beare, his voice dripping with suspicion. 'The buses leave in five minutes, with or without you.'

Alex gave Gerald one more shove against the wall. 'Nothing, sir,' he said, with a forced smile. 'I was just making sure Gerry packed a change of underwear. You know, in case he sees a ghost.'

Mr Beare eyed them both with distrust. 'Five minutes,' he said.

Gerald shouldered past Alex and headed for his cabin, his brain a lashing tempest.

Gerald now knew what he was up against. Whatever mystery lay behind the Triple Crown and the egg-shaped symbol, and whatever treasure was hidden at the Billionaires' Club, Gerald would have to go past Alex Baranov to get to it. But as he thundered along the path, he was at least able to crack a smile. In the grand hierarchy of threats that Gerald was facing, little Alex Baranov and his father came off a distant second to Sir Mason Green.

Dark clouds cloaked the sky as the last of the teams stepped from the buses outside an imposing stone wall that was coated green and grey with centuries of lichen, moss and neglect. Inside the outer wall, visible through a fine mist, stood the crumbling edifice of a once-mighty castle.

Sam paused on the bottom step of the bus and peered

out. 'What a miserable place for a summer house.'

'I doubt even Miss Whitaker would find this place interesting,' Ruby said. They stepped down and joined the rest of the students by a large pair of gates set into the outer wall. Mr Beare wandered among the teams, handing out the satellite devices. 'Once you find the hidden symbol, press the red button to record your exact location. Then make your way back to the courtyard to report in. Just to make it more interesting, the first team back here with the correct coordinates will enjoy a home-cooked meal.'

While Mr Beare was talking, Gerald kept a thoughtful watch on Alex Baranov. While Alex's teammates, Owen, Millicent and Gretchen, chatted in anticipation of the challenge ahead, Alex was silent. He had about him the cool reserve of a poker player holding a spare ace.

A sharp jab to the ribs dragged Gerald from his thoughts. 'Come on, daydreamer,' Felicity said. 'We have five minutes to grab whatever gear we want.'

She hooked her arm into his and pulled him to a long trestle table, where students were picking through a trove of equipment. Battery-powered lamps, coils of rope, hiking sticks, backpacks, water bottles, first-aid kits, snack packs. 'Take as much or as little as you think you'll need,' Mr Beare called out. Sam and Ruby were pulling on down-filled parkas.

'The symbol is hidden somewhere inside the castle, not at the South Pole,' Gerald said. 'Do you really need all this heavy-duty stuff?'

Ruby tossed him a jacket and a headlamp. 'We've decided we're not sleeping till we find it,' she said. 'That means searching through the night. See if you can keep up.'

Gerald pushed an arm through a sleeve and said to Sam, 'Is Ruby always like this in a race?'

'Oh no,' Sam said. He glanced at his sister as she elbowed her way past Millicent to grab a spare water bottle. 'Sometimes she can be really competitive. It can be kind of scary.'

Twenty-five teams poured into the vast castle complex. Gerald caught up to Ruby and Felicity and pulled them to one side. They waited by an ivy-covered column as the rest of the teams scurried into the crumbling maze of buildings. Within seconds they had all disappeared: into outbuildings, through the keep into the castle proper, down into cellars. The outer courtyard was deserted apart from Gerald, Ruby, Sam and Felicity.

'This is going to be a marathon, not a sprint,' Gerald said. 'We may as well take our time and do it logically.'

Sam looked at Gerald as if he had lost his mind. 'Were you not listening?' he said. 'There's a hot meal on offer here.'

Gerald took a beanie from his pocket and pulled it onto his head. 'Do you think Professor McElderry will be tucking into a home-cooked meal tonight?' he asked. A piercing wind whistled through the ramparts above their heads. Sam studied the tops of his boots. Gerald could not make out his mumbled reply.

Ruby pointed to the far corner of the yard. 'Let's start over there and work our way around,' she suggested. She took Gerald's gloved hand and led him towards the ramshackle remains of a stone outbuilding. Granite blocks lay scattered on the ground like a giant child's discarded playthings. 'Look, I know you're worried about the professor,' Ruby said to Gerald. 'We all are. But don't be too harsh on Sam, okay? He's trying to help.' She cast an eye back to her brother as he trudged along beside Felicity. 'Well, his version of help anyway.'

Gerald kicked at a rock and sent it skittering across the ground. 'I just feel this weight,' he said in a low voice. 'This weight of—' he sighed, '— this weight of expectation. We're not playing for a plate of baked beans on toast. Professor McElderry's life depends on us deciphering a coded message and a challenge that no one has ever completed before. It's too much.'

Ruby tightened her grip on Gerald's hand.

They walked in silence for a moment. Then Ruby spoke. 'Do you ever wonder what Mason Green wants so badly that he's willing to kill to get it?' she asked.

'The last thing he wanted was to rule the world,' Gerald said. 'It's hard to imagine this will be a big step down from that.'

'Then maybe we shouldn't be helping him.'

Gerald brushed his thumb across the back of Ruby's

hand. 'Tell that to Professor McElderry.'

Gerald stooped and picked up a rock about the size of a cricket ball. He brushed it clean of dirt and moss, then wound up and tossed it as hard as he could over the battlements. A second after it cleared the top rampart they heard the sound of shattering glass, followed by a shout of anger.

Gerald's eyes popped. 'Crud. I must have hit a bus.' He looked back towards the main gate and saw Sam and Felicity bolting towards them. He cast about and his gaze fell onto a set of stone stairs that disappeared into the ground. 'Quick,' he said to Ruby. 'Down here.' Gerald stumbled down the slippery steps, his boots shuffling across years of undisturbed moss and muck. A dozen steps down and he came face to face with a tangle of dead vines blocking the way.

'What's the holdup?' Ruby asked. Felicity scrambled down to join them. 'The bus driver is coming,' she said, catching her breath. 'And I don't think he's very happy.'

Gerald grabbed a handful of vines and yanked them to one side. 'You didn't happen to pack a machete, did you?' he asked.

Sam bundled down the stairs right into Felicity's back. 'Careful!' she called over her shoulder.

'Sorry,' Sam said. 'But one of the drivers has just stormed into the courtyard and he looks mighty cross.'

Gerald buried both hands into the curtain of foliage and shoved hard. He did not want to be pulled out of the challenge because of a broken bus window. He squeezed through the vegetation and blundered further down the stairwell with the others behind him. An earthy aroma of damp decay filled his nostrils as he fished the headlamp from his pocket. He flicked the switch and strapped it on. Yellow light fell onto the grimy steps ahead.

'Where's this taking us?' Ruby's voice followed Gerald as he ventured deeper into the dark.

'Away from grumpy bus drivers seeking revenge,' he said. 'I think there's an opening up ahead.'

The torchlight fell on an ancient oak door set into an archway in the stone. Gerald took hold of a heavy iron ring bolted into the timbers. He tensed his shoulders and pushed. The wooden portal disintegrated in a puff of dry rot, showering dust everywhere. Gerald staggered through the opening still clutching the iron ring. Ruby, Felicity and Sam stumbled in after him.

'What did you do to that door?' Ruby asked, gaping at the splintered remains, piled up like termite droppings on the floor.

Gerald looked back at her in surprise. 'I don't know my own strength,' he said. 'Remember that the next time you choose to annoy me.'

Three more beams of light filled the room as Sam, Ruby and Felicity flicked on their torches. 'I suppose this is as good a place as any to start looking for the symbol,' Gerald said.

A quick scout of the room turned up nothing.

'The only thing you'll find in here is a potential case of pneumonia,' Ruby said. 'Let's keep going.' She led them through a doorway in the far wall and into a narrow tunnel carved through the bedrock.

The four headlamps shone down a passage and disappeared into the darkness. They walked single file into the unknown.

'I bet no one has been down here for years,' Felicity said from the back of the line. 'Maybe decades.'

'Maybe centuries,' Ruby said. Her boots scuffed through a carpet of dust.

Sam tapped Gerald on the shoulder. 'You don't suppose there would be any rats down here, do you?' he asked.

Ruby laughed from the front of their little caravan. 'I'll keep an eye out for you, hero,' she said.

They passed a series of deep alcoves on either side of the tunnel. The headlamps illuminated racks of decaying wine casks and even a rusted suit of armour. But there was no sign of the egg-shaped symbol.

After what seemed hours of fruitless searching along the dank tunnel, Ruby suddenly stopped. The others piled into her back.

'What is it?' Felicity whispered.

Ruby squinted into the gloom ahead. 'I thought I heard something.'

'Rats?' Sam asked.

Ruby shook her head. 'You and your stupid rats.

No, numbskull. Voices. Come on.'

Felicity, Sam and Gerald bunched together behind Ruby as they crept along the passage to a narrow opening. Ruby paused. She flicked off her headlamp and motioned for the others to do the same. Darkness surrounded them.

Ruby peered through the gap, her eyes struggling to adjust.

Sam craned his neck over her shoulder. 'What do you see?'

Ruby shot up a hand and pinched her brother's lips together. 'Ssshhh.'

Gerald strained his eyes but could make out nothing.

Then Ruby's urgent whisper filtered back to him.

'I think it's Alex Baranov,' she said.

Chapter 16

Dim light seeped through from the opening at the end of the tunnel. Gerald crawled forward, crowding in behind Sam, trying to get a better view. They looked into a cavernous chamber hewn from the subterranean granite. Six battery-powered lanterns were dotted around the floor, barely illuminating the immense space and the vaulted brickwork ceiling. But it was enough for Gerald to see a rickety assembly of scaffolding shaped like a wedding cake teetering up to the ceiling. Halfway up the structure was Alex Baranov. Millicent, Owen and Gretchen stood at the base, staring up at him.

'Come down,' Millicent called. 'You're going to hurt yourself.'

Alex ignored her and clambered higher up the

scaffold, his headlamp lighting the way.

'What's he doing?' Gerald whispered to Ruby. This earned him a sharp *shush* and a clip around the ear.

Alex climbed on until he stood on a platform at the top of the scaffolding. He steadied himself with the palms of his hands flat to the ceiling beneath the apex of the central arch. His headlamp shone a pool of light onto the keystone that held the arch in place.

Ruby gasped. She grabbed Gerald by the collar and yanked his head up next to hers. 'Look,' she hissed, ignoring his grunts of discomfort. Gerald followed Ruby's pointed finger to where Alex Baranov was inspecting the face of the keystone.

And then he saw it.

The outline of an egg-shaped symbol was carved into the front of the keystone.

'Are you sure you locked the door behind us?' Alex called down to his teammates. 'I don't want anyone walking in on this.'

'Don't worry. No one is going to find you,' Gretchen called back, sounding bored. 'Can't we just record this on the satellite thingie and get back for dinner. I'm starved.' She plopped herself down on a low strut, sending a wobble up the wooden frame.

'Careful!' Alex cried, pressing his hands harder against the ceiling. 'This thing is unsteady enough without you sitting on it.'

Gretchen scowled up to him. 'Are you calling me fat?'

'No, I'm calling you stupid.' Alex carefully removed his backpack from his shoulders and, balancing precariously twenty metres above the stone floor, opened the top flap.

'What's he taken out?' Ruby whispered.

Gerald shoved her to one side, pushing her face into a wall. 'It looks like a mallet,' he said. 'A rubber mallet.'

Ruby pushed back, cracking skulls with Gerald. They both emitted muffled yelps.

'What's he want with a rubber mallet?' Ruby asked. Her eyes squeezed shut and her hands wrapped around the back of her head.

Gerald's eyes jolted wide. 'The symbol,' he said. 'I bet he's going to knock out the stone with the symbol on it.'

'Why would he do that?' Felicity asked.

'Alex said the symbol represents something,' Gerald said. 'Something that's really valuable. I think it might be the same thing that Mason Green wants us to find.' He rose to his knees.

'What are you doing?' Ruby asked.

'I'm going to stop him,' Gerald replied. 'Or Professor McElderry is—' He didn't finish the sentence.

Gerald shot from cover and into the open. He was across the cellar floor in an instant, brushing past Millicent and Owen where they sat, bored rigid, on the floor. He shouldered Gretchen out of the way, sending her spinning onto her backside in the dust, and launched himself up the scaffolding.

The structure creaked and juddered as Gerald clambered hand over hand up the wooden struts.

Alex, lining up to take a swing at the keystone, was almost shaken from his perch. He dropped to his hands and knees with a startled cry, landing on all fours amid a mess of off-cut masonry blocks and ancient wooden tools. A chisel tipped over the edge and tumbled to the floor. It ricocheted off a beam just above Gerald's head, missing him by centimetres.

Alex clung to the top planks and unleashed a stream of abuse. 'Stop it, you bloody fool!' he cried. 'You'll bring the lot down.'

Gerald paused halfway up, breathing hard. There was a manic gleam in his eyes. 'Tell me what's so important about that stone block and I'll stop,' he said. He did not take his gaze off Alex for a second.

Baranov glanced up to the stone that locked the arch in place, then down to Gerald clinging to the scaffolding below. 'Not a chance,' he said. Their eyes were locked in a wrestle of wills.

Gerald's mouth stretched into a grim smile, and he shook the bars like a wild chimp trying to escape from the zoo. Alex dropped to his belly, still clutching the rubber mallet. Chunks of stone tumbled from the top platform. Bodies dived for cover as the falling masonry exploded on impact.

Gerald looked down and saw that Ruby, Felicity and Sam had emerged from the hidden passage to watch the show. Gerald gave the scaffolding another almighty shake. A timber brace snapped free and cartwheeled to the floor. Then a cry echoed down from the ceiling.

'It's yours!' Alex's voice cracked with fear. 'You can have it!'

Gerald stopped the shaking. Alex peered over the edge of the top platform, his eyes showing white. 'You'll give it to me?' Gerald called up.

Alex glared death at him, but nodded. Gerald resumed his steady ascent. When he reached the top he found the other boy sitting amid a litter of building rubble, his arms wrapped around his knees.

'I'm sorry I had to do that,' Gerald said.

'You could have bloody killed me,' Alex spat back.

Gerald shook his head. 'I wasn't thinking clearly,' he said. 'But trust me—I have to complete this challenge.'

Then Alex—bluff, confident Alex Baranov—did something that took Gerald completely by surprise.

He started crying. Swollen tears rolled down his cheeks.

Gerald looked at the boy sceptically. 'Are you all right?' he asked.

Alex tried to swallow the sobs. 'Why do you even want it?' he asked, his voice cracking. 'What good is it to you? My father is going to kill me if I don't get it for him.'

Gerald pulled himself the last few steps to the top of the scaffolding. 'I hardly think your father is going to—'

Alex lashed out a hand and grabbed Gerald's jacket.

'You saw him,' he said. 'In Rice Crispies' office. You saw what he's like. You don't make a fortune in Russian oil by playing by the rules. He'll do anything to get his hands on it.' Alex clenched his teeth. 'Anything.'

Then realisation dawned on Alex's face. 'You don't know what's inside this stone, do you? Or what the symbol means.'

Gerald said nothing. He could feel his advantage slipping away.

Alex wiped his hand across his eyes, smearing tears down his cheeks, and laughed. 'Weren't you listening in that history lesson?' he said. 'This was James VI's summer house. A friend of his left something here for safekeeping.'

Gerald fumbled for a response but he was cut off by Alex's triumphant cry: 'It's Cornelius Drebbel's perpetual motion machine, you idiot!'

Chapter 17

Gerald's mind spun, whirring and buzzing as quickly—and about as effectively—as Sam's perpetual motion machine.

This is what Sergei Baranov was after, and the reason he did not want Gerald to try for the Triple Crown: a mythical contraption stolen from the collection of Rudolph II of Bohemia?

Then a sudden realisation tapped on the window of Gerald's subconscious: was the perpetual motion machine also the object of Sir Mason Green's desires?

Gerald's heart raced. It made no sense. How could an impossible machine that defied the laws of thermodynamics be worth Professor McElderry's life? He rattled his head to try to get his thoughts back on track. He could worry about the sense of it all later. All he had to worry about now was getting Drebbel's machine to Mason Green.

Gerald looked up to see that Alex had pulled himself onto his knees and held the rubber mallet back over one shoulder. Gerald flinched.

Alex caught the look on his face. 'Don't worry, Gerry. I'm not going to knock you off,' he said. 'Not yet, anyway. Here, come and be a help for a change.' He nodded towards a large stone block by Gerald's knee. 'You're going to have to lift that up and shove it into place once I've tapped the keystone out far enough.'

Gerald looked at the lump of rock. 'Why?'

'Because if you don't plug the gap the ceiling will collapse and bury us under eighteen tons of rubble,' Alex said. 'Is that enough of a reason?'

Then Ruby's voice drifted up from the floor far below. 'Gerald, what's going on up there?'

Gerald did not take his eyes off Alex. 'We're agreeing on a date for a sleepover,' he called back. 'What do you think we're doing? You might like to step back a bit.'

Alex flashed Gerald a mocking smile. 'Ready?' He raised the mallet from his shoulder and swung it square against the keystone. The impact sent a shudder through the scaffolding, like a shiver running down a giraffe's neck. Gerald dropped to his hands and knees, waiting for the structure to collapse under him.

But somehow the tower held true.

The keystone did not budge.

'Come on,' Alex said. 'Be ready. I'll get it this time.' He lined up again and delivered another whack to the stone. This time it moved out about ten centimetres. 'Lift the block ready,' he said to Gerald.

Gerald sucked in a breath and hoisted the stone onto his shoulder. It must have weighed twenty kilograms. A blaze of pain flashed through his collarbone. 'Give us a hand, then,' Gerald grunted.

Between them, Gerald and Alex worked the block in behind the loosened keystone, fitting it neatly into the gap. Alex whacked it with the mallet, smacking it hard up against the keystone. He paused to catch his breath. 'Someone cut that block to just the right shape,' he said. 'A few more good hits and the keystone will be free and this block will be in its place. The arch will be as good as new.'

Gerald took a careful pace back. The structure beneath his feet seemed to sway. He glanced down and was suddenly very aware of just how high they were above the stone floor. He saw Ruby staring up at him, concern written across her face.

There once was a girl named Ruby...

No! He had to concentrate.

Alex struck the block with a tremendous clout. The stone surged forward, spitting the keystone out like a watermelon pip. Gerald was taken by surprise as the heavy granite block fell into his fingers.

Fell *through* his fingers.

Gerald dropped it.

'Careful!' Alex yelled.

But it was too late.

The keystone smashed onto a plank at the top of the scaffold then spilled over the edge. Gerald and Alex watched as the keystone fell through the air and hit the floor far below like a bomb.

'You idiot!' Alex yelled. 'If that machine is broken…'

Gerald did not want to think of the consequences. He may have cost the professor his life.

Alex looked at Gerald. Gerald held his gaze for a moment. Then they both moved in a clattering dash down the side of the scaffolding. 'Ruby! Sam!' Gerald yelled as he rattled down the wooden frame. 'It's in the keystone. Quick!'

Alex yelled out for his teammates, urging them into action. 'Find it!'

Gerald and Alex jumped to the floor at the same moment and dashed to the pile of rubble. Gretchen and Owen were already on their knees, picking through the debris. Ruby and Sam dived in seconds later.

Alex pushed his way into the scrum, shouldering Ruby aside. She landed awkwardly on a sharp rock and yelped in pain. In a mad flurry of digging, Alex pulled a sturdy metal box from the wreckage and held it above his head in triumph.

'I've got it!' he cried.

The searchers stopped. All eyes were on Alex as he slid his fingernails under the lid, ready to prise it open.

'Stop,' Gerald said, breathing hard. He was on his knees, begging. 'You said you'd give it to me.'

Alex didn't take his eyes from the prize in his hands. 'Well, I guess I lied then.' He eased off the lid and let it fall to the ground with a clatter.

He looked in the box.

'Well?' said Gretchen. 'What's inside?'

Alex's voice was dry as desert sand.

'It's...it's empty,' he said. A look of absolute desolation washed across his face. The words had barely left his mouth when there was a creaking groan from above. Gerald looked up. It took a moment to register what was happening. By the time the first bricks were hitting the floor Gerald was on his feet and he, Ruby, Sam and Felicity were sprinting for the passageway.

The roof was falling in.

The headmaster's office at the Oates Outdoor Education Centre was crowded with dust-caked bodies.

On one side, in a sullen line, stood Gerald, Ruby, Felicity and Sam. On the other, equally sullen, were Alex, Gretchen, Owen and Millicent. Between the two groups stood Mr Beare who, while not sullen, certainly did not look happy.

Facing them all was Dr Crispin. And judging by the shade of purple his face had acquired, he was not happy at all.

'It is a miracle that no one was injured or killed,' the headmaster said, pacing the small amount of carpet left vacant in his office. 'What on earth were you all thinking, going into such a dangerous place?'

Felicity opened her mouth to answer, but Dr Crispin flung up a hand, cutting her off. He was mid-rant and in no mood for interruption. 'How would your parents react if you had been hurt, or worse? As it is I've got the Scottish Heritage Council baying for my blood. Can you imagine their response to all of this? You lot stumble into a previously undiscovered cellar under a heritage-listed castle and instead of reporting your finding you blinking-well destroy it. That castle may be a ruin but that doesn't mean you can ruin it some more.' The headmaster leaned back against his desk and wiped a checked pocket handkerchief across his brow.

Gerald stared glum-faced at Alex Baranov.

It had been an eventful afternoon. After the first of the stone blocks from the cellar archway started raining down like mortar shells, Gerald had managed to lead everyone back to the hidden doorway. They dashed along the passage, keeping just ahead of a roiling plume of dust that chased them though the tunnel. They shot out of the stairwell into the courtyard like a fusillade of cannonballs. Gerald gave a garbled explanation to

Mr Beare about what had happened while somehow avoiding any mention of the scaffolding, the rubber mallet or the keystone. But with a gaping sinkhole suddenly appearing in the centre of the castle grounds, swallowing up entire buildings, the second leg of the Triple Crown was abandoned. Everyone was marched onto the buses for the drive back to the camp. Gerald avoided taking the coach with the jagged crack across its windscreen.

Dr Crispin ranted on and on. Discipline this. Responsibility that. Gerald figured that if he said nothing, the headmaster would eventually run out of puff and everyone could go and get something to eat. But Dr Crispin, clearly rant-fit from a lifetime in training, was showing no signs of fatigue.

'And who came up with this year's Triple Crown challenge anyway?' he barked, turning his full fury to Mr Beare. 'Why were students at that castle to begin with? Who in their right mind would send a hundred hormone-addled teenagers into a castle? Can you answer me that?'

Mr Beare's pasty complexion faded to a sickly greyish hue. He groped for a response. 'Um...we used an external supplier,' he said. 'A company that specialises in this sort of thing.'

'Specialises in what, exactly?' the headmaster interrupted. 'Endangering students' lives and a spot of castle demolition on the side?' He seethed at the hapless maths teacher. 'Out!' he cried to the eight students. 'I need to continue this conversation with Mr Beare. Alone.'

Gerald did not wait for a second invitation. He darted to the freedom of the cold afternoon outside, followed closely by Ruby, Sam and Felicity. They huddled together by a frozen fishpond in the courtyard.

'Well that was about as much fun as a knee to the groin,' Sam muttered, bundling in close to the others to escape the cold. 'Who's for something to eat?'

Ruby wrapped her arms around herself and shivered. 'For once, I agree with Sam. Let's see what's on offer in the dining hall. Are you coming, Felicity?'

Felicity bounced on her toes, like an over-eager spaniel late for its afternoon walk. 'Yes. And I have something I really need to show you all. It's super important.'

Gerald looked at her with interest. 'What is it? You've been acting strange since we got on the bus back at the castle.'

Felicity gave him an impish grin. 'I'll tell you once we've got some hot food in front of us and there are no prying eyes about.'

They started towards the dining hall, but Gerald paused. 'You go on,' he said. 'There's something I need to do first.'

Gerald held back in the courtyard garden outside the headmaster's office, rubbing his arms to keep warm, until he saw what he was waiting for.

'Your father arranged all of this, didn't he?' Gerald crossed to Alex Baranov as the boy stepped from a covered walkway and onto the gravel path that led to the cabins. 'This challenge for the Triple Crown. It was all designed to locate the hiding place for Drebbel's perpetual motion machine, wasn't it.'

Alex buried his hands deep in his pockets and strode along the path, head down and saying nothing.

'It's a clever way to get a hundred sets of eyes looking for you,' Gerald said. 'First, you weed out the hopeless ones by setting a twenty-mile hike to find a symbol—a symbol that marks the place where the perpetual motion machine was hidden a few hundred years ago. Then you let the clever ones loose to try to find the hiding place. What was the third leg in the challenge? To retrieve the machine? How proud your father would have been when you were the one to do it. How did he convince Mr Beare to go ahead with the idea? Throw some money his way, did he? Isn't that the Baranov solution to everything?'

Alex stopped and swung around. 'Forget about it, will you?' he said. His eyes drilled into Gerald's forehead. 'My father thought the machine was hidden in James VI's castle but it wasn't there so it's no use banging on about it. My father has even less reason to be proud of me now.'

Gerald paused as an unexpected emotion washed through him. Was it pity?

Alex dropped his eyes to the ground. A fresh gust sent a flurry of leaf litter across the courtyard, whipping at Gerald's ankles. He suddenly felt very cold.

'I'll see you around,' Alex said in a low voice, then he turned to walk away. Gerald reached out and took his arm.

'I'm sorry about all of this,' he said, 'I have to get that perpetual motion machine or my friend is going to—', Gerald stopped and sighed. 'It has to do with Sir Mason Green,' he said. 'It's complicated.'

Alex stared down at where Gerald held him by the sleeve. 'Sir Mason Green?' he said. 'I hardly think he's going to cause you any problems.'

Gerald grunted. 'You don't know him like I do,' he said.

Alex shook his arm free. 'You're an idiot, Wilkins. Mason Green is my godfather.'

Gerald stared open-mouthed as Alex Baranov stalked off to the cabins.

By the time Gerald reached the dining hall, Sam was well into his second helping of lasagne. Ruby looked at Gerald with alarm as he dropped onto the bench beside her. 'You look terrible,' she said.

Gerald took a moment to respond. He was still trying to process what Baranov had just told him. He looked at Ruby, glassy-eyed. 'Sir Mason Green is only Alex Baranov's godfather,' he said.

Ruby and Felicity gaped back at him.

'His what?' Sam said.

'It looks like Mason Green and Sergei Baranov are closer than we thought,' Gerald said.

'Then why is one of them trying to stop you from finding the perpetual motion machine and the other is doing all he can to get you to do it?' Ruby asked.

Gerald held his head in his hands. 'If I knew that, I wouldn't be in this stupid situation,' he said. He rolled his eyes up to Felicity. 'What was it you wanted to show us?'

Felicity bounced in her seat and started babbling. 'You won't believe what I've found,' she said, her face alight with excitement. 'It's too amazing. Too, too amazing.'

Gerald had seen Felicity in full excitement mode before, but it was usually something to do with horses. After the day he had endured, he was not in the mood for a twenty-minute monologue about the latest from the Argentinean polo championships.

'Oh please,' he said with a heavy sigh, 'just tell us what it is.'

Felicity put a stout little book, bound in faded brown leather, onto the table in front of him. Gerald looked at it. 'And?' he said.

'It's a diary,' Felicity said, doubling the bounce rate in her seat. 'It was in the mess of broken rubble and stonework in the cellar after the keystone was knocked out. It must have been hidden inside the stone.'

'How did you get it?' Sam asked.

'It landed right at my feet,' Felicity said. 'Everyone else was looking for something much bigger, so no one noticed it.'

'Except for you,' Gerald said.

Felicity bounced some more. 'Except for me.'

Gerald picked up the book; it was barely bigger than the palm of his hand.

'Open it,' Felicity said to him, nudging Ruby with excitement.

Gerald flipped open the front cover. Written on the first page, in a fine scrawling hand, were the words: *This journal is the property of...*

Gerald's eyes flicked back up to Felicity, and he said in disbelief, 'This is the diary of Jeremy Davey?'

Chapter 18

Gerald carefully turned the pages in the little book. Each one was dense with handwritten scrawls. Every few pages there was a faded newspaper clipping, pasted in with glue that was cracked and brown with age. 'Why would Jeremy Davey leave his diary in the cellar of some rotten castle in Scotland?' he asked.

'For the same reason he threw a coded message in a bottle into the sea,' Sam said. 'He was a nutter.'

Ruby stirred sugar into her tea. 'Let's stick to what we know, shall we?' she said. 'Jeremy Davey stuffed a coded message into a bottle and tossed it into the sea sometime around October 1835. We don't know where or why. Now, almost two hundred years later, his diary turns up in the ruins of the summer castle of James VI, the boy king of Scotland.'

'I know some quite interesting things about him,' Sam said.

Ruby brandished her teaspoon in Sam's face. 'Keep quiet,' she said. 'I will insert this into your nose if I have to.' Sam stared defiantly at his sister but his head shrank back into his shoulders like a deflating pool toy.

Felicity pressed her fingers to her lips to stop herself from laughing. 'And the diary was in a keystone which, if you can believe Alex Baranov, was where the king was hiding a perpetual motion machine built by his good friend Cornelius Drebbel.'

'But the machine wasn't there,' Gerald said. 'Someone had already taken it.'

'Who? Jeremy Davey?' Felicity said.

'Possibly,' Ruby said. 'Whoever it was built that rickety scaffolding up to the ceiling, used those old tools to fashion a plug for the keystone and made off with whatever was inside that metal box that Alex found.'

'Then why leave the scaffold still standing?' Gerald said. 'Wouldn't you take it down so everything looked undisturbed? And why stick your diary there in its place? That's just bizarre.'

Ruby thought for a moment. 'Maybe once they found what they were after they just took off,' she said. 'No point hanging around once you've got the treasure. And as for the diary? Maybe he dropped it accidentally. We may never know.'

Gerald leafed through the pages, trying to make out the tiny handwritten passages. 'So why would Jeremy Davey take a perpetual motion machine? And was it even him?'

Ruby leaned across and took the book from Gerald. 'Whether it was Davey or not, we've got his diary. And it could give us a clue to the coded message. It's only a few weeks until you go to New York for the Billionaires' Club initiation, Gerald. We need to have it worked out by then.'

The conversation was interrupted by a rolling grumble from Gerald's stomach. He rubbed a hand across his belly. 'I need food, then I can think,' he said. 'But I have been tossing around one idea.' He leaned across the table and looked to Felicity, then Ruby and finally to Sam. 'Why don't you all come to New York with me?'

He was met by a chorus of surprise.

'I'm taking the Archer corporate jet anyway so it's easy enough for you lot to hitch a ride,' Gerald said. 'Obviously not to the Billionaires' Club—Alex and I are stuck doing that together.' He shook his head at the prospect of spending a night in Alex Baranov's company. 'But once I find the box that Green wants, it would be really good to have you guys around for when I deliver it to him. It would make me feel…I don't know…more secure. You just need to get your parents to agree. Mr Fry will be there to look after us. Well, at least until we ditch him.'

'But aren't we meant to stay here at the camp during the mid-term break?' Felicity said.

Gerald climbed off the bench and turned towards the kitchens. 'After what happened at the castle today, I get the feeling that Rice Crispies will be more than happy at the prospect of getting rid of us for a while.'

Before Gerald could move, Kobe Abraham ran into the dining hall and raced up to the table. 'Have you heard?' Kobe gasped, steadying himself on the table's edge while catching his breath. 'You know Marcus Budge? He's been caught smoking with some girl behind the boys' toilets. Rice Crispies is going ape.' Kobe sucked in more air. 'The teachers are going through all the cabins, searching for cigarettes and anything else they can find.'

'Is that a problem for you, Kobe?' Ruby asked.

Kobe took another breath. 'I've got some magazines stashed under my mattress that I'd rather Crispies didn't find.' He pushed himself off the table and dashed out of the hall.

Sam and Gerald looked at each other with a growing sense of panic.

Felicity eyed them curiously. 'Why are you two looking worried?' she said. 'You don't have any cigarettes, do you?'

Gerald and Sam stood from the table. 'No,' Gerald said, his pulse quickening. 'But there is one thing.'

'What's that?' Felicity asked.

'The vandalised remains of a priceless French

painting, rolled up in a tube under my pillow,' Gerald said. He and Sam eyed each other again, then bolted for the door.

By the time they reached the cabin, Dr Crispin and Miss Frobisher were completing their search. A small crowd had gathered to witness the scene. Charlie Blagden stood forlornly beside a pile of contraband, looking entirely unhappy.

'Chocolate hobnobs, kitkats, mars bars, chewing gum.' Miss Frobisher picked through the stash of sweets and biscuits. 'There's enough junk food here to open a corner shop.'

Gerald and Sam skidded to a stop on the gravel path, jostling into each other. Dr Crispin stood before the hapless Charlie, giving him a severe dressing down for hoarding snacks against school rules. The headmaster's voice cut like a whip through the still afternoon air. But Gerald did not register a word that was uttered. All he could do was stare at the way the headmaster punctuated his rant by slapping a cardboard tube into his open left hand.

'Is that it?' Sam squeaked in Gerald's ear.

'Yes,' Gerald squeaked back.

He could not take his eyes from the cardboard container, moving back and forth like a metronome.

Ruby and Felicity arrived just as Dr Crispin dismissed Charlie and turned his attention towards Gerald and Sam.

'Gerald Wilkins!' the headmaster barked. 'I would

like a word with you.' He shook the tube in Gerald's direction. From inside came the sound of something sliding up and down. 'This was under your pillow,' Dr Crispin continued. 'Are you hiding anything in here? Cigarettes? Matches?'

Gerald's pulse rate doubled. 'I don't think you'd believe me if I told you,' he said.

Dr Crispin's eyes narrowed. 'I see,' he said. He wedged his thumbs under the rim at one end of the tube and flicked off the red cap with a sharp 'pop'. A rolled bundle slid into his hand.

Gerald and Sam looked at each other in heart-attack inducing panic.

Dr Crispin unrolled the bundle and stared at the contents.

Gerald felt he was about to be violently ill. 'I can explain,' he began.

The headmaster raised his eyes and delivered Gerald an ice-pick stare. 'Can you, Wilkins?' he asked. 'Where do you even begin to explain this?'

Dr Crispin held up a detailed pencil sketch of himself. He was dressed in a ballerina's tutu and fishnet stockings, while pouring a large packet of Rice Crispies into a bowl. Gerald's signature was plain to see at the bottom of the drawing.

Gerald's eyes bulged. He recognised the sketch from his notebook. He opened his mouth and a stutter of *ums* and *ahs* stumbled out.

Dr Crispin glared at Gerald. 'I will not be made a fool of, boy,' he hissed. 'I don't care how much money your mother gives to the building fund.' He screwed up the sketch, shoved the tube into Gerald's chest and stormed off.

Gerald and Sam stared after him, then at the cardboard cylinder in Gerald's hands.

'What happened to the Delacroix painting?' Sam asked.

'I have no idea,' Gerald said.

They both looked up to find Ruby and Felicity laughing at them.

'They really don't deserve us, do they Ruby?' Felicity said.

'No, Flicka, they do not,' Ruby replied.

Gerald looked from one smug face to the other. 'What are you talking about?'

'You were so sure you could wander about with a piece of priceless art and not get caught,' Felicity said. 'I was worried something like this might happen so I took the Delacroix and hid it properly, and not just tucked under my pillow.'

Gerald could feel his cheeks reddening as he gave a mumbled thanks.

'Sorry, I didn't hear that,' Felicity said.

Gerald screwed up his face. 'I said "thank you",' he mumbled a little louder. 'But why did you have to replace it with that drawing I did of Rice Crispies?'

'To teach you a little lesson, Gerald Wilkins,' Felicity said.

Ruby put her arm around Felicity's shoulders. 'I think we might change the team motto to *Ruby and Felicity are always right.*'

Gerald looked across to Charlie as Miss Frobisher made him toss the cache of snacks into the bin. His stomach rumbled again. 'I could murder a chocolate hobnob round about now,' he said.

In the weeks before the New York initiation, Gerald pored over the message from Jeremy Davey. Despite long nights spent dedicated to the task at a lamp-lit table with bottomless mugs of hot chocolate, he was no closer to finding the keyword that would unlock the code. When he wasn't filling in endless alphabet grids, he was staring at a picture of Eugène Delacroix's *Liberty Leading the People* that Ruby had found in the library's encyclopaedia. He felt he knew every square centimetre of the painting, particularly the dull blue satchel that was slung over the young boy's shoulder—the original of which was rolled in a cardboard tube and hidden inside the hollow leg of his bunk.

Felicity took charge of the forensic investigation of Jeremy Davey's diary, combing through the document for any clues that might provide the keyword. She recruited help from the best resource available at Oates: Kobe Abraham.

When Gerald heard about Felicity's decision to enlist Kobe's assistance, he was not sure it was a great idea.

'Nonsense, Gerald,' Felicity said. 'Kobe is like a factoid sponge. He absorbs any piece of information put in front of him and links it with everything else he knows. He's a machine. Take this little gem.' Felicity opened the diary to a faded newspaper clipping.

Gerald shrugged. 'It's a list of names from an old newspaper,' he said. 'So what?'

Felicity frowned at him. 'You're lucky I'm not Ruby or you could be experiencing physical pain. This is from *The Times* in 1817. It's a list of people sentenced to transportation to New South Wales.'

Gerald shrugged again. 'Lots of convicts got sent to Australia back then. What's so special about this lot.'

Felicity pointed to one name on the list. 'Kobe thought this name looked interesting.'

Gerald peered at the list. 'Ralph Davey?' he said. He thought for a moment. 'Do you think it's a relative of Jeremy's?'

Felicity nodded eagerly. 'Kobe and I think he might be Jeremy's father. The date would fit.'

'So, his dad was transported to Sydney for stealing a loaf of bread. Does that get us any closer to the keyword?'

'What did I say to you about physical pain? Ralph Davey was not sent to Australia for stealing. Kobe also found this article, about Davey's trial. He was a Luddite.' Felicity made the statement as if it answered everything.

Gerald looked at her blankly. 'And a Luddite is what, exactly?'

Felicity flicked her hair behind her shoulders in the way she always did just before showing off some piece of superior knowledge. 'We learned about them in history class at St Hilda's last year,' she said. 'The Luddites were a group of craftsmen and textile workers who tried to hold back the industrial revolution in the early 1800s. They smashed up the machines that were replacing them. There were riots in the north of England. The protest leaders were hanged, or transported to Australia.'

Gerald's face remained blank. 'So Jeremy Davey's father was one of the Luddites sent to Australia because he burnt down a widget factory. How does this help us?'

Felicity flicked her hair again. 'Have you thought that his father's name could be the keyword? Or Luddite, maybe?'

Gerald's eyes widened and he opened his notepad to his many scribblings trying to crack the code. He tried *Ralph* and *Ralphdvey* and *ludite* in the grid. 'You have to drop any letters that appear twice,' he explained as he beavered away with a pencil, 'otherwise you end up with more than twenty-six letters which is, you know, not going to work.'

As it turned out, none of Gerald's guesses worked either. He tossed down his pencil in frustration. 'Well that got us absolutely nowhere,' he said. 'Did you and Kobe make any other grand discoveries?'

'Don't be like that,' Felicity said. 'We all want to rescue Professor McElderry. You're not the only one worried about him.'

Gerald felt a flush of shame. As his departure for New York drew closer, he was becoming increasingly irritable. There had been no further contact from Sir Mason Green and, if anything, the silence had been worse than the ordeal of sitting opposite the insane old man on a remote highland track sipping a cup of tea. Gerald's nerves were on edge.

'I'm sorry,' he mumbled. 'I'm just—'

Felicity put her hand on Gerald's arm. 'We did find one other thing,' she said. 'Most of the diary is Davey complaining about how hard it is to provide for his mother and younger brothers. It sounds like he was having to put food on the table for the whole family from quite a young age.'

Gerald drummed his fingers against his cheek, thinking. 'That fits with his father being transported, I guess,' he said.

'And then there's this,' Felicity said. 'It's another clipping. This one is about a voyage around the world being planned for 1831, for a ship called HMS *Beagle*. Davey has circled it. It says the ship was due to leave England and chart the west coast of South America before crossing the Pacific to visit—'

'Australia!' Gerald got in first. 'You think that's the ship Davey was on?'

'To go to find his father. That is exactly what Kobe and I think,' Felicity said. 'And then, around October 1835, the young midshipman Jeremy Davey got into some sort of trouble and tossed a coded message into the sea.'

Gerald looked down at his notebook and ran his fingers across the jumble of random letters that he had copied from Davey's note. If Felicity and Kobe were right that Jeremy Davey had written the message while trying to find his father, it somehow made Gerald's task that bit more noble. He had a sudden urge to know Jeremy Davey's fate.

Chapter 19

New York City! Gerald had seen a lot of the world in his eight months as a billionaire. London, New Delhi, Paris, Rome, Athens, Prague and quite a few points in between. And now, once again, his senses were dazzled, this time by the mad scramble of downtown Manhattan in evening rush hour. Lights blazed in shopfronts, casting a rainbow of colours onto the fresh blanket of late winter snow on the footpaths. Harried locals did battle with gawping tourists along the bustling boulevards, all with someplace to go and scant time to get there. Streams of people in overcoats and woollen hats swirled around the hotdog vendors and pretzel carts. Hawkers in sandwich boards stood on corners, trying to convince shoppers to venture down side streets for the latest fashion wear at sale prices. A jangling chorus of car horns echoed along the canyons of office towers and apartment buildings, like an orchestra tuning up in never-ending disarray, waiting for a conductor who would never appear. Police on point duty tried to keep the yellow cabs and the cars and the courier vans and the limousines and the buses and the delivery trucks and the postal carts and the tourist coaches moving smoothly in a stop-start crawl that was barely faster than walking pace.

In the middle of all the chaos, Gerald's limousine edged along Fifth Avenue. Gerald, Ruby, Felicity and Sam pressed their noses against the windows and gazed at the frenetic activity of the night outside.

'It's just like the movies,' Sam said in awe, 'only there's more of it.'

'Look at all those boutiques,' Felicity said, her eyes widening. 'I could do some serious shopping here.'

'Once we get the professor free from Mason Green, maybe we can spend a little time in the shops,' Ruby said. 'Right, Gerald?'

Gerald tapped on the glass partition behind the driver's seat. 'Once we rescue Professor McElderry, you can swing by the ankles from the top of the Statue of Liberty if you want,' he said. The partition slid down, revealing the back of Mr Fry's head. 'How far to go, St John?' Gerald asked.

The butler's jaw tightened at the use of his first name. 'Sir will arrive at the Billionaires' Club in a matter of minutes. I will then take your companions to the Royal Suite at the Plaza, where they are free to order room service until they split at the seams. I shall retire to the hotel bar, on high alert for unsavoury characters and a mere telephone call away should anyone require my assistance or the world suddenly come to an end, whichever occurs last.'

'Sounds great, *Sinjin*,' Sam said from the back seat. 'Do you think they'll have cheese burgers on the room service menu?'

Mr Fry sniffed. 'I should be astonished if they have anything else.'

The limousine pulled to the kerb outside a free-standing building that overlooked a small park, blanketed in snow. Gerald peered through the window at the red-brick structure and counted up twelve storeys. An iron fire-escape zigzagged down a side wall that faced a narrow laneway. A dozen dormer windows in the roof looked down over the bustling street below. Black wrought-iron flower boxes, empty for the winter, sat beneath the tall, narrow windows along the street frontage, every one of which appeared to be bricked over. The entire building exuded a cold indifference to the world.

Gerald climbed out of the limo and ducked his head back inside. 'Wish me luck,' he said. Sam gave him a thumbs up and Felicity blew him a kiss. Gerald turned to Ruby. She gave him a stern look.

'Do you have the note from Davey?' she asked. 'And the piece of Delacroix painting?'

Gerald patted his backpack and nodded. He was about to say goodbye when Ruby jumped forward and threw her arms around his neck. She squeezed warm and hard, then kissed him on the cheek. 'Be careful in there,' she breathed in his ear.

Gerald stumbled backwards into the night and watched as Mr Fry steered the limo back into the flow of traffic. He raised a hand to his cheek and, staring after the red tail-lights of the limousine, whispered, 'Scooby dooby doo…bee.'

The evening crowd hurried along the footpath of one of the world's most famous boulevards. Through the flicker of faces flashing past, Gerald spotted Jasper Mantle. He was wrapped in an overcoat and standing in the building's main doorway. Gerald swung his pack onto his shoulder and picked his way through the snow to greet him. As he got closer he saw that Alex Baranov was also there.

Gerald stood and stared at Alex. He was dressed entirely in black commando gear. His trousers were tucked into a pair of combat boots and his jacket seemed to have more pockets than a billiard table. The outfit was topped off with a black woollen beanie. The only things missing were camouflage paint and an assault rifle.

Gerald nodded at Jasper Mantle and hitched his pack tighter onto his shoulder. 'Did I miss the invasion?' he asked, 'or do I have time to get a gas mask and rations?'

Alex glared at Gerald but said nothing.

Mantle clapped his gloved hands together. 'Let's get inside and out of this chill.'

The front door was nothing grand: plain red and thick with street grime. Jasper Mantle pulled a key from his pocket, opened the door and led the boys into a dimly lit foyer. He bolted the door behind them, blocking out the buzz of the city.

Gerald sneezed hard. Twice. He rubbed his nose. 'It's very dusty,' he said. Another sneeze sprayed across Alex's back. Gerald did not bother to wipe it off.

Jasper Mantle flicked on more lights. They did little to improve the visibility, only serving to illuminate more dust. At the far end of the foyer was a single lift with an art deco semi-circular floor indicator with an arrow. It was the only thing in the room that could pass for decoration. There was not a stick of furniture, the walls were naked, and a small mound of junk mail on the floor inside the door suggested the Billionaires' Club was not the heart of New York's social scene.

Gerald looked at the dingy surrounds. 'It's not quite what I expected,' he said. 'You know, considering the neighbourhood we're in.' He had the prickly sensation of insects crawling over his skin and down his neck.

Jasper Mantle fished inside his overcoat pocket and pulled out a stubby brass key. 'Don't let the decor fool you,' he said. 'We keep the location of the club secret. You can imagine what a target we would be if we advertised. The lobby is maintained like this to deter any thieves who might make it inside the front door.'

Alex looked around with distaste. 'I would hope so. I have no intention of spending the night in a fleapit like this.'

Mr Mantle inserted the key into a lock by the lift doors and pressed the button. Far above them, cogs and wheels moved into action.

With a *clunk* the doors juddered two-thirds of the way open. The lift had stopped thirty centimetres short of floor level. Mr Mantle wedged his shoulder against one door and his hands against the other and shoved them fully apart.

'You'll have to excuse some of the facilities,' he said. 'It's a very old building. We haven't had cause to use it much lately.'

'Since 1830, apparently,' Gerald muttered. He went to climb in but Alex shoved him aside. He surveyed the interior of the lift and his top lip curled. 'What a dump,' he said.

It was going to be a long night.

'In you go, Gerald,' Mr Mantle said, following after him. 'Adventure awaits.'

The doors stuttered closed, and the lift shunted upwards. After a short journey it ground to a halt. The doors pulled back halfway: they were a good metre below the floor level. Alex pushed the doors fully open and climbed out. He reached down and helped Mr Mantle up and through the opening. Gerald held out his hand, but Alex looked down through the gap and laughed. 'I don't think so,' he said.

'You are a dipstick of epic proportions,' Gerald grumbled under his breath. He tossed his backpack between the doors and clambered out.

As he emerged into the light, it took him a moment to absorb his surroundings. 'Now,' he thought, 'this is more like a Billionaires' Club.'

The reception salon was straight from an eighteenth century French palace. Crimson silk lined the walls, resplendent with enormous oil paintings. Antique card tables surrounded by high-backed chairs were set around the room, laid out for games of chess and bridge. There were no windows, but eight oak doors were evenly spaced around the walls. A fire blazed in a grate beneath a grand mantelpiece, infusing the room with a snug cosiness that had Gerald hankering for his slippers and a corner of one of the plush lounges on the hand-woven oriental carpet.

He unzipped his jacket and let it fall in a heap to the floor behind him.

'Wow,' he said. It seemed the most appropriate thing to say.

Mr Mantle removed his gloves and tossed them into the bowl of his up-turned hat. He laid his overcoat along a leather banquette and gazed around with satisfaction. 'It has been a while since I've been here,' he said. 'The old place hasn't changed a bit.'

Alex's eyes widened, drinking in the scene. 'If you haven't been here for a while,' he said, 'then who lit the fire?'

Jasper Mantle eased himself onto a lounge and propped his feet on an ottoman. 'That is one of the many tricks of the house,' he said. 'It's a bit like the light inside the refrigerator. The fire goes on when the doors open—in this case, the elevator doors. We get a bill once a quarter from the gas company and leave it at that. The fire goes out when the last person leaves. It's the same with the chandeliers and lamps. Quite ingenious.'

Gerald pulled out a chair from a card table. 'So we just sit here all night?' he asked. 'Seems a bit pointless. Comfy, but pointless.'

Mr Mantle grinned broadly. 'As I told you at Oates, the club's founder, Diamond Jim Kincaid, was somewhat eccentric. He installed a few surprises in here.'

'By surprises you mean puzzles?' Gerald said.

'Puzzles. Booby traps. Dead ends. All sorts of mischief,' Mr Mantle said. 'Nothing too serious, of course—just a little fun. But it is written in our constitution that each new member must spend a night here to solve as many puzzles as they can. The more you solve, the further into the house you get. Some of the puzzles don't do anything when you crack them, but others unlock hidden doors, or give clues to other conundrums. The best anyone has done so far is get to the second floor.'

Gerald blinked. 'Are you saying that the Billionaires' Club has been around for almost two hundred years and no one except Diamond Jim Whatsisface has ever been above the second floor? What's up there?'

'No one knows for sure,' Mr Mantle said. 'But it's every club member's duty to try to find out. Wouldn't you like to be the first?'

'If it's that important, why do we only get one night to do it?' Alex asked.

Mr Mantle picked up his hat and tugged his gloves onto his hands. 'You don't become fabulously wealthy by playing at games all the time,' he said. 'This is a pleasant distraction that might test your lateral thinking skills and tickle your ego, but it's hardly going to make your fortune. I will leave you to it. I can't hang around here all night.' Mr Mantle allowed himself a polite laugh. 'That's your job.'

He crossed to the lift and consulted his watch. 'It's eight o'clock. I'll be back at eight in the morning to let you out. I look forward to hearing all about your adventures.' He climbed down into the lift and the doors faltered closed. The arrow indicator tracked him down to the ground floor.

Alex looked at Gerald.

Gerald looked at Alex.

Twelve hours to locate a hidden box, or Professor McElderry was a dead man.

'So, what's with the commando gear?' Gerald said.

'Is there a paintball arena on the fourth floor?'

Alex smiled. 'My father did this night twenty years ago,' he said. 'He gave me a few clues.'

Gerald shrugged. 'Well, go for your life, champion. Don't let me stop you storming the castle. I've got my own puzzles to solve.' Gerald wandered over to the closest door and tried the handle. It wouldn't budge.

'I've already tried them,' Alex said. 'They're all locked.'

Gerald grunted, then picked up his pack from the floor. He dropped cross-legged to the rug and flipped open the bag.

'What are you doing?' Alex asked.

'I told you,' Gerald said. He pulled out the message from Jeremy Davey. 'I have my own mysteries to work on. But if your dad told you how to get started, crack on.'

Alex stared at Gerald, then kicked a boot at the rug. 'He never got out of this room,' he muttered. 'He said I'd have to work it out for myself.'

'Then what's with the secret ops gear?' Gerald asked.

Alex's face flushed pink. He unzipped a pocket on his left sleeve and pulled out a chocolate bar. 'He told me you get hungry after twelve hours of sitting around doing nothing.'

Gerald looked at Alex in disbelief. 'All those pockets are full of snacks?'

Alex gave a self-conscious nod. 'Want a Twix?'

Gerald snuffled out a laugh. 'You little chocolate

soldier,' he said, and held out his hand. Just as Alex tossed the chocolate bar, a telephone rang. The Twix fell to the rug as Gerald's eyes darted towards a black bakelite phone on an end table. It emitted another jangling ring.

Gerald swapped a curious glance with Alex then crossed to the table. He picked up the handset from the cradle and lifted it to his ear.

'Hello?'

The line crackled. Then a familiar voice filled his head.

'Gerald? Excellent—this is Mason Green. Have you solved that code yet?'

Chapter 20

Gerald's knuckles were white as he clenched the telephone handset.

That voice.

It cut to the marrow.

'Gerald? I know you're there. I can hear you breathing. Have you deciphered the code?' Green demanded.

Gerald's heart raced. 'I've been trying—'

'Trying!' Mason Green shouted the word. 'Have I not made the stakes clear?'

'I know,' Gerald said, his voice pleading. 'I will do it.'

There was a long pause. When Green spoke again, it was in a tone of deepest displeasure.

'Is Sergei Baranov's boy with you?'

Gerald felt like he'd been punched in the chest. 'How

did you know?'

'I know, and that's enough,' Green said. 'What the devil does that fool Mantle think he's playing at, inviting that bleached weasel along? He'll ruin everything.'

Alex took a step towards Gerald. 'What's going on?' he asked. 'Who's on the phone?'

Gerald turned his back on him. Green's voice barked down the line. 'Don't tell him!' Then, quieter, 'Can he hear me?'

Gerald cupped his hand to the mouthpiece. 'Only if you keep shouting at me,' he said.

'Then listen carefully, Gerald Wilkins.' Green's voice dipped to a mortuary whisper and Gerald had to press the earpiece hard to the side of his head to hear. 'Sergei Baranov is a very dangerous man. You don't make your fortune on the oil fields of Russia by sending people flowers and baskets of muffins. I suspect he is after the same thing I am. And with the Baranovs, the apple does not fall far from the tree. Do you follow me? Unless I am mistaken, young Alex will follow along as you work your way through the various puzzles. He may even help you. But when you reach the final piece—the box—he will do all he can to take it from you.'

Sir Mason Green paused to let his words rattle around Gerald's skull. Gerald glanced over his shoulder. Alex Baranov stood just metres away, his commando boots planted wide and looking every inch the Russian assassin. Mason Green whispered again, 'If he is anything like his father, he will not hesitate to kill you for it.'

'I don't believe you,' Gerald said into the telephone. Alex was staring right into his eyes.

Green's voice rasped in his ear, 'What you believe, Gerald Wilkins, will get you killed. Know this: in the field of ruthless pursuit, the Baranovs make me look like a stamp-collecting schoolboy.'

'But...but you're his godfather,' Gerald whispered.

Green laughed. 'Then you should understand my character assessment of both Baranovs is based on detailed personal knowledge,' he said. 'Solve the code. Collect the box. Do that or the professor dies. Horribly. And then, I will come for you.'

A vision of Professor McElderry, stumbling dazed and lost in the Scottish highlands, flashed through Gerald's mind. 'You've been here before,' he said to Green. 'Tell me how to get started. All the doors are locked. What do we do?'

Green's laughter rang hollow. 'Gerald, on my initiation night I didn't get out of the room you're standing in now.'

And then the line went dead.

Gerald looked at the handpiece like it had just licked his ear.

'Terrific,' he said.

He looked at Alex. He had not moved.

'Who was that?' Alex asked flatly.

Gerald's mind raced. How much of what Green had

said about the Baranovs could be believed?

'Just a club member,' Gerald said, avoiding the other boy's eye. 'A friend of my great aunt's.' He replaced the receiver in the cradle. 'Wishing us luck.'

'What's his name?'

'You wouldn't know him.'

Alex stared hard at Gerald. He was clearly making his own assessments as to what should be believed. 'Did he tell you how to get out of this room?'

'No. He wasn't any help at all.' Gerald looked at his watch. 'We better get going. You start by the far door and I'll start over here.'

'What are we looking for?'

'Clues.'

'Like what?'

'I have no idea.'

Alex marched to a door at the far end of the salon. Gerald turned and crossed to a set of double doors at the opposite end of the room. He took hold of the brass handle on each and pulled. They could have been welded shut for the amount they moved.

'Terrific,' Gerald muttered.

Hanging on the wall next to the doors was a simple black picture frame, the glass obscured by grime. Gerald wiped his palm down the front, leaving a smudged view of the contents.

Beneath the fly spots and the dust was a notice, handwritten in thick black ink.

Know it henceforth that:
no person shall enter
or be given specific
cause to enter these
kept premises without
the approval or consent
herewith required by the
Regent of the club.
In making this ruling,
certain death for whom
ever befouls our Order.

> *Regent of the Billionaires' Club*
> *of New York, 1830*

'And have a nice day,' Gerald said. 'What a cheery welcome.'

Alex loomed over his shoulder. 'There's nothing back there,' he said, jerking his head towards the far door. 'What about here?'

'Locked solid,' Gerald said. 'Not even a keyhole.'

Alex nodded at the frame on the wall. 'What's that?'

'The club rules, by the look of it,' Gerald said.

Alex squinted at the old notice. 'What's that even mean?' he said. '*Certain death for whom ever befouls our Order?*'

Gerald shrugged. 'I guess they didn't like visitors.'

Alex yanked on the door handles. The portal stood firm. 'This is rubbish,' he said, aiming a kick at the floor.

'What are we supposed to do?'

Gerald scanned the room. 'Maybe there's a switch behind one of the paintings,' he said. He looked back at the notice in its black frame. 'Or behind this thing.' He lifted the bottom of the frame away from the wall. A haze of dust rained on his face, and he sneezed. And sneezed again. He glared up at the notice as if it was to blame for their sorry situation.

Then he saw it—seemingly lit up like the shopfronts of Fifth Avenue.

'Oh my gosh,' Gerald said. He stared open-mouthed at the sign.

Alex looked at him with suspicion. 'What?'

Gerald hesitated and turned his face. 'Nothing,' he said. 'It's nothing. I thought I saw something, but I was wrong.'

'Listen, Gerry. *Gerald*. You must realise that wherever either of us goes in this house tonight, the other one is going to follow,' Alex said. 'So if you can see a way of getting out of this room don't hold back. Otherwise we're both wasting our time.'

Gerald breathed deep. He knew Alex was right. And time was the one thing that Professor McElderry did not have to spare.

Gerald pointed to the faded lettering. 'There. On the notice.'

'What about it?'

'Take the first letter of each line and read down.'

Alex read the notice again, his lips moving silently. Then he said, 'K-n-o-c-k t-h-r-i-c-e?'

Gerald crossed to the double doors. 'That's got to be how we open these,' he said. 'We knock three times.'

'Don't be stupid,' Alex said. 'That's too obvious.'

'All answers are obvious,' Gerald said, 'when you know them.' He swung his pack to his shoulder and rapped his knuckles on the double door.

Once.

Twice.

Three times.

The hollow sound of the final knock echoed to the ceiling. Then somewhere in the hidden distance came a buzzing whirr. The shifting of gears. The popping of locks.

And the twin doors opened.

Gerald pushed the doors and they swung inwards with a disconcerting *creeeeaaak*. Beyond the doorway stood a wrought iron staircase that spiralled up into the darkness.

'What do you think?' Gerald said.

'You opened it,' Alex said, 'You go first.'

'Thanks. I can see you're going to be a lot of help.'

Gerald pulled on the shoulder straps of his backpack and started to climb. The clang of his boots on the metal steps rang up the stairwell. He had no idea what he was doing, but he was pretty sure that the club founders would regard it as befouling their Order.

Chapter 21

The spiral stairs wound tightly and the light from the reception salon struggled to penetrate the darkness ahead. By the time Gerald reached the top he could barely see in front of him. He stumbled onto a landing and stepped down hard, expecting another step to be there. A second later, Alex thumped into his back.

'Watch out,' Gerald said. He spread his hands in front of him, feeling about. 'I can't see a thing.'

There was no apology from Alex. 'There must be a door or an opening,' he said. 'Stairs don't lead to nowhere.'

'Try not to wet yourself, okay?' Gerald said. Not for the first time that night he wished that Ruby, Sam and Felicity were with him. If for no other reason, at least they had a sense of humour. Gerald's hands pressed up against a smooth and featureless wall. He ran his fingers down to where a doorknob ought to be, and they wrapped around a cold lump of metal.

'I've got something,' Gerald said. He turned the knob and pushed. The door creaked open. Out of the darkness, the interior of an enormous chamber lit up in a flash. A line of crystal chandeliers ignited, one after the other, like a string of Chinese firecrackers.

From the open doorway, Gerald and Alex stared in slack-jawed wonder at what lay before them. Flames erupted in an enormous stone fireplace, a bare grate transformed into a welcoming blaze in seconds. Wall lamps crackled into life. A music box the size of a barrel organ spouted a plinking version of *Für Elise*. It was as if the room was waking from a long winter's hibernation and stretching the cricks from its joints.

The room was twice the size of the ballroom in Gerald's Chelsea townhouse back in London and seemed to occupy the entire floor of the building. Wooden display cabinets and workbenches were laid out in rows, as if in an enormous workshop. At the end of each bench stood a tall wicker basket, stuffed with rolled-up documents. Gerald looked upwards to take in the scale of the place. The walls stretched up and kept on going. A broad mezzanine balcony extended around the walls, home to an enormous library of books, but there seemed to be no way to get up to it.

'Wow,' Gerald said. 'Just, wow.'

He followed Alex into the room. The moment Gerald stepped over the threshold, the door slammed shut behind them. He spun around and went to grab at the doorknob but instead snatched at air. Polished wood panelling on the back of the door matched the rest of the wall seamlessly. It was impossible to locate the opening.

'Looks like we're going to have to find another way out,' Gerald said. 'This is locked tight.'

He crossed to the nearest workbench. Wood-handled screwdrivers and other antique tools were laid out across the top. Gerald bent down to inspect a shiny silver sphere about the size of a cricket ball in a squat display stand. The moment he picked it up a tiny slot opened on the top and a brass flag sprang out. Engraved on the flag in neat block letters were the words, PUT ME DOWN!

Gerald almost dropped the ball in surprise. He replaced it delicately in its cradle; the flag popped back inside and the slot closed.

'What is this place?' Alex asked. He was at the other end of the room, looking up at a collection of ancient keys that was hanging in a frame on the wall. There were at least fifty keys, in all shapes and sizes.

Gerald looked at the tools and the boxes of screws, springs and rivets, spread across each bench top. 'It's like an inventor's playhouse,' he said.

Alex crossed to the fireplace and tapped a fingernail against the glass of a mantel clock, its hands set on the twelve. They did not move. 'This must be Diamond Jim Kincaid's workshop,' he said.

'What makes you think that?' Gerald asked.

'The enormous portrait of him above the fireplace,' Alex replied.

A grey-haired man with an alarming handlebar moustache stared out from an ornate frame with an expression that said the rest of mankind were, clearly, all idiots. A narrow wooden plaque on the bottom of the frame identified the subject as 'Diamond' Jim Kincaid.

'Looks like all that money didn't make him very happy,' Gerald said. His eyes dropped to the signature at the bottom right corner of the canvas. His heart skipped in his chest. Signed in blood red was: *Eug. Delacroix 1830.*

Gerald tried to keep his face blank.

Eugène Delacroix—the French artist whose *Liberty Leading the People* sat vandalised in the Louvre, the section hacked from its canvas rolled in a cardboard tube in Gerald's backpack; the painter whose work was supposed to lead Gerald to the box that would save Professor McElderry.

That Eugène Delacroix.

Gerald swallowed his breathing and walked as calmly as he could across to a workbench.

If there's a Delacroix painting here, the box can't be far away.

He had to remain calm. He had to think.

Gerald's hand shook as he pulled a document from one of the wicker baskets and unrolled it, trying to appear casual. The document was titled: *Design #35*. The paper was covered in line drawings of a bizarre device packed with cogs, gears and springs. Gerald's brow wrinkled. He pulled out another document. *Design #26*. This one had a giant flywheel with a hand crank. The drawings looked just like Sam's attempt at a—Gerald's eyes grew wide—'perpetual motion machine,' he whispered to himself.

He glanced at Alex, who was across the room inspecting the contents of a display case. *He hasn't noticed*, Gerald thought. *He doesn't realise what could be hidden in this room...*

Alex reached into the case to a metal box inside. But when his fingers were centimetres away the lid popped up, a mechanical hand stretched out and smacked him hard on the wrist, then zipped back inside. The lid banged shut.

'Ow!' Alex said, rubbing the back of his hand.

Gerald quickly rolled up the documents and stuffed them back into the basket. His eyes darted from workbench to workbench, taking in the gizmos spread around the room. But he could not see anything like the glossy black box that Mason Green wanted him to find. His gaze stopped on a waist-high cabinet, standing to the right of the fireplace. It took him a moment to realise that it was different from the other work surfaces in the room. There were no tools or bent springs, no contraptions or devices. There was only a polished steel casket, about sixty centimetres square and twenty centimetres high. Gerald edged over to get a closer look. On the front of the casket, two small screws held a tiny brass plaque in place.

Engraved on the plaque was: *Cornelius Drebbel 1572–1633*.

Gerald swallowed hard. *The* Cornelius Drebbel. Advisor to Emperor Rudolph II of Prague, friend of King James VI of Scotland and inventor of the perpetual motion machine.

Alex had picked up a hand drill and was winding the crank, watching as the bit twisted in the air.

Gerald turned to the metal box that bore Drebbel's name. He shuffled around so his back would shield any possible view Alex might have of what he was doing. Carefully, silently, *desperately*, he opened the top of his backpack. If Drebbel's perpetual motion machine was inside the metal box, Gerald could have it out and into his pack in seconds. Alex would not have a clue. Then all Gerald had to do was wait until Jasper Mantle let them out in the morning, and Professor McElderry was as good as saved.

Gerald took in a long, silent breath. Sweat beaded on his forehead.

He eased the lid up.

It swung smoothly from a hinge at the back. The only thing inside was a ball-shaped indentation in the lush silk lining, large enough to hold a good-sized eggplant. Gerald stared into the empty casket. If it was meant to house Drebbel's machine, it was no longer there.

Gerald screwed his eyes shut with frustration. First the empty keystone in Scotland and now this. Where was the perpetual motion machine? He was quickly pulled from his thoughts by the sound of a panel sliding open. There was a movement at the front of the cabinet and Gerald stumbled back as a mechanical man dressed like a pint-sized butler rolled onto the floor. The figure was no taller than Gerald's hips and it moved like a drunken penguin, but there was no mistaking the dapper black jacket and pinstriped trousers of a gentleman's gentleman. It was as if Mr Fry had been melted down and recast in stainless steel.

'What is that thing?' Alex peered around the side of the cabinet, his eyes growing wider by the second.

Gerald stepped clear as the mechanical half-man surged forward on unseen wheels. The robot's head, which appeared to have been fashioned from an ancient colander, spun in endless circles. Gerald was getting dizzy watching it.

'I think it's some kind of wind-up servant,' Gerald said. The robot turned and, with a buzz of clockwork gears, lurched back towards the cabinet.

'Looks like a rubbish bin in a suit,' Alex said, making sure to keep Gerald between the robot and himself. 'Do you think it's dangerous?'

'Only if you really hate being banged in the shins,' Gerald said. He dodged as the robot whirred past. It stopped, spun in place and rolled to Gerald's feet. Gerald jumped as the half-dome of the robot's head flipped back. Underneath was a blue silk pillow, upon which rested an envelope.

Gerald plucked up the note.

'What's it say?' Alex asked, still keeping a safe distance.

A blob of red wax bearing the initials *JK* sealed the flap. Gerald turned the envelope over. In copperplate handwriting on the front was: *To the interloper*.

He cracked the seal and pulled out a stiff ivory-coloured card. It read,

> *You have until the chimes count ten*
> *To unlock the stairway*
> *That leads to heaven*
> *Or, for you there will be sleep.*
> *Noxious to start,*
> *but eternally deep.*

'What does that mean?' Alex said. 'A stairway to heaven?'

Before Gerald could respond, the robot's head flipped back into place, and, with a burst of spinning gears, trundled into the cabinet. The moment the wooden panel closed behind the mechanical man, the clock on the mantel chimed—a single hollow toll. The hands, which had rested in place on the twelve, flicked into action; a second hand started tracing around the clockface. The music box stopped playing, and an eerie silence fell over the room.

'What's going on?' Alex said.

'I'm not sure.' Gerald looked down at the card in his hand. 'What happens when the clock reaches ten?'

The fire in the grate, which had been burning so majestically, suddenly vanished—snuffed out in an instant. Gerald and Alex stared at the empty fireplace. Then Gerald had a sickening thought.

'What's that hissing sound?' Alex asked.

Gerald started towards the grate. He was two metres away when he smelled it.

'Gas,' he said. He screwed up his face at the odour. 'Eternal sleep—this place is going to gas us!'

Alex stared at Gerald in disbelief. 'Gas us? Who's trying to gas us?'

'We can worry about who and why later,' Gerald said. He retreated from the fireplace with his hand over his mouth. 'We don't want to be here when that clock strikes ten.'

Alex's face registered the seriousness of the situation. He rushed to the panelled wall where they had entered the room and hammered his fists against the wood, desperate to find the hidden doorway. But it was impossible. The panels were unyielding, no matter how much battering Alex unleashed on them.

'That's no use,' Gerald called to him. 'There has to be another way.' He gagged at the smell that rolled from the fireplace. The clock on the mantel ticked on—two chimes rang out.

'Minutes!' Gerald said. 'The clock is chiming minutes!' Gerald looked at the card again. *Unlock the stairway that leads to heaven.* What did that even mean? Death? He looked to the banks of bookcases above them on the mezzanine and then to the wood-panelled ceiling high above. He scanned the room—the workbenches, the cabinets, the portrait of Diamond Jim Kincaid leering down at them as if enjoying their torment.

Alex ran to Gerald, panic in his eyes. 'I know,' he said, fumbling in a pocket. 'I know what to do.' Baranov pulled out a cigarette lighter: a chunky silver zippo. 'I can burn the gas away,' he said.

He flipped the top of the lighter open and raised his thumb over the flint wheel.

Gerald's eyes popped. He may not have been the best science student at St Cuthbert's, but he knew that one spark near that fireplace meant that being gassed would be the least of their problems. Gerald lashed out with his right hand and smacked the lighter from Alex's grasp. The steel block arched into the air with the top still folded back. If it landed the wrong way, he and Alex would be toast—and probably toasted.

He dived full stretch with his hand out, his eyes glued

to the falling lighter, and landed on the floor with an *oomph*. The zippo fell safely into his palm. Gerald took in a long breath of gas-tainted air, closed the top of the lighter and shoved it into his pocket.

The clock chimed three times.

Alex stared down at Gerald, fury in his eyes. 'What did you do that for?' he said.

'I'll explain in seven minutes,' Gerald said. 'Until then, no flames. Okay?'

Gerald righted himself and he looked desperately for any sign of an escape route. His eyes fell on the collection of keys on the far wall. 'Unlock the stairway...' he whispered to himself. He didn't wait to explain to Alex and dashed across the room.

The box frame housing the keys was about a metre across and almost two metres high. Gerald dragged a stool from a nearby workbench and climbed onto it. He reached up and grabbed the frame with both hands. It was heavier than he expected and as he shoved it up, trying to free it from the hook, it slipped. The box fell through his fingers and the base smashed onto the floor. Glass exploded across the boards. The frame buckled and toppled forward like a felled oak, landing face down with a crash.

Gerald cringed at the sound, and then he looked up at the wall where the keys had been hanging. A grid of fifty keyholes stared back at him.

Fifty keys for fifty keyholes.

Gerald jumped from the stool and dragged the remains of the box frame out of the way.

'Come and help,' he called to Alex. Gerald looked down to the pattern of keys scattered on the floor, then up at the keyholes. 'I just hope they haven't got out of order.' He pointed at the furthest key. 'Hand me one at a time,' Gerald said to Alex. 'Don't touch anything else.' Gerald climbed back onto the stool and took the first key from Alex. Stretching as high as he could, he inserted it into the top right keyhole. It went in smoothly, and turned.

'Hand them up in order,' he said to Alex. 'Quick.' The clock on the mantle chimed four times.

Gerald and Alex looked at each other. 'Really quick,' Gerald said.

One after the other, Gerald pushed the keys into place, turning and unlocking the grid of keyholes. Gerald had no idea what it would achieve—it might only start the barrel organ again—but it was the only option they had.

The stench of the gas was nauseating. Alex looked like he was about to vomit. 'Hurry,' he gasped at Gerald.

The clock chimed five times.

Gerald shoved in another key and turned. Only two keyholes left. He looked to Alex. The expression on the boy's face told Gerald that something was not right. Alex looked distraught—he held up three keys.

'Three?' Gerald said. He didn't have time to think

about the consequences. He fumbled the first—a heavy iron piece that seemed hundreds of years old. It slid into place. But it wouldn't turn. Gerald grunted as he tried to force the head around, but it refused to budge.

'Try another one,' Alex said.

Gerald pulled the key out and shoved it in the next hole. This time it turned smoothly.

Two keys.

One hole.

The one in his right hand looked like it might be the one. He slid it in place and hefted the shank around. It moved smoothly through ninety degrees and stopped.

Gerald stared up at the grid of fifty keys in fifty holes. He slipped the spare one into the pocket of his jeans.

The hiss of the gas was all they could hear. He looked around, hoping that somewhere a panel had popped open and they could escape.

There was nothing.

The gas still poured through the fireplace.

Then, from high above, came the sound of splintering timber.

Gerald threw his head back to see a section of panelling fall free from the ceiling. Sheets of wood veneer slipped from their mountings and tumbled like autumn leaves. Alex leaped clear. The boards crashed to the floor, taking out a workbench and scattering its contents across the room.

Gerald pressed his back against the wall. Plaster dust

added to the foulness of the gas that ate into Gerald's nose and eyes. He hacked up a cough that threatened to pop a lung.

Alex lifted himself off the floor, his sleeve to his mouth. The two of them gazed up at the ragged section of ceiling. For a moment neither of them recognised what they were looking at, but then it hit Gerald like a slap to the face.

A door.

There was an ordinary wooden door set flat into the ceiling.

The clock chimed six times.

Gerald jumped from the stool and raced to Alex. 'That has to be the way out of here,' he said, gagging.

'How are we supposed to get up there?' Alex asked.

Gerald grabbed the edge of a workbench. 'Help drag this to the wall. We should be able to get to the balcony.'

They hefted the bench underneath the mezzanine walkway. Gerald and Alex scrambled on top but the balcony was still too high. Gerald looked around and saw the stool that he used to reach the keyholes. He jumped back to the floor and raced to fetch it. It was like jumping into a swimming pool brimming with slime. The smell was horrendous. He held his breath, grabbed the stool and handed it to Alex, who climbed on top and, at full stretch, was able to reach the bottom of the iron balustrade. He pulled himself up and hooked a foot between the railings. Seconds later he was over the handrail and onto the balcony.

Gerald leaped onto the stool and stretched high, straining up onto his toes. His fingertips brushed the underside of the metalwork. 'I…can't…reach…'

The gas swirled higher. Gerald's head was spinning. If he fell now, there was no waking up tomorrow. His eyes were losing traction in their sockets, sliding backwards. His knees buckled. He could feel himself drifting away.

Then, a strong hand snapped around his left wrist just as his head fell back, his eyes lolling about like dumplings in soup. Gerald gazed drunkenly up to see Alex leaning over the balustrade. He strained, a grunt wrenched from his chest, and he hauled Gerald onto the mezzanine. They landed heavily, collapsing against a bookshelf. Three leather-bound volumes fell loose, thumping one after the other onto Gerald's head.

The blows were enough for him to regain some sense. He wiped a hand over his face. 'Thanks,' he said to Alex with halting breath. 'At least the air is better up here.'

'Not for long,' Alex said. 'Three minutes to go. And that door is still a long way up.'

Gerald propped himself on his elbows and looked up. The door was set flat into the ceiling, about three metres out from the wall, the closest side roughly in line with the outer edge of the balcony.

'We need a ladder,' Alex said.

'What would we lean it up against?' Gerald said. He struggled to his feet. 'There must be another way.'

Alex was swaying, his head bobbing. 'I don't feel so good,' he mumbled.

Gerald moved too late to grab him. Alex staggered against a bookcase. He flashed out a hand to steady himself and latched onto a brass light fitting. The length of metal pipe came away from the wall and he crashed into the shelves, sending books cascading to the floor. He crumpled on top of them, like a scarecrow knocked from its perch.

'Are you okay?' Gerald was by Alex's side. He took the length of piping from his hand.

Alex blinked hard. 'No, I'm not,' he said. 'Thanks for asking.'

'I was more worried that the flame from the lamp was going to light the gas,' Gerald said. He held up the brass pipe—then stalled in thought. His eyes darted around the mezzanine. There were at least twenty identical fittings set into the walls. None of them was alight.

Gerald pulled the lampshade from the fitting in his hand. There was nothing on the end. No wick, no bulb. The fitting was an S-shaped length of solid brass—with sharp corners, not rounded at the bends.

The clock on the mantelpiece chimed eight times.

Gerald rushed to the wall bracket where Alex had torn off the light. It was a brass plate about ten centimetres across, with a looping, clockwise-pointing arrow engraved on the front in fine filigree. Gerald slid the light fitting back into place.

'What are you doing?' Alex's breathing was tight, laboured.

Gerald grabbed the free end of the brass rod with both hands. 'These things aren't lights,' he said. 'There's no gas line, no wiring. So what are they for? Decoration?'

Alex bowed his head between his knees. 'Does it really matter?'

'Kincaid liked his wind-up toys,' Gerald said. 'Let's see what this does.' He leaned on the brass rod. It moved smoothly around, turning clockwise, in the direction of the arrow. Gerald cranked the handle like he was trying to start a vintage car. The far end of the next bookcase along started to swing out, arching back towards Gerald through ninety degrees before it juddered to a halt, perpendicular to the wall. He kept cranking and the shelves started to cantilever, sliding back one by one to form a flight of seven stairs up the side of the wall.

'It's too short,' Alex said. 'We can't reach the door from the top of that.'

Gerald ran to the next light fitting and reefed off the glass lamp cover. He cranked the handle. The far end of the neighbouring bookcase lurched outwards, swinging across the balcony to be parallel to the first set of shelves. Then the bookcase moved straight up, gliding on tracks hidden in the pattern of the wallpaper. When the bottom shelf was level with the top of the first bookcase, it too cantilevered back, extending the staircase to fourteen steps.

Gerald traced his eyes across the gap from the top step to the door in the ceiling. 'This is our way out of here,' he said.

The clock chimed nine times.

He stumbled to the next light fitting and turned the handle. As a third bookcase swung out from the wall, Gerald looked back over his shoulder and shouted to Alex, 'Start climbing. One more after this and we should reach the door.'

Pinpricks of colour sparked in Gerald's eyes like flickering Christmas lights. The gas was thickening. Breathing was near impossible.

The bookcase moved up the wall, then tilted back to join the rest of the stairs. Gerald staggered to the next set of shelves. This one should do it.

He turned the handle, struggling to get feeling into his fingers. It was as if his body was shutting down, withdrawing troops from the perimeters. The fourth bookcase swung out, then climbed high up the wall. Gerald looked up to see Alex directly above him, on his hands and knees. The handle cranked six more times and the final piece in the staircase snapped into place.

Gerald stumbled through the clutter of spilled books onto the stairs. He dropped to his hands and knees and hauled himself up on all fours.

The staircase reached to just below the ceiling, right next to the door. Alex lay on the top step, his head resting on his arm.

Gerald slid in beside him and shook his shoulder. 'Come on,' he urged. 'We're almost there.'

Alex peeled back an eyelid and stared vacantly at Gerald.

'It's no use.' His voice was barely a whisper. 'The door. It's...locked.'

Gerald stared at a keyhole next to the door handle.

And from far beneath them, the clock began to chime.

Chapter 22

The clock counted down the seconds. Gerald struggled to focus on the door that stood between his life and his death.

Dong, dong, dong...

Was that five? Or six? Concentrating was impossible. Gerald was aware of Alex Baranov by his side and of the doorknob above his head. And that was all. His world had collapsed to just those two things.

Dong, dong...

He could no longer smell the gas, could not distinguish it from normal air. His eyes were open but he could barely see. It was like staring down a funnel.

His mind flitted to his mother and father, to Sam and Ruby. He would never have the chance to say goodbye to any of them. Or to tell Ruby how he really felt, even if he could find the words. He had kept that much locked up inside. And now it was too late.

Locked up inside.

Locked.

Need to open.

Need...a...

Key.

Gerald's eyelids flickered.

A key?

From deep within his oxygen-starved brain Gerald somehow mustered the wit to slide his hand into the pocket of his jeans. He pulled out the last key from the display case. He gripped the end and with an unsteady hand pushed it into the keyhole in the door.

It was received like an old friend.

He turned the key and the door dropped open. Fresh air gusted into Gerald's face. The sudden infusion of oxygen was a tonic. He dragged Alex up by the collar to sit next to him.

'Wake up!' He slapped Alex hard in the face. He slapped him again. Then a third time. Alex slurred a mumbled. 'Whazzit? Whassamatter?'

Gerald was laughing now. 'Oh, that felt good!' he said out loud. He wound up and smacked Alex again. 'Wakey, wakey!' The last hit was more for Gerald's benefit than for Alex's. 'Come on,' Gerald said. 'Time to go.'

A set of sliding stairs dropped through the doorway in the ceiling, reaching down to the top of the bookcase. Gerald shoved Alex in the back and heaved him up. He could smell the gas gathering around them once more.

Gerald climbed up after Alex, and they emerged into a dark room. A waft of gas vapour chased after them. Gerald looked about and saw a trapdoor hinged at the floor. He swung it shut over their escape hatch. The door sealed tight, preventing any gas from sneaking through the cracks.

Gerald collapsed onto his hands and knees and breathed the clean air. It was like drinking a glass of iced lemonade on a summer's afternoon.

Alex slumped onto the floor, his hands over his eyes. His lungs pumped like bellows at a forge. After a while, his breathing steadied.

'Why?' he asked. 'Why would they try to kill us?'

Gerald sat on the floor, his legs out in front of him. 'If you're going to be a junior billionaire,' he said, 'you're going to have to get used to this type of stuff.'

Alex lifted his hands from his face. 'What are you talking about?'

Gerald laughed. 'The members of the stupid Billionaires' Club aren't trying to kill us,' he said. 'Mr Mantle and the others don't know what's inside most of this building. We're probably the first people to make it this far into the club since Diamond Jim Fungusguts opened for business. That room down there,'—he nodded at the hatch in the floor—'was in perfect condition when we arrived. It was untouched. Not so much now.'

'But Mantle said someone got to the second floor,' Alex said.

'If they did, they didn't get out the same way we did.'

'But why would someone set a trap like that?'

Gerald was convinced that Kincaid had set the snare to protect the perpetual motion machine, either Drebbel's original or one that Kincaid had managed to build on his own. But he was not about to share that theory with Alex Baranov. 'People go a bit bizarre when it comes to defending what's theirs,' Gerald said. He hoped he sounded convincing. 'Especially mega-rich people.'

'We have security in our house in London,' Alex said, 'but we don't go to the point of gassing intruders. Who would do that?'

A vision of Sir Mason Green appeared before Gerald's eyes. 'I can think of a few people,' he said. He shook his pack from his shoulders and pulled out a water bottle. He took a long drink and tossed it to Alex, who caught it with a nod of thanks. He drank and wiped his mouth with the back of his hand. 'You saved my life down there,' he said.

'You did the same for me,' Gerald said. 'If I'd fallen off that stool there was no way I was getting up again.'

Alex unzipped a pocket on his sleeve and dug inside. 'Twix?'

Gerald nodded and accepted the snack. For a

moment, the two of them were content to savour the taste of chocolate.

'So, why have you been trying to stop me from coming here?' Gerald looked sidewards at Alex. 'The pillowcase over the head. The slingshot at the horse. Why try to keep me away?'

The question seemed to catch Alex off guard. He studied Gerald's face for a moment. 'What's the quickest way to win any competition?' he asked Gerald.

Gerald shrugged. 'How?'

'Have your opponent quit before it has even started,' Alex replied. 'My father says everything in life is a competition. To win, someone must lose. And for him, losing is not an option.'

'That's a pretty miserable way to look at life,' Gerald said.

Alex swallowed the last of his chocolate. 'You've met my father,' he said.

Gerald stood shakily and made his way through the gloom towards the nearest wall. He ran his hands along velvet wallpaper until he found what he was looking for. 'There's a lamp here,' he said to Alex. 'Should I risk lighting it?'

Alex sniffed the air. 'I can't smell any gas,' he said. 'And we need to see to find a way out of here.'

Gerald pulled Alex's zippo from his pocket. He flipped the top and took a deep breath. His thumb hovered over the flint wheel—and he struck it. Sparks flew and a flame danced in the darkness. Gerald paused—there was no massive explosion—and he turned on the gas tap on the lamp. A thin hiss sounded from inside the lampshade. He held up the lighter and, with a soft pop, the lamp flashed into life. Then in a chain reaction, wall lamps lit up around the room.

Alex swallowed a gasp at what was revealed. 'Far out,' he said.

Gerald could only agree. It was far less grand than the room they had just escaped from. But what it lacked in scale it more than made up for with its fittings. The red velvet walls were hung from floor to ceiling with picture frames. Hundreds, probably thousands, of picture frames. And they all contained the same thing.

'Butterflies,' Gerald said. 'Zillions and zillions of them.'

Butterflies. Moths. Flying creepy-crawlies of countless varieties and varying degrees of ugliness. Insects from the size of two outstretched hands to those barely bigger than the pinhead that held them on the display cards. The room was a storage house of specimens of the world's airborne bugs, pressed under glass and frozen in time.

Gerald trailed along one of the walls in a state of wonder. 'Looks like Diamond Jim was a butterfly collector as well as a tinkerer,' he whispered. He had no idea why he should be whispering but the setting seemed to call for it. 'What Jasper Mantle wouldn't give to get his hands on this.'

The vast collection appeared to be sorted geographically. One section was dedicated to the countries of Europe and Africa, another to North America. Gerald drifted along like a migratory moth, passing by the countries of South America: Chile, Argentina, Brazil (lots and lots of butterflies from Brazil), Colombia, Ecuador. He paused in front of a section labelled Galapagos Islands. Each insect was carefully recorded with its name written beneath it. The Galapagos Sulphur butterfly. The Galapagos Silver Fritillary. The Painted Lady. The Monarch. The Large-Tailed Skipper. Then, his attention was captured by a single frame—about forty centimetres square—that stood empty. From what Gerald could see on the walls around him, this was the only gap in Kincaid's collection: the only specimen he had failed to acquire. Gerald leaned in close. Beneath the vacant frame were the words: XERXES BLUE.

'That's the butterfly that Jasper Mantle is always going on about,' Gerald said. 'It looks like he's not the only one who couldn't track one down.'

Alex grumbled impatiently. 'This is all very fascinating, but it doesn't get me any closer to finding the perpetual motion machine, does it?'

The hair rose on the back of Gerald's neck. He turned to face Alex.

It was time to get some answers.

'What's so special about this machine of Drebbel's?' Gerald said, advancing on Alex. 'Why is Mason Green ready to kill to get his hands on it?'

Alex saw the look in Gerald's eyes and retreated a step. 'Look, Gerald, I want to help you. My father wants to help you.'

Gerald took another pace. 'Yeah, because he's such a sweet-hearted guy.' Then a thought suddenly pierced Gerald's brain. 'Your father made his fortune from oil,' he said.

'So what?'

'The last thing an oil man wants loose in the world is a machine that runs on nothing,' Gerald said. 'He wants to destroy it.'

Alex retreated further. 'What are you talking about?'

'What did your father say about eliminating the competition? What bigger competitor to the oil industry would there be than a machine that runs forever without any fuel?' Gerald laughed. 'As if I needed Mason Green to tell me. You can't be trusted.'

Alex backed into the wall, knocking a collection of New Zealand moths to the floor. Gerald advanced. 'You're going to rob me and take off with the one thing that can save my friend's life.' Before Gerald could take another step, Alex's hand darted inside one of the zippered pockets of his jacket. He pulled out a thin block of black plastic and flashed it before him.

Gerald pulled up and stared at Alex's extended hand. 'You're going to attack me with a fountain pen?'

Alex's mouth formed an unsteady smile. He tilted

his head to the side, then flicked his wrist. In a blur of movement, the black rectangle transformed into a menacing blade.

Gerald's eyes jolted in their sockets.

Alex stepped out from the wall. 'It's a butterfly knife,' he said, almost apologetically. 'Appropriate in the situation, I guess.' He herded Gerald across the room and against the wall. Then, with a quivering hand, Alex pressed the flat of the blade under Gerald's chin. 'You need to find that machine.'

Chapter 23

Gerald touched his hand to his jaw and inspected his fingers. A thin line of blood streaked his palm.

The tip of the blade danced at his throat. Alex's hand was shaking. Gerald stared into eyes that betrayed their owner's nerves.

'If you want that machine,' Gerald said in the most confident voice that he could raise, 'you'd better help me look for it.'

Alex glared back at him, then lowered the blade. Gerald let out a long, slow breath and turned to his backpack, lying open on the floor. He crouched and shot a glance back at Alex. The knife was still in his hand, like the sting on a scorpion's tail. Gerald was banking on Alex being more nervous than nasty—a boy blundering about in his father's cumbersome boots. He jerked his head towards the other end of the room. 'See if you can find a door or some way out over there,' he said.

Alex did not move. 'I think I'll stay where I can keep an eye on you,' he said. 'I don't want you running off.'

Gerald scanned the wall of insects in front of him. Apart from the hatch in the floor where they had first entered the room, there didn't seem to be any way in or out. Gerald wandered back along the walls, past the South American butterflies, beyond North America and on to Africa.

'What are you looking for?' Alex followed Gerald like a suspicious shadow.

'I don't know,' Gerald said. 'Something that looks out of place.' He stopped in front of a collection of butterflies and moths from France. The Provence Chalk-Hill Blue. The Lesser Purple Emperor. The Two-Tailed Pasher.

He moved to the wall and ran his fingers across the wallpaper between the framed display boxes. 'That's odd,' he said.

'What's that?' Alex asked.

'Do you see how the velvet lies flat in the space between these frames?' Gerald said. 'Like it has been brushed smooth.' He looked further along the wall. 'But not over there. Or there. It's only in this section here, with the French butterflies.'

Alex shrugged. 'So?'

Gerald studied the patchwork nature of the display

boxes in front of him. He reached out and grabbed a horizontal frame.

'Hey!' Alex said. 'The last time you touched something we were gassed almost to death.'

Gerald did not bother to look around. 'You'll just have to trust me, won't you.'

'What are you doing, then?'

'Have you ever heard of the French painter Eugène Delacroix?'

'No.'

'I didn't think so. But you do French at St Custard's?'

'Yeah. So what?'

'How would you translate Delacroix?'

Alex thought for a moment. 'I dunno. *De la croix*... of the cross?'

Gerald nodded. 'That's what I thought.' Then he rotated a frame of pink butterflies through ninety degrees. Its edge brushed the wallpaper flat as it turned. The frame reached the vertical and seemed to snap into place. Gerald ignored Alex's protests and adjusted more frames where the wallpaper had been brushed flat, turning them left and right. The pattern on the wall was transformed.

'This last one,' Gerald said, reaching high, 'and that should do it.' He turned the frame and it slotted into place with a soft click. Gerald stood back to survey his work: the shape of a giant cross, made up of a mosaic of framed butterflies. There was a light buzzing sound. Then a section of wall popped back, like a door on a hinge.

Gerald pushed on its edge and, perfectly weighted, it swung in smoothly to reveal another set of spiral stairs.

'How did you know to do that?' Alex asked, his eyes widening.

Gerald lifted his foot onto the bottom step. 'Someone had to do something,' he said. 'Puzzles don't solve themselves.'

Then he started to climb. Alex moved in close behind him. The stairwell wound up and up, taking them higher into the house of puzzles.

At the top of the stairs a gas lamp mounted by a wooden door shone a pale light over a small landing.

Gerald glanced down the staircase. Alex was directly below him, the butterfly knife still in his hand.

This could be his only chance.

Gerald lunged at the door and shouldered it open. He dived through the gap and spun on his heel, throwing all his weight behind the door to slam it shut behind him. The impact rocked the wall. Gerald's hand darted to the doorknob, searching for a lock or a key. There was none.

Fists pounded on the door from the other side. Alex screamed blue murder. Gerald latched on to the doorknob with both hands and pressed his shoulder into the wood.

But the knob began to turn, slipping through his grip. Gerald clenched his teeth and squeezed his hands like a vice. It was no good. The handle edged around, opening the latch millimetre by millimetre.

Gerald's eyes darted about, searching for something to stop Alex from getting into the room. They landed on a sturdy iron bolt, attached to the top of the door. All he had to do was push it home. But to reach it he would have to take a hand off the doorknob.

Alex's cursing reached a new level of toxicity, and the handle slipped further in Gerald's grip. He had to move now, and he had to move fast.

Gerald shot his right hand high, like a shell from a cannon. The heel of his hand jammed against the base of the bolt. The iron shaft shifted sharply upwards, but not before the door exploded open. Alex rammed his way into the room, sending Gerald flying backwards.

He landed hard on an oriental rug, the air knocked from his lungs. Before he could right himself, Alex was on top of him. Knees and hands held Gerald to the floor, pinned and as powerless as any of Kincaid's butterflies.

Gerald strained to roll free but Alex was too strong. He slumped back onto the rug and glared up at his victor.

Alex smiled. A tangle of blond hair fell across his forehead. Then he smacked Gerald hard across the face. The blow raised a glowing red welt on Gerald's cheek. 'Just repaying the favour,' Alex said. He pushed himself up, grinding his knees into Gerald's biceps on the way.

Gerald swallowed a yelp of pain. He refused to give Alex the satisfaction of crying out loud.

'Don't try that again,' Alex said.

'Or what?' Gerald said. He held a hand to his cheek

and sat up. 'You'll fillet me like a fish? Even your family couldn't keep you out of prison for that. Stop being an idiot and help me find this machine. Then you can run back to Daddy for a pat on the head.'

'Don't speak to me like that!'

'Again,' Gerald said, 'or what?'

The two boys eyed each other. Then they noticed where they had landed.

The place looked like it had been shipped, piece by piece, from a Parisian garret. Piles of artists' canvases were stacked against one wall. A dusty overcoat lay discarded across an even dustier chaise lounge. A gentle light filled the space. It took Gerald a moment to realise it was coming through a bank of dormer windows that ran the length of the room. It was his first glimpse of the outside world since he had walked into the bizarre confines of the Billionaires' Club hours before. He could feel the vibrancy of Fifth Avenue seeping through the glass from twelve storeys below.

Gerald climbed to his feet and crossed to a large canvas on an easel by the closest window. A grey drop cloth was draped over it. Gerald tugged on a corner and the cloth tumbled free, clouding him in dust. He emitted a colossal sneeze, then looked at the canvas and gasped.

Standing before him was a full-sized painting: *Liberty Leading the People*.

Gerald's mouth dropped open. His eyes darted to the bottom right corner of the painting, to just below the satchel slung from the young boy's shoulder. There, in blood red, was the name: *Eug. Delacroix 1830*.

The roll of canvas tucked into Gerald's backpack weighed heavy on his own shoulders. 'What's this doing here?' Gerald said. His eyes soaked in the detail of the French masterpiece. He slid off his pack and pulled out the cardboard tube that Mason Green had given him. He unrolled the section of canvas and held it up. It matched the painting perfectly. 'So is this a copy?' Gerald wondered aloud, 'Or is the one in the Louvre the copy?'

A sudden thought flashed through his mind and he walked to the back of the easel. The reverse side of the canvas was stark white.

'Interesting,' he said.

His thoughts were interrupted by a shout from Alex Baranov. 'Over here, Gerry. Come and make yourself useful.'

Alex stood in a far corner of the studio looking at a large wall cabinet that reached from the floor to the ceiling, similar to a display case in a department store. When Gerald got closer he saw that the shelves were lined with identical boxes: a grid twenty high and twenty across. The boxes were all painted a gloss black, the same as the one on Mason Green's desk at the Rattigan Club all those months before.

Gerald's heart pounded.

The key to Professor McElderry's life was hidden inside one of those four hundred identical boxes. Gerald mouthed a silent wish that Alex did not realise the significance of what he had found. He scanned the expanse of boxes, and his eyes lit on a gap in the grid. Nine rows up, seven in from the left. The alcove was empty.

'I spotted that as well,' Alex said coolly, following Gerald's gaze. 'Strange that one is missing, don't you think? I expect that's the one Sir Mason had in his possession before he went on the run. So, which one has Drebbel's machine in it, do you think?'

Gerald closed his eyes in despair.

'Honestly, Wilkins. Who do you think told my father about the machine in the first place: the tooth fairy?' Alex said. 'Green wasn't asked to be my godfather for his moral guidance. This was a partnership, until he went and got himself in trouble with the law, the old fool.'

Gerald shook his head. 'He speaks highly of you as well,' he said. 'Something about a bleached weasel.'

Alex grunted and pulled one of the caskets from the case. He turned it in his hands, inspecting it from all angles. 'It's locked,' he said, pointing to a small gold key plate on the front. He slid the box back into its place. 'Mason Green and my father were business partners for years, long before you inherited your pile. Don't think for a second that you have any advantage over me in this venture. Drebbel's machine is in one of these boxes. We've just got to figure out which one.'

Gerald gave Alex a sideways look. 'So it's 'we' now is it?' Gerald said.

'Don't get above yourself, Gerry. Only one of us is walking out of here with the right box. Care to wager who that might be?' Alex crossed to a shabby desk and rifled through the drawers. 'There must be a key here somewhere.'

'How are we going to know which is the right box?' Gerald asked.

'By opening all of them, you idiot. Instead of asking stupid questions, how about looking for the key.'

Gerald scuffed across to a table next to the display cabinet. It was pushed up against the wall and scattered with the artist's tools: tubes of paint, thumbtacks, a palette, mixing knives, a bulbous glass decanter stuffed with brushes. Gerald picked through the odds and ends on the table with no real hope of finding anything of use. He gathered up the paint-stained brushes from the flask, like taking flowers from a vase. He peered down the neck.

'Holy crud!'

Alex looked up from where he was searching the desk. 'What is it?'

Gerald raised his head and blinked. 'I think there's a key in this thing.'

Alex almost knocked Gerald to the floor as he shouldered him out of the way. He wrapped two hands around the decanter and peered down its neck. At the bottom was a tiny golden key attached to a brown fob the size of a pea. 'It is! Wilkins, you've done well.' The opening to the decanter was too narrow to reach in so Alex went to pick up the flask to tip it over.

It wouldn't budge.

'Blast it!' he said. He tried to shake the base of the decanter. 'It's cemented to the table.' He tried again with frustration. 'It won't move. Why would anyone glue it down?'

Gerald picked up a brush and elbowed Alex aside. 'Let me have a try,' he said. He poked the handle down the narrow neck. 'Maybe I can hook it with this.' Gerald prodded the handle through a fine chain that looped the key to the fob. But when he tried to slide it up the side of the decanter, the key slid off and tumbled back to the bottom. 'The neck is too narrow,' he said. 'I can't get enough of an angle.'

Alex snatched the brush from him. But he had no more success than Gerald. Every time he managed to hook the keychain, the brush choked in the slender neck and the key slid free.

Alex threw the brush hard against the wall. 'Damn it! I'm just going to have to break it.' He looked about for a suitable object but couldn't find anything. In desperation, he seized the largest paintbrush he could find and clubbed it against the side of the decanter.

The thick glass emitted a low-pitched *dong*, but stood firm.

Alex cried out in frustration. Gerald was worried he would blow a valve.

Alex cursed and swept an arm across the table top, sending paint tubes and other bits and pieces scattering over the floor. He grabbed the lip of the table and went to toss it into the air. But the table wouldn't budge.

'The stupid thing is bolted to the floor!' Alex clamped both hands around a table leg and strained. His neck muscles coiled like restless pythons in a sack.

The table did not move a millimetre.

Alex threw his hands in the air and fell back from the source of his torment.

Gerald looked at the table and the decanter, anchored in place. 'Interesting,' he said.

'It's not bloody interesting,' Alex fumed through clenched teeth. 'It's bloody infuriating. Why would anyone do something like this?'

Gerald peered down the neck of the decanter at the golden key. 'Maybe there is a way.'

He grabbed up his backpack from the floor and pulled out his water bottle. Alex put out his hand to take a drink, but Gerald batted it away. 'Not for you,' he said. 'For this.'

He took the lid off the bottle and poured the contents into the flask.

'What is that going to achieve,' Alex said, 'apart from a wet key?'

Gerald kept pouring. 'Watch,' he said.

The pea-sized fob on the keychain began to bob with the rising water level.

'It's floating!' Alex stared as the fob rose from the bottom of the flask and dragged the key up with it. 'That's genius.'

Gerald smiled to himself. 'Yes,' he said. 'Yes it is.' He poked a finger through the mouth of the flask and hooked the chain.

'Cork,' he said, nodding at the fob. 'Clever, yes?'

Alex went to snatch it but Gerald whipped his hand clear. 'No,' he said. 'I think I've earned the right to open the first one.'

As Gerald took a step towards the cabinet of boxes something caught his eye. He stopped and stared at the wall behind the table.

'What's the problem?' Alex said. 'Pick a box and get on with it.'

Gerald tried to process what he was seeing. Something that, for some reason, looked familiar. On the wall behind the decanter was what appeared to be an inky stain. Perhaps the remnants of where a painter had wiped dry his almost-clean brushes. But on closer inspection the pattern morphed into something quite recognisable.

'It's the boxes in the cabinet!' Gerald said.

'What are you talking about?' Alex asked.

Gerald pointed to the smudged drawing on the wall. 'Squint your eyes. It's the same pattern as the grid of boxes.'

Alex lowered his head to be level with the image. 'You're right. Hey! There's an 'x' in one of them.'

Gerald nudged Alex aside. 'It's marking the empty space. The one with the missing box.' He jerked his head up towards the display cabinet. 'You don't suppose that this is a map showing which box contains the machine, do you?'

Alex didn't move. His eyes were fixed on the glass decanter. It was Gerald's turn to ask, 'What's the problem?'

A smile spread on Alex's face. 'It is definitely a map showing which box to choose. But not the one that's gone missing.'

'What do you mean?'

Alex grabbed Gerald by the collar and shoved his head in front of the decanter.

'Hey!'

'Stop complaining,' Alex said. 'And look.'

Gerald stared straight ahead. His eyes widened. Looking at the wall through the water-filled decanter, the image transformed from a smudged ink stain into a sharp and very clear likeness of the cabinet of boxes. But the 'x' was in a different square—the cubicle three down and four from the right.

'The water must bend the light,' Alex said. 'No wonder the stupid bottle and table are bolted into place. The only way to see the picture properly is for everything to be lined up in the right spot and then only if the jug is full of water.' He slapped Gerald hard on the shoulder. 'Nice work again, Gerry. Looks like there's more than one key to this puzzle. That's why Mason Green had the wrong box. Whoever took it in the first place used the picture on the wall. They didn't work out the water part.'

Alex lashed out and grabbed Gerald's right wrist. He squeezed hard until Gerald's hand popped open.

'Ouch!'

Alex grabbed the key. 'I'll be taking that,' he said and crossed to the cabinet. He counted three down and four in from the right, slid out the glossy black box, inserted the key and turned it.

The lid popped open and Alex stifled a gasp. Nestled in a bed of coarse black silk was a silver oblong the size of a large eggplant. A band of tiny rivets ran along its length.

'It's the symbol from the Triple Crown,' Alex said. 'It's identical to the shape that was carved into the keystone in the castle cellar in Scotland. The symbol that represents—'

'The perpetual motion machine,' Gerald said. 'That's it?'

Alex lifted the silver egg from the case and cradled it in his hands. 'Heavy,' he said. 'Does it open? Should I just twist it?'

Gerald stared at the glittering object in Alex's hands—the prize that would win Professor McElderry's freedom. If he did not act now, his friend's life was as good as gone.

'I'll buy it off you,' Gerald said.

Alex's eyes moved from the egg-shaped machine to

Gerald. He took a moment to study Gerald's expression. 'How much?' he asked.

'Anything,' Gerald said. 'Name your price.'

Alex raised an eyebrow. 'You have an interesting approach to negotiation.' He paused, his eyes laser-like on Gerald. 'All right. If it's that important to you, you can have it.'

Gerald let out a slow breath. The weight of anguish that had bound up his being for the last months started to fall away.

Alex placed the egg back in the box and locked the lid. 'Fifty billion dollars,' he said.

The sounds of Fifth Avenue filtered up from twelve storeys below: car horns, traffic, a shout.

Gerald wasn't sure he had heard right. 'How much?'

'Fifty. Billion. Dollars. No—make it a hundred billion, if you want it that much.'

'But I don't have that much money. No one does.'

The smile returned to Alex's face. He slid the golden key into one of his pockets and zipped it shut. 'Then I get to keep it.' He tucked the box under his arm. 'Like I said, Gerry: everything is a competition. And a Baranov never loses.' He turned to the line of dormer windows. 'I expect there's a way to the fire escape from here. I have a car and driver waiting downstairs. I'd offer you a lift to the airport,'—he raised his nose in the air—'but I don't want to.' Then he went to the closest window and unlocked the latch.

Gerald's vision turned red. He couldn't let this happen. The professor's fate could not be decided this way. He launched himself across the floor at Alex, catching him around the ribs and knocking the box from his grasp. It flew free and clattered onto the floor, chipping its gloss exterior. Alex lurched to the side, stunned. Gerald twisted, desperate to take Alex to the ground. The two boys hit the rug, slamming into a side table. They rolled in a clinch, legs thrashing. Gerald winced at a knee to his ribs and a punch to his gut.

The wrestling match was over in seconds.

Alex stood on Gerald, pinning him down with a combat boot to the throat. Every time Gerald moved, he pressed a little harder. Gerald struggled to breathe and finally he gave up, like a fish too long out of water.

'You really are an annoying little tick,' Alex sneered down at Gerald. He emphasised his words by pushing on Gerald's neck as if it was an accelerator pedal. 'Are you familiar with the carotid arteries, Gerry? They run up either side of the neck and take blood to the brain. Funny thing is, if you restrict them your brain doesn't get the oxygen it needs to function.'

Gerald could feel Alex's boot pressing harder against his neck. Numbness spread across his face.

The last words Gerald heard were, 'And then you pass out.'

Chapter 24

Gerald woke to a blast of icy wind in his face. He lay on his side on the rug and blinked away the mist that shrouded his eyes. Thin curtains at the windows fluttered inwards like washing on the line. It took him a moment to realise that Alex was gone. Gone, along with the glossy black box and the perpetual motion machine.

Drebbel's machine.

The last hope for Professor McElderry.

And Gerald had let it slip through his fingers.

With a weary breath, he sat up and held a hand to his neck. The skin was scuffed raw from the sole of Alex Baranov's combat boot. Gerald muttered an oath. What was he to do?

Call the police?

And tell them what? Two boys were fighting over something that neither of them was entitled to? Gerald laughed to himself. He could hardly see the New York Police Department rushing to investigate that.

A sudden tiredness washed over him. He looked at his watch. Three o'clock in the morning. Five hours before Jasper Mantle would arrive to let him out. And five hours before he could expect some contact from Sir Mason Green. What would Gerald tell him? That the perpetual motion machine was on its way back to England in someone else's bag?

Gerald got slowly to his feet. His head was still foggy as he limped across to his pack. He knelt to scoop its contents back into place when his hand fell upon the square of canvas from the Delacroix painting.

He paused, laid the canvas flat on the floor and studied the detail of the messenger bag. 'Fat lot of good this has been,' Gerald thought. 'Supposed to help me find the black box.' He flipped the canvas over, and looked at the smudged pattern on the reverse side. 'Now the professor is good as dead.'

And then he saw it.

The rush of blood to his brain almost knocked him sidewards, as effectively as any blow from Alex Baranov's boots.

The smudged pattern on the back of the canvas square.

The inky stain on the wall behind the decanter.

They were almost identical.

Gerald snatched up the piece of painting and stumbled to the table. He picked up two thumbtacks from the assortment of junk that Alex had scattered across the floor. His hands were shaking as he pinned the canvas square over the pattern on the wall.

He took in a deep breath then looked through the water-filled decanter. The smudged stain on the canvas refracted into a clear impression of the grid of black boxes. But this time a different hole was marked. Gerald's heart raced—the square on the grid three up from the bottom and seven in from the left contained an egg-shaped symbol, ringed with a band of dots: the mark of the perpetual motion machine. Gerald grabbed the edge of the table with both hands to steady himself. He swallowed hard.

Alex had taken the wrong casket.

Gerald's eyes darted across to the wall of boxes.

Three up. Seven across from the left.

He hauled the box out and marvelled at the heft of it in his hands. He ran a finger over the lock at the front. Alex had pocketed the key, but Gerald was not worried—he could keep it. Gerald had the box that Mason Green desired. And that was all that counted.

Gerald scooped up his backpack and tucked the box under his arm. He didn't spare the Billionaires' Club a second glance as he climbed out the window into the frosty morning. He clambered down the fire-escape stairs. It was only as he neared the footpath that Gerald realised he had no way of contacting Mason Green. After all he had been through with Alex Baranov, he was left with the wooden box but still no way of freeing the professor. Gerald paused midway between steps and catapulted a curse-strewn tirade into the air to join the thrum of traffic noise rising from the street.

He was answered by an unexpected voice.

'That's no way to speak to your friends.'

Gerald leaned over the railing and stared to the street below. His gaze was met by the upturned faces of Felicity Upham and Ruby and Sam Valentine.

'You really should see someone about that anger problem of yours,' Sam continued. 'It's really unattractive.'

A huge smile lit Gerald's face. He scampered down the last few flights, his boots knocking snow from the iron steps and creating a mini blizzard that chased him all the way to the street. He leapt over the final three stairs and landed in the tangled embrace of his friends.

'What are you all doing here?' Gerald asked amid a flurry of questions about his adventures during the night. 'How did you know to come?'

Ruby pushed herself free of Gerald's arms and looked at him with mild confusion. 'What are you talking about?' she said. 'We got your message at the Plaza. We came straight away.'

'I was halfway through a dusk-to-dawn zombie movie marathon and a cheeseburger the size of my head,'

Sam said, exposing a sliver of gherkin between his front teeth, 'so this better be important.'

It was Gerald's turn to look confused. 'I never sent you any message,' he said, shifting the wooden box from one hip to the other. 'I was lucky to get out of this stupid place in one piece. I didn't have time to send a message to anyone.'

A frown creased Felicity's brow. 'The note was quite specific,' she said. 'Someone slipped it under the door to our suite. We were to meet you here at the foot of the fire escape straight away.'

Gerald looked around them. The zigzag of iron stairs had deposited him in a narrow alley that ran along the side of the building, just off the bustle of Fifth Avenue.

'If you didn't send the message,' Ruby said, 'who did?'

Her words were barely out when a large metal grate in the footpath beneath their feet gave way, swallowing them like a midnight snack.

Gerald opened his mouth to scream, but the sudden drop seemed to wedge his stomach into his throat, blocking any chance of noise escaping. The combination of no ground at his feet together with the pull of gravity sent terror into his heart and a chill wind up his trouser legs that caused instant clenching of eyes, teeth and buttocks.

He landed awkwardly, his knees buckling under him. He sensed a body dropping close to his left, then two more to his right. Gerald opened his eyes to find himself buried to the armpits in a giant nest of shredded newspaper.

For a moment, no one spoke. Gerald still clutched the black box to his chest, as if cradling a small child.

'What just happened?' Sam's voice filled the dimly lit space.

Gerald looked around. They appeared to have fallen into a cavernous cellar and landed in an industrial vat the size of a backyard swimming pool. Above him, Gerald could make out a tangle of grey metal pipes and rusted steel girders that disappeared into the gloom up towards the street. To their right, in a storage cage against a brown brick wall, were a large red boiler and an assortment of junk. And to their left was—

'Well hail, hail! The gang's all here.'

Gerald spun his head to see Sir Mason Green standing over them with a smug grin on his face. 'I am so glad you are all right,' Green continued. 'It was the devil's own job trying to calculate how much paper to shred to provide you with a comfortable landing. It's a good seven-metre drop from the street and I really couldn't have you shattering anklebones or popping knee joints. That would have been most inconvenient. So I erred on the side of caution.' He lowered a rope ladder into the vat and beckoned Gerald across.

Gerald twisted his way through the mass of shredded paper, holding the wooden box above his head. 'Now I know how a guinea pig feels,' he muttered. He finally made it to the side, took hold of the ladder in one hand, tucked the box under his arm and climbed out.

'I could hardly afford to damage the contents of that casket,' Green said. 'Not after you went to such lengths to secure it for me. It wasn't too much trouble, I trust?'

Gerald stared at the box in his hands. Ruby, Felicity and Sam dragged themselves to the side of the vat. 'You have no idea,' he said. 'Why all the fuss over a perpetual motion machine? Is it really that important?'

Sir Mason Green stiffened as if all the joints in his body had frozen. His eyes locked onto the wooden casket. 'Oh, Gerald, it is more important to me than you can possibly imagine. I hope you have the correct one. I understand there are a few from which to choose.'

Gerald tightened his grip on the black box. 'There's a couple fewer now,' he said. 'Alex took one as well.'

Green's eyes seemed to glow in the dim light of the cellar. 'I was wondering how you fared with Baranov the younger. Did he prove as outrageously deceitful as his father?'

Gerald ran a hand across the rough graze that Alex's boot had burned across his throat. 'You have your faults but you are a good judge of character,' he said. 'Alex pulled a knife on me and took off with a box. It had a silver egg in it that looked just like the symbol for the perpetual motion machine. But I'm pretty sure it was the wrong box.'

Green laughed with gusto. 'I am absolutely certain he has the wrong one,' he said. 'Now tell me, Gerald, did that piece of the Delacroix painting prove useful?'

Gerald nodded. 'How did you even know about that?' he asked.

'I didn't. At least, not for sure,' Green said. 'There were rumours that Delacroix left a hidden design on the canvas that might point to the perpetual motion machine. But I had no idea how it might work.'

'There's a whole artist's studio on the top floor,' Gerald said. 'Are you saying Delacroix painted there?'

'Apart from being a collector, Jim Kincaid was a patron of the arts,' Green said. 'If gossip is to be believed, he brought Delacroix to New York to get him away from the dangers of Paris after the revolution of 1830.'

'That makes sense,' Ruby said. 'I'm fairly sure Delacroix's painting inspired the design of the Statue of Liberty.'

'So, while Kincaid was in his workshop trying to reinvent Drebbel's machine, Delacroix was upstairs working on *Liberty Leads the People*,' Gerald said. His brain raced. 'Kincaid was storing all his attempts at recreating the machine in those black boxes. I bet he had one spot set aside for Drebbel's original and Delacroix recorded the location in a puzzle on the back of the canvas.'

'But how do you know the box Alex took isn't the right one?' Sam asked.

'Because, Mr Valentine, I have located the only key for the correct box. The fact young Baranov was able to open his casket is all the proof I need that the poor boy is on his way to present his father with a sad attempt at Cornelius Drebbel's engineering masterpiece.' Green chuckled to himself. 'Sergei will be livid.'

'Why would Alex's father want this machine so much?' Felicity asked.

'To protect his oil business,' Gerald said. 'He wants to make sure no one else can use the machine to compete with him.'

'You are partially correct,' Green said. 'If I know Sergei Baranov, he wanted to keep the machine in a Siberian bunker until his oil supplies run low, then open the Baranov Perpetual Motor Company and make a fortune selling the technology. Except, of course, he doesn't have the machine.' Green reached out to take the box from Gerald. 'I do.'

Gerald whipped the casket away and shoved it into Sam's hands. 'Not until we know Professor McElderry is safe,' Gerald said. 'That was the deal.'

Green stared at Gerald for a moment, then crossed to a wooden bench and picked up the handset of an old rotary telephone. He dialled a single number and waited.

'Professor?' he said into the mouthpiece. 'Can you show your face, please?' He put the receiver back in its cradle and turned to Gerald. 'I will keep my end of the bargain,' he said. His eyes locked onto the box in Sam's hands. 'I hope for all your sakes that you have managed to do the same.'

Gerald felt something brush against his fingers. Ruby was rubbing the back of his hand. 'What happened in the club?' she asked.

'Let's get the professor out of here and I'll tell you all about it over a mountain of pancakes, whipped butter and maple syrup,' Gerald said.

Sam placed the black box at his feet and nudged it with his boot. 'If Sergei Baranov wants to dominate global energy with this thing, what's your scheme?' he asked Green. 'Why do you want it?'

Sir Mason arched his fingers. 'Nothing as mundane as that,' he said. 'I have a far more creative plan for my little machine.'

Gerald glanced at his watch. 'What's taking the professor so long?' He stared hard at the silver-haired billionaire. 'What are you up to?'

Green raised an eyebrow in mock indignation. 'Up to?' he asked. 'Why ever would you think I was up to something? The cellars under the Billionaires' Club are vast. The building above us is twelve storeys. From my cursory investigations down here, the complex may have as many levels beneath the street. It has a labyrinthine quality about it—so many criss-crossing corridors and stairways. The cellars are a puzzle in themselves. Another of Diamond Jim Kincaid's eccentric touches.' Green extended his arms wide and turned a slow circle. His jacket billowed open, and Gerald started at the handgun tucked into Green's waistband. 'It's draughty and dank and be it ever so humble, it is certainly no place like home, but it will do for my time in the city,' Green said. 'A handy bolthole to keep tabs on you while you retrieved my treasure box.'

'You're welcome to it,' Gerald said. 'As long as it buys the professor's freedom.'

Sir Mason smiled coolly. 'Once I have the box, the professor is free to do whatever he pleases.'

Then, from a shadowed doorway at the rear of the cellar, a figure shuffled into the room. Professor Knox McElderry of the British Museum—his red beard combed and trimmed, his brown herringbone suit shambolic as usual but neat enough—stood blinking in the soft light. He had the air of a large brown bear that had just emerged from a long winter's sleep, not certain which way to turn first.

'Professor McElderry?' Ruby said softly, not wanting to startle him. 'Are you all right?'

McElderry blinked again, his shaggy eyebrows knitting into a single auburn hedge across his forehead. He looked at Ruby for a moment before a glimmer of recognition showed in his eyes. A gruff rumble rolled from his throat.

'Miss Valentine?'

Ruby's face lit up. 'Oh, you remember!'

Mason Green held up a hand, gesturing for the professor to stay where he was. 'Your friend has been off the Voynich juice, as it were, for a few weeks now,' Green said. 'He was only on it for the trip to Scotland so he wouldn't make a fuss. I should bottle the stuff and sell it to new parents. But as you can see, he is fit and well.' Before Gerald could say anything, Sir Mason tuned to the professor and said, 'Can you excuse us now, McElderry? I have some business to transact. If you would be so kind as to return to your quarters until I summon you again.'

The professor blinked once more and shuffled back into the shadows.

Gerald looked after the disappearing form, aghast. 'Where's he going? What's wrong with him?'

'He will be free to leave at the appropriate time,' Green said. 'I've waited long enough. Let me open my little treasure chest.'

Gerald gave Sam a nod. Sam picked up the box. 'Careful, boy,' Green said. 'I can't have it damaged.' He pulled a small golden key from his trouser pocket and knelt by the casket. The key slid into the lock, then Green shot a glance at Gerald. 'Let's hope for the professor's sake that you have chosen well,' he said.

Gerald swallowed. Beads of sweat formed on his forehead.

Green turned the key. The tip of his tongue flickered

across his lips. He took the lid by the sides and tilted it back.

For a moment, no one said anything. The only sound was the drip from a leaking pipe somewhere in the cavernous space above them; a slow, mournful drip, drip, drip…

Gerald's eyes slowly closed.

The box was empty.

Chapter 25

Mason Green stared into the bare gloss interior of the wooden box as if he had been snap-frozen. Only his steadily reddening face gave any indication that he was still alive.

No one spoke.

No one moved.

The leaky pipe in the ceiling sounded its sorrowful tone.

drip...

drip...

drip...

Finally, Gerald ventured a thought. 'I could go get another box and—'

Sir Mason Green erupted in volcanic fury. He grabbed

the box, wound up like an Olympic hammer thrower and hurled it into the exposed brick of the nearest wall. The casket shattered into a storm of splinters, spraying needles of ebony everywhere. Then he snatched up a table lamp, yanked the power cord from the socket and, with a swinging heft, sent it to the same fate. Coloured glass showered through the air in a kaleidoscope of destruction. Green turned his rage onto anything not bolted down—chairs, books, boxes—all the while emitting a guttural '*Noooooo*'.

Gerald took a pace back and beckoned Sam, Ruby and Felicity to follow. Quiet as cats, they retreated into the shadows as Sir Mason Green raged on, unchecked and unstoppable. A blizzard of broken furnishings filled the air.

Then Gerald saw it: the doorway in the gloom through which Professor McElderry had disappeared. He grabbed Sam by the shoulders and shoved him through it, then ushered Felicity and Ruby after him. The four of them clattered into a narrow tunnel-like corridor, walled with grimy brown bricks. The air was sour with mould and disuse. The only light came from a line of dim bulbs that were fixed in wire cages at regular intervals along the ceiling, snaking into the distance.

Sam led the way, running deeper and deeper into the unknown. They dashed around bends and down stairwells, past alcoves and doorways, all the while the clamour of Sir Mason Green's fury becoming softer and softer behind them.

Sam suddenly stopped.

'What's the hold up?' Ruby asked, catching her breath. 'Green will run out of stuff to throw soon enough, and then he'll notice we're gone.'

Sam looked back at them, his face flushed. 'There's a crossroad,' he said.

Ruby elbowed past Felicity to get to her brother. 'What do you mean "crossroad"?' she said. 'We're under a building, not trying to navigate a motorway.' But then she saw what Sam was referring to: an identical brown brick passage running across the corridor, with a line of caged lights tracing into the distance in each direction.

'Should we call out to the professor?' Felicity suggested. 'He can't be far away.'

'And tell Green exactly where we are?' Ruby said. 'I don't think that's such a great idea given the mood he's in.'

'I agree,' Gerald said. 'Confronting an enraged psychopath is one thing—an enraged psychopath with a gun is another thing altogether.'

'So what do we do?' Sam asked. 'Left, right or straight ahead.'

The four of them clustered in the eye of the cross-roads, each staring along a different route. Gerald strained his eyes, as much to wring his brain into finding a solution as to see into the distance. He was on the verge of popping a blood vessel when the answer came to him.

'We need to split up,' he said.

Ruby, Sam and Felicity turned to look at him as if he had just suggested they all put their tongues in a light socket.

'Are you nuts?' Sam said. 'Who knows where all these passages lead. If we all head off in different directions we might never see each other again—or anyone else for that matter.'

'I hate to say it, but Sam's right,' Ruby said. 'There's no telling how long and twisted these corridors get.'

'I'm with Ruby,' Felicity said. 'We could be wandering around down here forever.'

'I'm not saying we go four different ways,' Gerald said. 'Hear me out. Now, what are we looking for?'

Felicity shrugged. 'Professor McElderry, of course.'

'That's one thing,' Gerald said. 'But we're also looking for a way out. If Mason Green is happy to let the professor wander around down here by himself then it's a safe bet that McElderry doesn't know how to get back to the street. It's no use us finding him and not being able to get out of here.'

'What about the way we came in?' Sam said. 'Can't we get out back there?'

'There are two problems with that,' Gerald said. 'I couldn't see any ladder or stairs to get back to the street. And there's a gun-toting psychopath back there.'

Ruby chewed on her bottom lip. 'So what do you suggest we do?'

Gerald tightened the straps of his backpack. 'Sam and Felicity go one way. Ruby, you and I go another. If one of us finds the professor, bring him back here. If one of us finds a way out, we come back here. Either way, we should meet back at this spot in thirty minutes.' Gerald tore a blank page from the notebook in his pack and rolled it into a loose tube. He lit the end with Alex's zippo and let it burn for a moment before stubbing it out on the floor. With the scorched end he marked a large sooty cross at the intersection of the four corridors.

'X marks the spot, all right?' he said. 'If we're lucky, when we next see each other we'll have both the professor and a way out.'

There was a general murmur of agreement. Then Sam piped up. 'What about rats?' He peered uncertainly down the corridor to the left.

'That's why you're teamed with Felicity,' Gerald said. 'She won't tease you as much as Ruby would.'

Felicity laughed. 'That's right,' she said. 'Nowhere near as much.' She took Sam by the arm. 'Come along, my hero. Let's go kick some tiny furry butt.'

Gerald watched as they wound out of sight, then turned to Ruby. 'Which way do you want to go?'

'As long as we keep track of where we've gone,' Ruby said, 'either way is as good as the other.'

A sudden fusillade of swearing echoed through the network of tunnels, seemingly coming from all directions at once.

'I think someone has noticed we're gone,' Gerald said. He took Ruby's hand and stepped into the corridor to the right. 'We better hurry. I'd like to get out of this labyrinth as soon as possible.'

Ruby tightened her grip on Gerald's hand. 'Lead the way then, Theseus.'

Gerald looked back at her blankly. 'Who?'

Ruby dropped his hand like it was a day-old haddock. 'Never mind,' she said. 'Let's see where this takes us.'

Gerald watched as Ruby strode ahead. He sighed— he would never understand girls.

Another string of blistering abuse sounded through the passageways. Gerald broke into a trot to catch up with Ruby. They soldiered on in silence until the corridor branched in two.

'Which one do you want to take?' Gerald asked, still smarting from whatever he had done to annoy Ruby.

'I think with mazes the trick is to always turn to the right, isn't it? That's how you get to the centre,' Ruby said.

'What have mazes got to do with anything?'

'This is the house of puzzles, right?' Ruby said. 'Who's to say these cellars aren't part of some giant puzzle that has to be solved.'

Gerald thought for a moment. After his experience in the rooms up above, there was every reason to suppose that Ruby was right. 'But what if you don't want to get to the centre?' he said. 'What if you want to find the way out?'

Ruby shrugged. 'You turn to the left, maybe?' She snatched up Gerald's hand one more time. 'Let's go, minotaur brain, before Green catches up.'

Gerald was going to ask what a minotaur was but thought better of it.

Another burst of cursing flooded the bricked corridors, this time louder and very much closer than before.

Ruby and Gerald broke into a run.

The path branched again—they took the left branch. It led them down a short flight of stairs, which they took at a jump, then into another offshoot to the left.

'This is getting us nowhere,' Gerald panted, chancing a look over his shoulder. 'Will we be able to find our way back to Sam and Felicity?'

Then Mason Green hobbled out of a passageway about ten paces ahead of them. He walked straight across their path and into the corridor opposite. Ruby and Gerald skidded to a halt and stared down the passage that Green had entered just as the back of his silver head disappear around a bend.

They paused there a second, staring down the empty corridor, when Green's face re-emerged to look back at them. Also looking at them was the business end of Green's handgun.

The bullet shattered into the brick wall a split second after Ruby had pulled Gerald clear. This time there was no neat plan of left hand turns. Gerald and Ruby pelted down any corridor they could find. Left. Right. Up stairs.

Down ramps. Anywhere, just as long as Mason Green's gun was as far away as possible.

Another shot rang out—it was impossible to tell from where—when Gerald and Ruby stormed into a long passage. This time there were no intersecting tunnels, just smooth walls and a floor that seemed to slope ever so gently upwards.

'This must take us somewhere,' Gerald said.

'It better,' Ruby panted. 'Because if this is a blind alley I don't fancy retracing our steps.'

They rounded a bend just as another shot echoed along the brick walls. Then came a shout—from not as far away as Gerald would have liked. 'I know where you went, Mr Wilkins.' Mason Green's voice was full of purpose. 'And I'm coming after you.'

Ruby squeezed hard on Gerald's hand. 'Hurry!'

The corridor curved, then ended abruptly in a blank wall of bricks. Gerald and Ruby skidded to a stop.

'A blind alley,' Ruby said. She looked to Gerald. 'We're trapped.'

Gerald turned to run back the way they had come but he halted at the sound of boots, advancing steadily up the corridor towards them.

Chapter 26

The blind passage seemed to close in on Gerald. He pressed his hands flat to the end wall, as if pushing on a solid brick barrier would somehow produce a path to freedom.

'What are we going to do?' Ruby whispered. 'The only way out is straight back to Mason Green.'

'And his gun,' Gerald said. He balled his right hand into a fist and pounded the wall in frustration. All that did was shoot pain up Gerald's arm and into his skull. He nursed the offending fist with his other hand, spun around and slid his back down the wall until he was sitting on the cold stone floor, cursing his luck.

Ruby dropped next to him and placed a comforting hand on his shoulder. She went to speak, but the advancing footsteps made anything she had to say pretty much redundant.

'It will all be okay,' Ruby said softly. 'I'm sure of it.'

Gerald's head slumped. He was not sure of it at all.

Then he saw the writing. The letters were pressed into a brick at the base of the blank end to the passage. Gerald rolled onto his stomach and squinted to make out the words. '*What gets wet the more it dries?*' He blinked up at Ruby. 'It's a riddle.'

His eyes darted to the adjoining brick. The alphabet was laid out in a neat grid of two rows: A to M and N to Z, each letter pressed into a carved square. Gerald sucked in a sharp breath.

'What is it?' Ruby asked.

'It's like a keyboard,' Gerald said. He pushed gently on the 'A'; it depressed a millimetre. He sat upright and took Ruby by the shoulders, his eyes wild. 'I bet if we type in the answer to the riddle, something will happen.'

'Like what?'

'I don't know. A door will open, another clue will appear—that's how the house works.'

The footsteps echoed closer up the passage. Ruby grabbed Gerald's jacket sleeve tight. 'What gets wet the more it dries?' she asked. 'Um—a cat washing itself.'

'That makes no sense,' Gerald said.

'At least I'm trying.'

Gerald concentrated. How could anything get wet as it dries? 'Uh—sand on the beach? Sweat on a hot day.

A fish's bum?'

Ruby looked at Gerald blankly. 'A fish's bum? Really?'

'Shut up,' Gerald shot back. 'I'm thinking out loud.' Then it hit him. 'A towel!'

'Brilliant,' Ruby said. 'Type it in.'

The voice of Mason Green came around the bend behind them. 'You may as well come out, Gerald. There is no exit down here. And, as you may have guessed, I have a gun.'

Gerald frowned and put the answer into the tiny clay keypad. Each letter clicked as he pressed it.

T O W E

When Gerald pressed the *L* a hollow *clunk* sounded behind the wall. Then a jagged opening appeared along the mortar between the bricks, as if a giant jigsaw piece had worked itself loose. The section swung in, revealing a continuation of the passage.

Ruby plunged through the opening as Gerald clambered to his knees. He was halfway through behind her when he paused. He had left his pack on the stone floor in the corridor. Gerald turned to reach for it but Ruby took him by the jacket and dragged him through to the other side. A second later the brick section swung back into place, and clicked secure as if it hadn't moved for centuries.

Gerald slumped on the floor, waiting for his eyes to adjust to the dim light. Ruby grabbed him and hauled him to his feet. Before he could protest she had a finger to his lips, shaking her head to warn him not to speak. Then Gerald noticed a spot of light shining from the brick wall onto Ruby's cheek. She pulled him across until Gerald saw a small peephole in the mortar. He peered through and stifled a gasp. On the other side of the wall stood Sir Mason Green.

Ruby's lips brushed Gerald's ear. 'I don't think he's very happy,' she whispered.

From the other side of the wall came a howl of rage as Sir Mason Green let fly with a military-grade stream of swearing.

Gerald's eyes popped. 'Wow,' he whispered back to Ruby. 'That's impressive.'

Ruby smothered a giggle beneath her fingers and leaned in close. 'He must know a swearword for every letter of the alphabet.'

'Just as long as he doesn't notice the alphabet at the bottom of the wall,' Gerald said. He ducked his eye back to the peephole. 'Dammit,' he said. 'He's taking my backpack.'

'Is there anything important in it?' Ruby whispered.

'Just my notebook and all those guesses at Jeremy Davey's coded message,' he said. Then Gerald sucked in a breath. On the other side of the wall, Sir Mason Green was staring at the knapsack in his hand. Then he slowly raised his eyes to glare right at the peephole.

Right at Gerald.

In a flash, Green rushed to the wall, running his hands across its surface, searching for any opening, any chink in the bricks. For a moment, Green's eye hovered a bare centimetre away from the peephole, looking directly at Gerald. The width of a brick away, Gerald held his breath.

Then, just as swiftly, Green turned and was away down the corridor.

Gerald pulled his face from the wall and he slumped back against the bricks with relief. 'He's gone,' he said. Gerald looked down to find Ruby grinning at him. 'What's so funny?' he asked.

Ruby's smile widened. 'You were very clever working out that riddle, you know,' she said.

Gerald's cheeks flushed.

'But not as clever as I am,' she continued. She pointed to a sign screwed to the wall. It was shaped like an arrow, pointing further along the passage, and had the words CENTRAL PARK painted in neat capital letters.

'Our way out of here,' Ruby said with pride. 'This tunnel must run all the way under Fifth Avenue and open out somewhere in the park. If Sam and Felicity have found the professor our work here is done.'

She beamed up at Gerald again. His cheeks turned a deeper red. There was a stirring in the pit of his stomach. Gerald looked into Ruby's eyes.

'There once was a girl named Ruby—'

Ruby put a finger to Gerald's lips. 'Not really the

time,' she said. 'We've still got a minotaur to track down, Theseus. Let's try to get this door open again.'

The colour drained from Gerald's face and his eyes dropped to his shoes. 'Oh, okay…'

After a few minutes of searching, Ruby's hand fell upon a metal lever set into the wall. She pressed her eye to the peephole to see if the way was clear, then pulled the handle. The section swung in and Ruby led the way through the gap.

They retraced the path to where they had last seen Felicity and Sam, making sure to remember the way back to the exit.

'How long have we been gone?' Gerald asked as they neared the intersection in the passageways. 'It must be longer than half an hour.'

They slowed to a walk and stopped at the ashen cross on the floor.

There was no sign of Sam or Felicity.

Gerald was about to ask 'What do we do now?' when there was a hissed whisper from further down the corridor.

'Gerald! Ruby!' They looked up to see Felicity crouched in a doorway where the passage curved. They rushed to her.

'We've found a way out,' Gerald said to Felicity.

'And we've found the professor,' Felicity said. 'Though, he does seem a bit confused.' She took them through a zigzag of passages. 'We think Mason Green has given him another bizarre potion,' she said. As they rounded a bend Gerald recoiled, screwing his eyes shut and turning his face away. 'What is that smell?'

A pungent green mist curled from a doorway just ahead. Gerald slapped a hand over his mouth and nose; the smell was eye-watering. He could not find words to describe the odour but if a cheese factory could fart that would go part of the way to just how vile the stench was.

Felicity tugged at his arm. 'Come on,' she said. 'You'll get used to it.'

Gerald paused in the doorway, his hand still over his nose. He stared into a spacious room. Large white tiles lined the floor and walls. Stainless steel benches were covered with beakers, flasks and titration tubes. Messy scientific scrawl covered a large whiteboard. And next to the largest workbench stood two people: Professor Knox McElderry, wearing a stained lab coat and holding a beaker containing a bubbling iridescent blue concoction, and a very anxious Sam Valentine, clutching forceps clamped around a test tube.

'Hold it still, damn you,' McElderry said as he went to tip the brew into the tube. 'I can't afford to spill any.'

The forceps wobbled in Sam's grip, and a drop of the mixture spattered onto the floor. Instantly, a mushroom cloud of purple vapour rose from the tiles. McElderry leaped back and snatched the test tube and forceps from Sam's hands. 'Try not to breathe that in,' the professor said, stoppering the beaker on the bench and taking another step back from the sizzling puddle on the floor. 'It could stunt your growth.'

Sam's face went from anxious to petrified. 'I'm sorry,' he said, shuffling in behind Felicity for protection. 'It just slipped.'

'Tell that to the people of China when that drop of super acid makes it down there,' McElderry said. His face coiled into a ferocious scowl. 'You may well be the stupidest boy in the world. Has anyone ever told you that?'

Gerald took a step towards the professor. 'You have,' he said. 'At least a few times.'

With a flurry of beard, McElderry swivelled his head to glare at Gerald. 'Have I?' he said, taken aback for a moment. Then he returned his suspicious gaze to Sam. 'How very astute of me.'

Gerald crossed to the professor and placed a hand on his shoulder. McElderry spun and glowered at him. The look in his eyes stunned Gerald: the pupils were so dilated that there was almost no iris visible, just two sink holes into the bottomless depths of McElderry's mind.

'Uh, professor, it's time to go now,' Gerald said. He tugged gently on McElderry's sleeve. 'Time to go home.'

McElderry baulked, leaning back. 'Can't you see I'm working on something important?' he growled. Then he blinked, which seemed to make his pupils grow even larger, and blinked again. 'You're the Wilkins boy, aren't you?' he said.

Gerald's face brightened. 'That's right,' he said. 'I'm Gerald—we met at the museum. You knew my great aunt, Geraldine.'

McElderry's brow furrowed, as if he was digging into the far recesses of a long-lost filing cabinet of recollections. 'Geraldine Archer,' he said. 'I did know her.' He looked again at Gerald. 'Gerald Wilkins. I know you too.' Then, as if a long dry riverbed had been flooded with memories, the professor took Gerald by the shoulders. 'You're right. We must get out of here immediately.'

McElderry dragged Gerald through the door. Ruby, Sam and Felicity rushed after them.

'We know a way out, Professor,' Gerald said. 'It's just up ahead.'

'I know a short cut,' McElderry said, not looking back. 'Far quicker. Far quicker.'

The professor's grip on Gerald's arm tightened as they bustled around a tight corner, then another, and up a short flight of stairs to a heavy wooden door. McElderry threw it open and ushered Gerald through with a sharp shove in the back.

Gerald launched through the opening and skidded to a stop. He hardly had a chance to get his bearings before Sam, Ruby and Felicity bundled into the back of him.

They all looked up to find that they were back in the original cellar where they had fallen from the street.

And glaring at them from the middle of a floor strewn with broken furniture and shredded paper was

Sir Mason Green.

Professor McElderry gave Gerald another prod between the shoulder blades. 'There, Sir Mason,' he said. 'Gerald Wilkins and his friends, just like you asked for.'

Sir Mason Green smiled, and raised his gun.

Chapter 27

Sir Mason Green snapped the padlock shut and tested the cage door. 'That should keep you in one place,' he said, 'while I figure out what to do with you. Now, if you'll excuse me, the professor and I have some business to discuss.' Gerald watched Mason Green usher Professor McElderry through the door at the rear of the cellar. He laced his fingers through the wires and rattled at the lock and hinges, but the door stood firm.

'Locked tight,' he said. 'We're stuck.'

The cage formed an airy box: three walls and a roof of thick intermeshing wire bolted against an unyielding brick wall in the corner of the cellar. The storage space had the look of a junk shop gone to seed. The floor was stacked with dusty wooden tea chests and random steamer trunks plastered with the faded stickers of sea voyages of years gone by: New York, Havana, Montevideo, La Libertad, Tahiti. A roll of mouldering carpet was propped against a water-stained grandfather clock, its hands forever marking twelve. Even a ship's wheel leaned awkwardly, and a little sadly, between a low bookcase stacked with decaying paperbacks and a filing cabinet that was missing a drawer. A large red boiler, squat and impressive, sat against the wall like a rust-caked Buddha with a robust chimney pipe that stretched from its top, through a narrow opening in the cage roof, and disappeared into the inner-gizzards of the club's heating system. A manufacturer's plate bolted to its rounded belly proclaimed in cast iron lettering: *Product of Kincaid Foundries, Coopertown, Pennsylvania.*

Ruby, Sam and Felicity sat in a disconsolate group, each perched on a tea chest, their chins cupped in their hands, as if waiting to be sold along with the rest of the junk. 'What is going on with Professor McElderry?' Ruby said. 'He seemed pretty normal, and then he takes us straight to Green like some trained chimpanzee.'

'Did you see the look on his face when Green thanked him?' Felicity said. 'If McElderry had a tail he would have wagged it. Pathetic.'

Gerald shook his head and frowned. 'He must be under the influence of some drug,' he said. 'But instead of being a zombie lurching around the place he's able to do whatever Mason Green needs him to do. Sam, what

279

was that blue stuff in the beaker?'

Sam screwed up his face at the memory of the stench that had filled the laboratory. 'The only thing he said was not to get any on my clothes. Or fingers. Or anywhere else for that matter. It was like whatever he was working on was the most important thing in the world. Nothing else mattered.'

Gerald scoured his brain for anything that might make sense of the situation. The only conclusion he could reach was that the professor was the victim of another potion from the poisoner's cookbook that was the Voynich manuscript. 'Whatever the reason he's acting this way, Professor McElderry still needs our help,' he said.

Felicity jumped down from her tea chest and wandered towards the rear of the storage cage, kicking at boxes and trunks as she went. 'In case you missed it, we could do with some help ourselves,' she said. 'It's still hours before Jasper Mantle is due to turn up and let you and Alex out of the house.'

'And what's he going to find when he does get here?' Ruby said. 'An empty room and no sign of either of you. No one has any idea where we are. We might as well have been swallowed up by the earth.'

'We can't wait for someone to come rescue us,' Gerald said, rounding on Ruby. 'We have to rescue ourselves.'

'And how do you suggest we do that?' Ruby said.

Gerald narrowed his gaze. 'Whatever it is, we need to do it before Green comes back. We're wasting the time we've got while he's not here.'

'Then don't let us slow you down, oh fearless leader,' Ruby snapped.

Frustration rose in Gerald's belly. He flashed out a hand and grabbed Ruby by the sleeve. She had dismissed him one too many times that day. Ruby's response was instant and explosive. She thrust both her hands against Gerald's chest. 'Don't!' she cried.

The force of the shove took Gerald by surprise and he stumbled backwards. His foot caught the corner of a steamer trunk and he lost his balance. He threw out his hands for support. They landed flat against the boiler.

Ruby's eyes widened with horror. 'Oh no—'

Gerald's face contorted. He peeled his outstretched palms from the red steel and held them up to Ruby.

'I'm so sorry,' Ruby said, dread in her face. 'Oh, what have I done?'

Gerald's mouth opened wide...

'Well, there's a strange thing,' he said. 'The boiler's stone cold.'

Ruby unleashed a storm of fists onto Gerald's chest. Gerald held up his arms to ward off the blows and laughed. 'You're not so worried about hurting me now, are you?' he said, as the punches continued. 'Serves you right for being rude to me. Again.'

Ruby gave Gerald one last punch and glared at him. Gerald thought he caught a twinkle in her eyes. 'I hate you, Gerald Wilkins,' Ruby said. She tried to suppress a grin but the corners of her mouth twitched upwards.

Felicity popped her head around from behind the boiler. 'Hey, there seems to be a riddle of some sort on the back of this thing.'

Gerald's head bobbed up like a dog spotting a squirrel. He looked at Ruby.

'A riddle?' they chorused. Gerald and Ruby dashed to the back of the cage.

They found Felicity kneeling on the floor, peering up at a cast iron plate riveted to the boiler's underbelly. 'It's a bit difficult to read,' she said. Ruby eased in next to her, sliding onto her stomach.

'Let's see,' she said. '*Who makes me does not need me; who buys me does not use me; who uses me will never see me.*'

There was a long silence, broken when Sam said, 'Well that's just stupid. Who buys something then never uses it?'

'You've clearly never seen my mother at the Boxing-Day sales,' Gerald said. 'What's that circular thing next to the riddle?'

Ruby looked to the left. 'It's a dial—like a combination lock but with letters instead of numbers. There's five concentric rings and a central hub, each with letters spaced around the outside.' She pushed her fingers against the outermost ring and twisted. 'And they turn! I think we have to work out the riddle and dial the answer.'

'What happens if we get it right?' Sam asked.

'If it's anything like the last riddle Ruby and I saw, it could get us out of here,' Gerald said.

'And if we get the answer wrong?' Felicity said.

Gerald tilted his head to the side. 'I hadn't thought of that.'

'Whatever it does, the answer has six letters,' Ruby said.

'What are the letters around the outside ring?' Felicity asked. 'That will at least give us a clue to the first letter in the answer.'

Ruby squinted again. 'It looks like there's every letter in the alphabet there,' she said.

'Terrific,' Gerald said. 'So what's the solution to the riddle?'

'*Who makes me does not need me*,' Ruby read again. 'That could be anything. People make stuff to sell all the time that they don't use themselves.'

'How about the last line?' Felicity said. '*Who uses me will never see me.* Who can't see things? Blind people?'

Sam shrugged. 'Or dead people.'

Ruby turned on her brother. 'Don't be an idiot. We're trying to solve a—'

'The answer is 'coffin',' Sam said. 'It's obvious.'

Ruby turned to read the riddle again.

'Genius,' she said. She dialled the outermost ring so 'C' was at the top, then soon had COFFIN spelled out from top to the centre.

'Done,' Ruby said. She looked about expectantly but nothing stirred.

'Maybe you need to press in the centre button for it to work,' Gerald said.

Ruby pushed the hub. It shifted in about a centimetre with a sharp *click*.

Then a sheet of metal dropped from the back of the boiler, flat on top of Ruby's head.

She let out a howl and wrapped her hands over her crown, rolling onto her back.

Gerald leaned over Ruby and peered into the dark interior of the boiler. He reached inside and pulled out an ornate gold key on a gold chain. He held it up and the key spun slowly, glinting in the light. It was about five centimetres long with two cross arms forming an X at the tip.

'That's the strangest-looking key I've ever seen,' Sam said. 'What do you think it opens?'

Gerald cast his eyes around the cage, searching for a keyhole. 'Hey Ruby, could you keep the moaning down?' he said. 'I'm trying to concentrate.'

Ruby peeled open an eyeball and stared death at Gerald. She was about to give him something to really concentrate on when a jangling ring filled the cellar.

Gerald poked his head out from behind the boiler to see a black telephone on a bench by the far wall. The phone was one of the few survivors of Mason Green's tantrum.

The telephone continued to ring.

Gerald ducked back and helped Ruby up from the

floor. 'This will bring Green running,' he said. 'We better shift to the front of the cage so he can see us. The last thing we need is him poking around back here.'

Seconds later the silver-haired billionaire walked into the cellar. He shot a quick glance at the cage and, satisfied that its occupants were still in place, hurried to the phone. He snatched the handset from the cradle and pressed it to his ear.

'Yes?' he said. He listened intently for a moment, his face darkening. 'Empty,' he said. 'If it was ever in the box, it is not there now.'

Sam elbowed Gerald in the ribs. 'Who's he talking to?' he whispered.

Green's voice strengthened. 'I have told the professor to stop work on the potions. The full translation of the manuscript is his top priority. Along with the coded message from Jeremy Davey. It must hold the key to all of this.' Green listened for a moment, his head bobbing in agreement. 'Of course. Do you take me for a fool? The curiosity machine takes precedence. The final mechanism is still a mystery to us.'

Gerald cocked his head. *The curiosity machine?*

Mason Green paused and turned to stare directly into the cage. 'I agree,' he said. 'They serve no further purpose. I will—'

A sudden outburst down the phone line cut him off. Someone was giving Sir Mason Green a royal roasting.

Green glanced towards the cage and, seeing four sets

of eyes observing everything that was happening, turned his back to them.

'Who's giving him a bollocking?' Sam said. Then, after a moment's thought, 'Does he have a boss?'

The idea that Sir Mason Green might take orders from someone else struck Gerald with such force that it took him a moment to realise Felicity was tugging on his jacket sleeve, as if trying to tear it off at the seams. With her other hand she was pointing to something on the side of the boiler. Gerald leaned closer to see. It was a neat cross-shaped hole in the sheet metal. Felicity grabbed Gerald's hand—the golden key still dangled from his fingers.

Mason Green still had his back to them and the phone to his ear.

Gerald put the key into the hole and turned it.

A jagged crack appeared in the bricks at the rear of the cage, and a section of the wall popped ajar. Gerald shoved the key into his pocket and ushered Sam, Felicity and Ruby through the opening. He glanced over his shoulder at Green, who was still occupied on the phone, and ducked through. As soon as he was on the other side, he pushed the brick portal closed and turned, beaming, to find Sam, Felicity and Ruby frowning back at him, arms crossed and brows furrowed.

'What's the matter?' Gerald whispered. 'I got us out of the cage.'

Ruby's eyes narrowed. 'Oh yes, we're free at last,' she said.

Gerald looked about him. They had escaped into a space the size of a broom closet. A single gas lamp flickered beside a yellowed sheet of paper fixed to the back wall. Gerald pushed past Sam to get a closer look. 'This is just like the mechanical drawings that Kincaid had in his workshop upstairs,' he said. 'But this is much bigger than the perpetual motion machine.' He ran his fingertips over the title, written in neat block letters at the top of the sheet.

THE CURIOSITY MACHINE.

'This must be what Green is looking for,' Gerald whispered.

The diagram showed a complex schematic of gears and widgets, handles and dials, cranks and pistons. Gerald unpinned the page from the wall and held it under the lamp to get a better look. 'This is amazing,' he said. 'What do you think a curiosity machine does?'

'Generate pointless questions?' Ruby said. 'Do you really think that's important just now?'

Gerald ran his eyes across the tangle of ruled lines and technical writing. 'I don't know,' he said. 'Maybe this house of puzzles has a few more secrets to reveal.'

Gerald turned at a sharp jab to his ribs. Ruby had her eye to a peephole in the bricks that looked back into the storage cage. 'Shush. Mason Green has just got off the phone.'

Gerald glanced back at the plans, folded them into a neat square and zipped them into his jacket pocket.

'What's he doing?' he asked.

'He's looking this way. Ruby whispered.

'Do you think he'll notice we're gone?' Sam said.

The scream that pierced the bricks and the shrill cry of *I'll kill them!* was all the answer they needed.

Chapter 28

Ruby pressed her face to the bricks. Her voice dropped to the merest hint of a whisper. 'He's coming this way.'

'What are we going to do?' Felicity whispered back.

Gerald looked to Felicity. She held the fingers of one hand across her mouth, as if trying to plug a leak. Sam was crouched on one knee, his head slumped forward. Ruby was motionless at the peephole, both hands spread flat to the bricks on either side of her face.

Gerald stood by the rear wall. His knees were shaking; he was like a little boy standing before the schoolyard bully. If Mason Green found them, there would be no escape this time. The sound of boxes crashing to the floor came through from the other side of the wall. Shouts.

More crashing. A single gunshot. Yet more crashing.

The wobbling in Gerald's knees intensified.

After an age, the sound of Green's fury abated, and Ruby turned slowly around, her face grim.

'He's gone,' she said. 'But who knows for how long.'

'What was he doing out there?' Sam asked.

'He unlocked the cage and turned the place upside down,' Ruby said. 'He found the open panel at the back of the boiler. He almost exploded with that little discovery. That's when he fired the gun. He's gone now, probably to check on the professor.'

'Terrific,' Sam said. 'Now we've gone and made the madman with a gun even madder.'

'There is some good news though,' Ruby said, the hint of a grin on her lips. 'He left the cage door open. We're free.'

Some stability returned to Gerald's knees. 'It's time we got out of here and told the police about Green's hiding place,' he said.

Ruby looked at him with surprise. 'That's a remarkably sensible suggestion,' she said, 'coming from you.'

Gerald shrugged. 'When all else fails, try being rational.'

'What about Professor McElderry?' Felicity asked.

'If we see him between here and the exit feel free to invite him along, but if he's under some magic spell he might take some convincing,' Gerald said.

Ruby found a metal lever by the wall and wrapped

her hand around it. 'We need to do this quickly,' she said. She pulled and the brick section opened. They poured through, vaulted the wreckage left from Green's fury and ran out of the cage. Gerald swooped on his backpack that Green had dumped by a workbench and hoisted it to his shoulder.

Four sets of boots scuttled along the stone floor of the corridor.

Gerald was last in line as they weaved their way through the cellar maze. They passed over the ash cross on the floor where they had first parted ways, and Gerald felt a glimmer of hope that freedom was close by.

Ruby darted around a corner to the left, then stopped. Sam almost ran into her. 'What is it?' he asked. 'Why are you stopping?'

Ruby glanced back the way they had come, then turned to look further down the corridor. 'This doesn't look right,' she said. 'I must have taken a wrong turn.'

'Which turn was wrong?' Sam asked. 'There have been a lot of them.'

Ruby's face flushed. 'I'm not sure,' she said.

Gerald stepped in before Sam could say anything to aggravate the situation. 'Let's just retrace our steps until something looks familiar,' he said. 'We can't have gone too far off track.'

They turned to go back when Felicity called out to them from halfway down the passage. 'Look at this.'

She pointed to a pair of bas-relief sculptures in the

wall: one of a devil's face, the other of an angel. Beneath each sculpture was a brass handle set into the bricks, with an arrow indicating a clockwise turn. Under all of this was a wooden door, less than a metre high.

'It's another puzzle,' Ruby said, inspecting first the devil, then the angel.

'What are you supposed to do?' Sam asked. 'Pick the one you like the most?'

'Or the one that the puzzle maker thinks you'll pick?' Gerald said. 'Whatever it is, it doesn't matter. We know a way out. We've just got to find it and quick. I don't want to see Mason Green again today. Or ever.'

He turned to head back up the passage. Staring at him from the end of the corridor was a tall, silver-haired man with a pistol in his hand.

'Steady, Gerald,' Sir Mason said in a cool voice. 'Anyone would think that you didn't like me.'

Gerald spun around and, for a crazy second, thought about running. But then Professor McElderry stepped into the opposite end of the corridor.

They were trapped.

There was a moment of tense silence, then Ruby spoke up, staring straight at the professor. 'You remember us,' she said. 'Try to think. Try to see through the haze of drugs that you've taken.'

McElderry took an unsteady pace forwards.

Ruby's voice rose. 'Try to remember. Please.'

The professor stopped and swayed on the balls of his

feet, as if he had entered the room and forgotten why. His eyebrows knitted together. After a moment they relaxed and Professor Knox McElderry took a determined step down the corridor. 'It's all right, Sir Mason,' he said in a clear voice. 'They won't get past me.'

Ruby's shoulders dropped.

Gerald turned to see Mason Green advancing on them. He shrank back as the professor and Green herded the four friends into a cluster in the middle of the corridor.

Felicity grabbed the handle under the angel. 'Should I give it a try?' she asked.

Mason Green aimed the handgun at Felicity's head. 'That is enough, Miss Upham,' he said. 'This house has sprung enough surprises on me for two lifetimes. Take your hand away from the switch, thank you.'

Felicity did not move. She turned her eyes to Ruby. 'What should I do?'

A brick an inch above Felicity's head exploded as Mason Green fired two quick shots into the wall. The sound reverberated in the confined space. Felicity screamed and dropped to her knees, her hands covering her head. Ruby and Sam rushed to her.

Gerald stared at Green, who was wreathed in a swirling cloud of gun smoke. 'I am through with kidding around,' Green said. 'You will all come with me.'

Gerald held up his hands, as if surrendering. He knew what he was about to do was a massive risk, but he had no choice. 'I've got the plans for the curiosity machine,' he said as boldly as he could. Gerald had no idea what the machine did or why Green wanted it, but the effect of his announcement was electric. Sir Mason's face flushed red; the gun dropped to his side.

'How could you possibly—' he began.

Felicity raised her head and glared at the man. 'You foul human being,' she said, then lunged at the switch beneath the angel. She jerked the handle to the right.

The floor along the length of the corridor juddered violently, as if shaken by an earthquake. Bodies were thrown from their feet like struck tenpins. Gerald tumbled onto his back, his hands flailing as he tried to find something stable to cling to. Another shot exploded from Mason Green's gun. Then, with a violent lurch and a wrenching roar, the floor fell away. It split across the middle and dropped as if hinged at each end, forming two steep slides that plunged into a black abyss. Gerald's stomach lurched and he closed his eyes as he slid straight over the edge.

All was darkness.

Gerald heard his name being called—it might have been Ruby or Felicity, he couldn't tell. He was overwhelmed by a sense of weightlessness, as if he was floating amongst the clouds in some ethereal play land. He was falling; he was flying.

And then he stopped. A brutal tug on his shoulder yanked him and his eyes popped wide open. Gerald jerked his head about in dazed confusion. His breath caught in his throat. He looked down to see his feet thrashing and a bottomless black pit yawning beneath him. He twisted his head up to find the sloping floor of the corridor metres above him. A searing pain in his armpits told him his backpack had caught on something. He craned his neck and saw it: a rusted iron rod jutting out from the side of the pit. He was dangling in space.

'Gerald!'

It was Ruby.

Gerald strained around to see Ruby flat on her stomach, clinging to cracks in the steeply sloping floor and scrambling to stop from sliding into the black hole. Further along the corridor, Sam and Felicity held each other in a desperate embrace, pressing the soles of their feet onto opposite walls and forming a human bridge across the passage.

Professor McElderry and Mason Green were both sprawled on the floor, further up each end of the corridor. They both looked too panic-stricken to move.

'Gerald!' Ruby cried again. 'Are you all right?'

Gerald struggled to lift his head. A sharp pain ripped into his sides. The iron rod that held his backpack could give way at any movement. He looked up as high as he could. The sculptures of the devil and the angel looked down at him in seeming bemusement.

'Ruby,' Gerald called back. 'You need to turn the handle under the devil. And you need to do it quickly.'

Gerald lurched to the side. One of the shoulder

straps slipped in its buckle, sending him into a teetering swing across the chasm. 'Really quickly!' he shouted.

Ruby twisted her head to stare into Gerald's eyes. 'I'll try. But if I slip you better catch me.'

Gerald managed a weak smile. 'Always,' he said.

Ruby sucked in a breath and wedged one foot against the far wall, bracing herself.

'You can do it,' Gerald urged. The shoulder strap slipped another centimetre, shunting him sideways. 'Remember your gymnastics.'

Ruby pushed with her hands and launched herself upwards. She pressed her other foot against the near wall and straddled the corridor in an arched split. Slowly, she leaned forward, her outstretched fingertips crawling spider-like across the bricks towards the devil carving. Then, with a heave, she wrapped her fingers around the brass handle. 'I've got it!' she cried.

'Turn it!' Gerald yelled back, just as the shoulder strap pulled free. His right side fell away and he dropped hard, swinging wildly from the left strap. 'Hurry!'

'But Green still has the gun,' Ruby called back.

'Turn the handle!' Gerald screamed.

Then Mason Green's voice joined the clamour. 'Stop, Miss Valentine, or I will shoot you.'

'Turn it!'

Ruby twisted the handle.

The corridor juddered even more violently than before. Sam and Felicity cried out as the floor fell away beneath them.

Gerald's head slumped. 'Crud,' he muttered.

A thunderous rumble rolled along the corridor. Hidden sluices at either end of the passage opened and unleashed a torrent of water. Twin tidal waves swept into the enormous funnel formed by the sloping floor. The barrel of one wave swept Mason Green clean away, sending him spinning straight under the human bridge of Sam and Felicity and into the maw of the chasm. Gerald caught a glimpse of him as he disappeared into the velvet blackness, his screams receding and lost to the roar of the water that poured down the giant spout.

Gerald clung to his backpack, buffeted by the waterfall that broke over his head. He caught the sound of Ruby crying out. The only word he could understand was 'professor'.

A moment later there was a flurry of movement above him. Gerald tilted his head to see Professor McElderry dangling over the edge of the sloped floor, his legs swinging into the emptiness.

Then Gerald saw a way to save them both. He threw out his right hand and, as his body swung across, latched onto the professor's waistband.

'Hold on, Professor,' Gerald called out, water gushing into his mouth. 'I've got you.' He shook his head to clear the spray from his face. 'We can save each other.'

McElderry turned his head and looked straight into Gerald's eyes. 'Gerald,' he said, 'you're as stupid as your friend.'

Gerald's mouth dropped open but the professor cut him off before he could speak. 'Did you ever once ask if I wanted to be saved?' McElderry said. He lashed out a shoe and knocked Gerald's hand away from his belt. Then he raised his arms from the floor and let the torrent sweep him over the edge and into oblivion.

Chapter 29

Gerald watched helplessly as the professor dropped past him. There was no screaming or wails for help. Professor McElderry went to his fate as calmly as a baby drifting to sleep.

But his kick had sent Gerald into a whirling spin. At any moment he expected to be joining McElderry in a plunge into nothingness.

Then, as if a tap had been turned off, the river stopped. Gerald looked up as the last drips spilled over the edge. With a grinding of gears, the floor began to rise back into place. Gerald waited until the stone surface had reformed beneath his feet, and he let the section carry him back up to the corridor, unhooking his tattered backpack from the iron rod as he went past.

Ruby, Sam and Felicity swooped onto him in a rolling embrace, wrapping him in their arms. After everyone was assured that everyone else was all right, Gerald took a step back and his hands dropped to his knees. He was drenched and shivering. And his heart ached at Professor McElderry's fate.

Why did he give up like that? Let himself be swept away?

Gerald's head fell between his shoulders, and his gaze landed on the small door under the angel and the devil: it had popped open a centimetre.

They all stared at the gap.

'What do you think?' Felicity said.

There was a long silence. Then Gerald turned towards the end of the corridor. 'Mason Green was right,' he said. 'Enough puzzles for one day.'

Ruby quickly found their way back to the exit. She tapped in the TOWEL combination and pushed open the entrance to the tunnel out of the cellars.

'Is that it for Mason Green?' Sam asked as he followed his sister along the narrow passage. 'Could you even see where all that water was going?'

Gerald trailed his friends along the dimly lit path, following the sign towards Central Park. 'It was a black hole,' he said. 'They were swallowed up.' Gerald shook his head in disbelief. The professor had actually wanted to be washed away. 'What was he thinking?' Gerald said to no one in particular. A shiver rolled down his spine.

'We could have helped each other.'

Ruby waited for Gerald to catch up. She took his hand and held it tight. 'You were lucky he didn't take you down with him,' she said.

'He must have been under the influence of one of those potions,' Felicity said. 'It's the only explanation.'

'But that's the thing,' Gerald said. 'I don't think he was affected by whatever drugs Green had been feeding him. He remembered my name. He remembered Sam. And there were his eyes.'

'What about his eyes?' Ruby asked.

'When he stared at me, just before he let himself be washed away, his eyes were completely fine. I'm sure he was back to normal.'

'Except for throwing himself off the top of a water-fall,' Sam said. 'Normal apart from that.'

Ruby gave Sam an annoyed look, then turned back to Gerald. 'We'll call the police. They might be able to find them.'

Gerald shook his head. 'I couldn't care if Mason Green was flushed into the bowels of the earth.'

They walked in silence to the end of the passage. There was a metal grille not much bigger than a cat flap at the bottom of the end wall. Sam unscrewed the four wing nuts at the corners and worked the grille free. He dropped to his hands and knees and crawled in. Felicity was halfway through the opening when Sam's cries filtered back to them.

'Ow! Ouch! *Getoffit*!'

Ruby squeezed in behind Felicity, as if packing into a rugby scrum. 'What is it?' Ruby called. 'What's the matter?' Then she paused, a suspicious expression forming on her face. 'Is this to do with rats?' she asked.

Sam's voice came back to them again, this time a high-pitched squeak. 'Rats? What rats?'

'No, you dunderhead. There aren't any rats. What are you squealing about?'

There was a lengthy pause. 'Uh—there's a bunch of flying bugs in here,' Sam said with more than a touch of wounded pride. 'Some of them got in my hair.'

Ruby blew a long burst of air between her lips, a little like an overheating steam engine just before it explodes. 'My brother, the thrillseeker,' she said. 'Let's go, Flicka. Hercules in there might need some help with his hair.'

Moments later they were standing in what seemed to be an enormous hot house, full of exotic tropical plants and thousands upon thousands of —

'Butterflies!' Felicity said as one landed on the top of her head. She glanced at Sam. 'This is what you were scared of?' she asked.

Sam's cheeks turned pink. 'Some of them can give you a nasty scratch,' he mumbled.

Gerald turned a slow circle to gaze at the soaring palm trees and the flights of gossamer above them. 'Does this remind you of somewhere, Felicity?' he asked.

'I was just thinking that,' she said as they started along a winding path. 'Mr Mantle's butterfly house, but a lot smaller of course. Where are we, do you think?'

'I'd guess it's the Central Park Zoo,' Ruby said. 'We're almost back to civilisation.'

'I hope that civilisation comes with breakfast,' Sam said. 'I'm starving.'

They reached a large glass door. On the other side were posters promoting upcoming winter events and how to get the most from your day at the zoo. Sam pulled on the door, but it was locked.

'Looks like we're here till opening time,' Felicity said. She found a plastic chair by the entrance and sat down. 'Might as well make ourselves comfy.'

'Why would you lock the door to the butterfly house?' Sam said, dragging a chair next to Felicity. 'It's not like all the bugs are going to stage a breakout.'

'I suppose it's to keep people out,' Ruby said.

The first rays of morning sun cut through the glass walls, casting a golden hue throughout the enclosure.

'What type of idiot would break into a butterfly house?' Sam asked.

'Apart from us, you mean?' Ruby said.

'Butterfly collectors, maybe,' Gerald said. He pulled up a squat stool, tossed his backpack on the floor and nestled in beside Ruby. He started to shiver. Sam wrapped his jacket over his friend's shoulders to keep him warm. 'People like Jasper Mantle travel the world trying to complete their collections.' Gerald continued. 'Except he's only one short of getting the lot and he's not likely to find that one in a public zoo.'

Felicity yawned. It had been a long night. 'What was its name again?' she asked.

Gerald leaned back to rest against Ruby's legs. 'It's the Xerxes Blue,' he said. 'I haven't had the chance to tell you, but there's a massive butterfly collection up in the Billionaires' Club. It must have belonged to Diamond Jim. But he didn't have any more luck than Jasper Mantle with the Xerxes Blue. There was an empty frame on the wall, just waiting until he found it—a bit like the empty box for Drebbel's perpetual motion machine. I guess collectors like to plan ahead.'

Gerald stopped.

He sat upright, as if he had just swallowed a particularly hot peppermint.

'What is it?' Ruby asked.

Gerald grabbed up his backpack. It was sodden from the drenching back in the cellars. He tipped out his notebook. The covers were wet but the pages inside were mostly dry.

'The message from Jeremy Davey,' Gerald said, searching inside the bag for his pencil. 'The keyword.'

Felicity moved from her chair and knelt next to Gerald. 'I'd forgotten all about that.'

'Mason Green hadn't forgotten about it,' Gerald said. 'He was talking about it on the phone, remember?

The professor was going to work on deciphering the code. On finding the keyword. But it has been staring us in the face all along.'

'What do you mean?' Ruby asked, moving to the other side of Gerald.

Gerald pointed with the end of his pencil at a page in his notebook. 'See? The very first letters in the coded message are XERS BLU. Jeremy Davey was telling us the keyword and we were too stupid to figure it out. Felicity, what was the boat that Davey was going on?'

'The *Beagle*. What about it?'

'Where was it sailing to?'

Felicity thought for a moment. 'Um, around the bottom of South America and across to Australia,' she said.

'Hold on,' Sam interrupted. 'Is this *the* HMS *Beagle* you're talking about? The same ship that Charles Darwin was on when he did all his botany stuff at the Galapagos Islands?'

Gerald clapped Sam on the shoulder. 'The Galapagos Islands is where the Xerxes Blue butterfly comes from. Jeremy Davey picked a keyword for his message from the name of a rare butterfly that he must have seen on the journey with Darwin.'

Ruby prodded a finger in Gerald's ribs. 'Well, what's the message say, genius?'

Gerald quickly drew up a fresh grid.

A	B	C	D	E	F	G	H	I	J	K	L	M	N	O	P	Q	R	S	T	U	V	W	X	Y	Z
X	E	R	S	B	L	U	A	C	D	F	G	H	I	J	K	M	N	O	P	Q	T	U	V	W	Z

He studied the original message: *Xers blu c axtb pxfbi pab cilbnixg hxracib jl snbeebg xis rjiocuibs cp pj pab sbkpao eqp hy rjiorcbirb co cgg xp nbop c xh lclpy hcgbo ib jl rqgkbkkbn cogxis c sj ijp fijv cl c sbobntb nborqb oj c nbgy ji pab dqsuhbip jl pab jib vaj lciso paco hbooxub hxy yjqn ojqg eb nxcobs ji eqppbnlgy vciuo.*

In a minute he had solved the puzzle. Gerald pushed his pencil behind his right ear and read the one-hundred-and-fifty-year-old words of Jeremy Davey: *I have taken the infernal machine of Drebbel and consigned it to the depths but my conscience is ill at rest. I am fifty miles NE of Culpepper Island. I do not know if I deserve rescue so I rely on the judgment of the one who finds this message. May your soul be raised on butterfly wings.*

Gerald, Ruby, Sam and Felicity were silent. The only sound was the rustling of thousands of wings, opening to absorb the morning light.

'The infernal machine of Drebbel,' Gerald repeated.

'The perpetual motion machine,' Sam said.

Ruby shook her head. 'Davey had it all along.'

'He must have taken it from the keystone in the castle in Scotland,' Felicity chimed in. 'Maybe that's why we found his diary there.'

'The son of a luddite transported to Australia,' Gerald said. 'He would hate the idea of a machine that could run forever. Just like Sergei Baranov does.'

'So he steals the machine and takes it on the *Beagle*, but to do what?' Ruby asked.

'Maybe he wanted to take it to his father in Australia so they could destroy it together?' Sam said. 'Like Alex and his dad.'

'But on the way something goes wrong,' Ruby said. 'Jeremy is marooned. He throws the machine into the ocean, but then has second thoughts: maybe he shouldn't have destroyed it.'

'So he writes a note asking for help and puts it in a bottle, but because he's torn about whether he did the right thing he writes it in code,' Gerald said. 'A cry for help, but an uncertain one.'

He leaned back and stared at the final words of a young man who died trying to reach the father who had been taken from him.

'It would have been handy knowing all that before we came to New York,' Sam said. 'It might have saved a bit of hassle.'

Gerald snorted. 'It would have got Mason Green off my back,' he said. 'I think he was actually going to kill us this time. He must have wanted that machine so badly.'

'Which one?' Sam said. 'The perpetual motion machine or the curiosity machine?'

'Yeah, what's that all about?' Ruby said. 'Green's eyes really lit up when you said you had the plans.'

Gerald patted his jacket pocket and felt the folded

paper inside. 'That's one puzzle I'm happy to leave unsolved,' he said.

'Aren't you the slightest bit curious about where the perpetual motion machine is?' Felicity asked. 'Davey's note basically tells you where to find it. Don't you want to go on an exotic expedition to the Galapagos Islands?'

Gerald gave her a sympathetic look. 'Now, why on earth would I want to do something like that?' he said.

It was early afternoon by the time the zoo authorities, the police and the FBI were through with their questions. A heavily armed search-and-rescue team had scoured the tunnel leading to the cellars of the Billionaires' Club, but there was no sign of Professor McElderry or Sir Mason Green. An inspection of the booby-trapped corridor triggered by the angel showed that it led directly to the New York stormwater system.

'It empties into the East River,' a bullet-headed police sergeant reported back. 'If they were reasonable swimmers they might have survived.'

Jasper Mantle arrived at the zoo in a purple-faced flurry some hours after he had opened the doors to the clubhouse to find neither Gerald nor Alex anywhere to be seen. He was horrified to hear of the ordeal that Gerald had been through; however, he was placated swiftly when Gerald told him about the extensive butterfly collection.

Mantle made an excuse about an urgent meeting he had to attend and disappeared down Fifth Avenue in the direction of the club.

Mr Fry had a car waiting to take everyone back to the Plaza. He had spent the time while the police were questioning Gerald pacing up and down outside the butterfly enclosure, growing increasingly harried. Gerald gave him a reassuring pat on the shoulder. 'We can keep this our little secret, Mr Fry,' Gerald said. 'I don't think my parents need to know all the details of what happened last night. You know, how all the children in your care managed to end up in a life-threatening situation. It can only cause problems that neither of us wants.'

Mr Fry gave a slow nod. 'As ever,' he said, 'young sir is wise beyond his years.'

Gerald wrapped a blanket around himself, and they all emerged into the afternoon. The sky had clouded over and a light dusting of snow was scattering across the rolling hillocks of Central Park. Gerald turned to his butler. 'It's a nice afternoon for a walk. How about you lead the way back to the hotel, St John?'

Mr Fry's eyes flickered towards the waiting limousine and its heated interior, parked just metres away.

'Or,' Gerald said, 'I could always tell my parents about your child-minding abilities.'

Mr Fry's jaw tightened. 'Wise beyond his years,' he mumbled and strode off along a path towards the soaring tower blocks of midtown Manhattan.

Sam and Felicity fell in behind Mr Fry but Gerald held Ruby back for a moment.

Ruby gave him a sideways glance as they walked side by side through the park. Snow danced earthward as gentle and light as any butterfly. Ruby bumped him gently with her shoulder. 'What are you going to do when you see Alex Baranov back at camp?' she asked. 'It sounds like he was pretty nasty.'

Gerald shrugged. 'I'll probably just ignore him. I figure any revenge I could take would be nothing compared to the roasting he'll get from his father when he presents him with a dud perpetual motion machine.'

They walked in silence for a while, then Ruby bumped his shoulder again. 'It's never boring when I'm with you,' she said.

The snow began to fall a little heavier. A sizeable flake landed on the tip of Ruby's nose. Gerald stopped and took Ruby's hand. If it was going to happen, it had to happen now.

'What is it?' Ruby asked, peering up at him. Gerald reached out a finger and brushed the flake from the end of her nose. Ruby stifled a murmur of surprise.

Gerald fixed his eyes on hers. The world around them blurred. He reached into his pocket and pulled out the gold key that they found in the boiler and put the chain over Ruby's head. 'I want you to have this,' he said.

Ruby put a hand to her throat and stared at the key in her palm. 'Thank you,' she said, biting her bottom lip.

Gerald brushed his hand down Ruby's cheek. It flushed red in the cold.

He opened his mouth.

Limerick time.

But before he could begin, Ruby had her forefinger across his lips. 'I've written a poem for you,' she said.

Gerald's heart stopped beating.

Ruby smiled up at him, and spoke:

> *'There once was a boy from Australia*
> *Keen for snogging and paraphernalia*
> *But when push came to shove*
> *His confessions of love*
> *Were destined for hopeless failure.'*

Ruby rose to her tiptoes and kissed Gerald gently on the cheek. Then she jogged off to catch up with Felicity and Sam.

She got ten metres, looked back at him and smiled, then ran on.

Gerald stood in the snow and put a hand to his cheek. He could still feel Ruby's lips on his skin.

'I swear,' he said to himself, 'as long as I live, I will never understand girls.'

Acknowledgments

With thanks to:

- Mum and Dad, with love and appreciation.
- As always, to Jane Pearson for her skill and endless patience.
- Stephanie Stepan, to whom all horse-related action contained within is dedicated.
- James Phelan for introducing me to the real puzzle house of New York. Seriously. Got to nytimes.com and search 'Puzzle House'.
- My wife Kathryn, our son Sam and daughters Ruby and Ella, who remind me of what is important in life.
- Oh, and Pippin the cat.